Scratched

Scratched

The Anderson Brothers Series
Book 2

MARIE LONG

To Big Bro #2
♪ House Music All Night Long! ♪

Acknowledgments

My creativity and writing ability would not have been made possible without my Lord and Savior, Jesus Christ. I thank Him every day, first and foremost, for everything He's done.

Thank you, Mom and Dad, for your love and continued support in everything I do. To my big brothers, thank you both for always being there. I love you, always.

I appreciate all my friends, online and IRL, for keeping me motivated to write. You guys are awesome.

Thank you to the *amazing* Red Adept staff for the top-notch work you have done on this book. I cannot recommend you guys enough.

Thanks to my friends of the Dragon's Sandbox. Your suggestions and detailed critiques have helped me so much with my writing.

Thank you to the reviewers and bloggers who have volunteered their time to read and review this book. I greatly appreciate every one of your honest, helpful, and valuable reviews.

A very special thanks to *you*, the reader, for giving the Anderson Brothers a chance to capture your heart just as they have captured mine.

Scratched

Chapter 1

I PULL UP TO THE DRIVEWAY OF DOMINICK'S DUPLEX AND wait while he and Denise get out. I'm mad about what went down last night. But fortunately, Dom was there to save her from that shit. If I see that guy William again, I'll kill him for Denise *and* for my baby brother, who had to experience the mental trauma all over again. I know Dom. As tough as he thinks he is, his mind is still fragile. He must've suffered one of his recurring flashbacks when he rescued Denise at the party.

Where she was almost raped.

I wish I could have taken a good, clean shot at William, too, that fucking bastard. But it was Dom's fight.

Dom taps the driver-side window, shaking me out of my thoughts. Rolling down the window, I'm met with a light breeze of the mild Seattle night that kisses my face. I stare at my brother, concerned and hoping tonight's ordeal doesn't send him off the deep end. He's got a lot of anger boiling inside after putting up with our father's abuse for all those years. It's a miracle I've been able to help him keep it under control for this long.

But still, he's like a ticking time bomb, and it worries me, especially with Denise there. She's been through enough, and she doesn't need his "issues" on top of what she already has to deal with. I know Dom likes her—*loves her*—but I don't think she knows what he's gone through.

"Thanks, man, for all this," Dom says.

I scrutinize the two of them. "You sure you two will be okay?"

Dom nods. "Yeah, man." He looks over his shoulder at Denise, who smiles in return.

She's got a beautiful smile. There's a glow about her that brings out the best in my brother. I hope she can help him quell his demons.

"All right," I say then stare out the windshield at nothing in particular. "I got a call while I was waiting at the hospital for you guys. Got this huge gig at a radio station down in Portland next Wednesday, so I'll be gone. But I'll be back by Friday."

Dom grins. "Wow, Kev, that's great! I'm happy for you, man."

"Thanks." I look back at him. "Take it easy, li'l bro, okay?"

He nods, his smile fading. "You, too."

I reach out the window, and we do our secret handshake that we've been doing since we were kids. Back then, it reminded us that we were inseparable no matter how bad it got.

I drive off into the night, glancing in my mirror to see Dom and Denise head inside the house. I won't see my little brother for a few days, but that doesn't mean I'm not going to call and check up on him.

Sunday night, I pack and head south on the interstate toward Portland. It's less than a three-hour drive, and I could've just left early on Tuesday, but I want to meet up with some of my deejay friends on Monday, some of whom I'll most likely crash with.

And there are other things that I need to take care of as well.

Twenty minutes into my drive, I detour east to Renton to a place I hate going back to. It's been a little over six months since I last visited, and the guilt inside me says I should stop in and at least say hello. I pull into the driveway of a little blue house that sits back among a cluster of trees. My headlights shine on the back of a white SUV parked in front of me. *Uncle Adam's here.*

Getting out the car, I slip on my earbuds and start up the music player in my back pocket. House music fills my ears, calming my nerves. A narrow, pebbled, flower-lined walkway leads up to the front door of the decades-old home. The scent of azaleas—Mama's scent—fills my nose, and I pluck a blossom and twirl it between my fingers. Each time I return, this place seems so new to me. So foreign. Maybe it's because I've been trying hard to forget the past. All that's left of "home" is pain. And my mother.

Warm light from the living room's curtained window casts a dim glow over the outside bushes. The small white light of a TV flickers. I ring the doorbell, and moments later, the door swings open. Uncle Adam's giant six-foot-six frame fills the doorway. A broad smile parts his dark, haggard face.

The music still going, I pull the earbuds out, and they hang down the front of my shirt.

"Kevin!" Unc steps out and embraces me in a big bear hug.

I tense up for a moment then relax and return the hug. Having worked on cars and construction all his life, Unc is strong and his body feels like a brick wall.

"'Sup, Unc," I say, pulling out of his arms.

He peers past me and frowns. "Still no Dominick, huh?"

I shake my head. "Naw, he's got some things going on, but he's handling it."

Unc heads back inside, leaving the door open for me. "Your mother had an accident in the garden yesterday. Sprained her ankle."

"Damn. Is she okay?"

"Yeah, it's just a minor strain. But the doctor told her to take it easy. I'm taking care of her for the weekend."

After our father—that coward—committed suicide, Mama was left alone and scared. That was when Uncle Adam stepped in. It's hard to imagine, even now, that this man is my father's brother. Unc is nothing like my father. Many times I've wondered if Uncle Adam was really my father instead of that other son of a bitch.

He's your dad, like it or not, Unc had said. *But don't think for a moment that I am like him. You three might as well be my sons, and I love you all very much.*

Uncle Adam really did love us, still does, and I don't think I ever heard those words uttered from my real father's mouth.

Unc leads me through the living room, where the TV is tuned in to an old sci-fi movie. My throat tightens as the familiar sights, smells, and sounds of my childhood fill my senses. The tail of the cat clock hanging on the drab grey wall in the kitchen still grinds steadily back and forth. Framed photos from family trips line the narrow hallway leading to the master bedroom, along with ones of Dominick, Michael, and me as babies and schoolchildren. At the end of the hall, a large family portrait hangs prominently. We seem happy, with Mama holding baby Dom and smiling, but that happiness was all a front. At the sight of it, I choke back angry tears.

I sneer at the way Pops appears in that portrait. His smile looks fake, plastered on, as if he knew exactly what he was going to do to his family.

"Kevin," Unc calls, pulling me back to the present. I didn't realize I'd been standing and staring for so long.

I snap my head to him. "Sorry. I just . . . "

He stands at the door to the master bedroom, his hand on the knob. "No, son. Don't you dare apologize. This is your home. Now, go see your mother." He opens the door.

I swallow then moisten my lips. The room has changed since I first left home. The old white draperies have been switched for teal ones. The once-drab white walls are re-painted to a sea blue with white trim. The furniture has been rearranged, and some new furniture added. The twin walk-in closets have been reconstructed into a single big one. I helped Uncle Adam with the painting and construction on that job. It was a fun project and helped ease the pain a little.

The bedside lamp sheds its warm glow over Mama's bronze face. She's sitting up in bed, her bandaged foot propped up on a pillow, her eyes focused on the thick, dog-eared Bible open in her lap. She got serious with the religion stuff after Pops died.

Her big brown eyes meet mine, over the top of her reading glasses, as I approach her bedside. Beaming, she book-marks her Bible and sets it aside. "Kevin? Oh, honey, you're back!"

"Hi, Mama," I mumble, hugging her and kissing her on the cheek. She's almost fifty, but the only wrinkles on her face are around her eyes and are probably due to all the crying she's done over the years. She still smells like Mama—all flowery and sweet. I close my eyes and feel them start to burn as memories take over. How could that son of a bitch of a father hurt this beautiful woman? And how could Dominick and I ever be mad at her for what she did? I forgave her, but Dom . . . well, his demons still run rampant.

I look at her swollen foot and ankle. "Uncle Adam said you had an accident. Are you okay?"

"Yes, baby. I was planting some new flowers and stepped on a spade. Carelessness on my part." She holds my hands and takes me in fully. "How are you doing?"

Sitting on the edge of the bed, I stare at her small, calloused hands over mine. "I'm fine. I'm on my way to Portland, so I thought I'd stop in and say hi."

"What's happening in Portland?"

"I've got a radio gig down there on Wednesday."

"Oh." The excitement on her face dulls. "Still doing that deejay stuff, I see."

"Yeah, and this upcoming gig could be my big break."

"So you're not going to finish college?"

I purse my lips. I really didn't want to drop out in the first place, but I had a personal obligation to Dom. Since *that day,* I've swore on my life to protect him, and to always be there for him whenever he needed me. I can't concentrate on school while worrying about him all the time. "I don't know yet," I finally reply.

"Kevin, you're twenty-four years old. It's not too late to finish. Maybe you can try out for the team again, get your basketball scholarship back, and—"

"Mama . . . "

"Baby, I don't want to see you throw your life away. You have so much going for you. The Lord blessed you with a talent, and you're not using it."

I scowl. "I'm not throwing my life away, Mama. I'm happy doing what I'm doing. I'm living comfortably with what I earn from my deejaying."

"But you need a college education. You're not going to get a decent job at a high school level. What happens when you get tired of deejaying? Then what? Going to get some dead-end job, living paycheck-to-paycheck for the rest of your life? How will you support yourself and your wife? Your children?"

"Whoa." I pull my hands from hers. "Wife and kids? You're thinking a little too far into the future, Mama. How about we think about the here and now?"

She smiles softly. "I want grandbabies someday, Kevin. Is there a special someone that's caught your eye?"

"Uhh, not really." It's partly true. I meet tons of girls every time I work, but most of them become a blur. Except this one girl named Trinity Brown. She's cute, deliciously chubby, follows me to my downtown gigs, and is always the first in line to get into a club I'm spinning at. She's someone I can never forget.

"Well," Mama says, "one day you will meet that special person, and you'll need to find a better way to support the both of you once deejaying is no longer your passion."

I stiffen. *Fuck that.* "I'll never get tired of deejaying. Music is my life. It's the only thing that keeps me sane right now. You should be happy for me."

She clasps her hands together on her lap. "Baby, I don't want you or your brothers to be satisfied with just getting by in life."

I clench my jaw. Being a deejay isn't "just getting by in life." It's a fun and exciting life for me, and I wouldn't want any other kind of job.

But then I think maybe it's *not* too late to try out for the team. And I only need seven more credits to graduate. "I'll think about going back. I'll talk to Coach Langley about trying out again."

The smile returns to her face. "Oh, baby, that's all I ask. Please don't throw your talent away. Maybe one day I'll see you on TV playing pro."

I laugh. "I'm not *that* good, Mama. The pro guys are no joke. Anyway, I can't rely on basketball my whole life. I'll eventually get too old to play, or I might get injured. Either way, my career would only be temporary."

"That's why you need to finish school—so you can get a good job to fall back on. That business degree will go a long way, Kevin."

"Mama." I exhale slowly. "I know what I wanna do with my life. It may or may not be what you intend, but I promise I'll use my God-given talents to go as far as I can."

"Thank you, baby." She leans over and kisses my forehead. "How's Dominick?"

I avert my gaze and look anywhere but at her. I can't tell her about what happened to Dom and his girl the other night. "He's fine."

"He hasn't come to see me since he graduated from high school," Mama says. "He's only called a handful of times. I try calling, but he doesn't answer. I miss my baby boy."

"He's still mad, Mama."

"At me?" Her eyes start to get glassy.

I don't reply.

"He thinks I don't care about him, doesn't he?" She covers her mouth, and a tear rolls down her cheek. "I tried. I really tried. I just wanted my family back. Lord Jesus, I just wanted my family back." She closes her eyes and sniffles, more and more tears falling.

My vision wavers and blurs, and I pull her into an embrace. She cries on my shoulder. "Mama." My voice quivers, and I blink away some tears welling up in my burning eyes. *No, damn it, I have to be strong for her, since Pops couldn't be.* But hearing her sobs and feeling her warm tears causes some of my own to fall. I quickly wipe them away with the back of my hand. "You'll get your family back one day. It's just . . . these things take time. A long time. I'll try talking to Dom more. I'll try to get him to come see you." *But not now. God, not now.*

I pull her away and wipe the tears from her cheeks with my fingers. A small smile touches her lips.

I cup her face in my hands. "No more, tears, Mama. I hate it when you cry. You've gotta be strong, okay? Be strong for all of us."

She nods and sniffs.

I release her then get up from the bed. "I should go."

"Kevin." She grabs my hand, and I look back. "Stay the night, please."

I draw my hand away firmly. "I can't, Mama. I'm meeting some friends in Portland tomorrow afternoon."

"But it's late. I don't want you driving on that interstate alone at night. Please, baby."

I look up at the ceiling and sigh. She always knows how to get to my heart when she uses that *needy mom* tone. "All right. But I gotta leave by nine tomorrow morning."

She beams. "Oh, that's fine, Kevin. Thank you."

I smile halfheartedly and leave the room. Returning to the living room, I discover Uncle Adam asleep on the couch with the TV still on. I quietly head toward the kitchen. *Might as well find something to eat before I go to sleep.* When I reach the breakfast nook, I halt. My eyes zero in on a spot on the wall near the baseboard. The paint in that spot is a shade lighter than the rest of the wall.

I remember that spot all too well. It's the same spot the back of my head hit after Pops grabbed me, choked me, cut me, and threw me against the wallboard. I blacked out from the impact and thought I'd died.

I place my hand to that spot on my head then move it down to the side of my neck, where my father sliced me with a box cutter. Even though I've covered up the scars with tattoos, they remain visible in my mind.

I raid the fridge and wolf down a plate of chicken and rice. Uncle Adam's still asleep by the time I finish, so as I head to bed, I turn off all the lights and the TV. The hallway leading to our bedrooms seems like an endless dark tunnel. I walk by the first room and flip on the light. It's Dom's, and it's every bit the same as he left it, only a little emptier. Posters of motorcycles and his favorite hip-hop artists hang the walls, and some of Uncle Adam's old mechanics books line the small bookshelf in one corner. Motorcycle magazines lie piled on the desk and on the seat of the pushed-in chair. The bed is made, and there's not a single article of clothing to be seen, my only indication that Mama was in here at some point.

I turn off the light and move past the bathroom to the next room—Michael Jr.'s. I clench my jaw as I flip the light switch. I don't know why I decided to come in here. Everything about that coward pisses me off. It's fitting that he bears our father's name. Serves him right. Michael's room is tidy as well, thanks to Mama. His walls are bare, other than a "Basic Striking Points" chart that shows all the vital areas on the human body and a shelf lining one of the walls, displaying dozens of martial-arts trophies and gold medals. A pair of dumbbells and a steel bench press bar with two twenty-pound weights are tucked under his bed. A picture of me and Dom as kids sits on the night table.

Fuck this. I shut off the light and leave.

I turn on the bedside lamp in my room. My old basketball posters are barely held to the walls with age-old tape. The bookshelves are bare. I used them to hold all the vinyls I collected when I was first learning how to mix. I pull open the closet. Only a few of my middle- and high-school clothes hang there, organized by color and pressed—more of Mama's doing. In the corner of the closet, I spot a bag, which holds my old two-channel mixer and turntable. Smiling, I pull out the bag and plop down on the bed with it. I uncover the equipment, which no longer works due to over-usage. This shit's junk compared to what I own now, but I guess I'll keep it around a little longer for its sentimental value. I stuff the equipment back into the bag and set it on the floor next to the bed.

Sticking the earbuds back in my ears, I switch to a new song on my player and lie back. I instinctively reach my hand under the bed, groping for the basketball I've always kept there. Palming it, I pull it out. The ball had seen its uses in the many pickup games I've played in at the parks. It's the same ball that got me my full-ride scholarship at the University of Washington. I toss the ball up with a perfect free-throw technique and catch it. I *do* miss the game. Sometimes I feel bummed that I've lost my scholarship.

But I'll never regret quitting school to save my brother.

Chapter 2

THE CROWD CHEERS AS I INCREASE THE TEMPO ON MY LAST set of the night. With one of the headphones' ear pads cradled against my ear with my shoulder, I set a drum loop through the mixer from Turntable A, while I scratch and juggle the current tune on Turntable B. This is a release from the stresses of reality. People dance and shout, drinks in their hands, going crazy. The sea of dancing bodies sparkles and glints under the strobe lights and mirror ball. Women smile at me, dressed in their finest, hoping their goods will get my attention. Try as they might, they're all a blur. I'm too caught up in the energy of this place to care about women. This is my life, the life of a deejay, and I wouldn't change it for the world. I never want to wake up from this musical high. I gaze out at the crowd. It's Friday night. The spring semester is over, and it's summer vacation for the UDub students. All of Seattle's Finest are out to party.

Including Dominick and his girl, Denise. It's been five weeks since the incident, and they've grown closer than ever.

I bob my head to the beat, mixing in another song to match the driving bass thump that vibrates the floor. Couples get closer, gyrating with their hips and asses and everything else. Denise spins around, and Dom holds her close in his arms. He kisses her neck as the two of them bump and grind to the beat. My eyes cut to the rest of the crowd, zeroing in on the little band of female groupies at the foot of the stage near one of the floor speakers. They're definitely groupies, because I see them at almost every one of my downtown gigs. Unlike some of the crude drunks who eye me like dessert, these chicks are okay. Especially Trinity, who's dressed in jeans and a white camisole to show off her curvaceous body. She dances beautifully, her big tits and ass bouncing as she moves. She and her friends always hang out in the same spot by the stage, flirting and casting suggestive glances at me while I mix.

I meet Trinity's gaze, and she bites her nails and averts her eyes. I can't help but smile at that. She's even sexier when she's embarrassed.

But damn it, they're all just groupies. I can't waste my time being around girls who only care about the persona and not the guy behind it. I thought it was cool at first, but it got old fast.

Two a.m. hits, and I wrap up the night. The emcee makes his announcements, and everyone starts leaving. That doesn't stop some of the girls from yelling their numbers at me, and some even try to make their way onto the stage. But the bouncers are there in a heartbeat and drag them off. Trinity and her friends fall to the back of the crowd, trying to be the last ones out. They smile and wave, making little kissy faces at me. My eyes glued to Trinity, I wave back and wink, the silent gesture making the girl glow. They're soon corralled by the bouncers and led to the exit. I get a brief look at Trinity, from afar, as she walks away. What I wouldn't do to have my hands all over that gorgeous round ass.

"That show was *sick*, bro!" Dom yells, interrupting my fantasy. His face is lit up like an excited little kid.

My brother hops up onto the stage and starts helping me break down my deejay equipment. One of the bouncers frowns and makes his way over to us, but I give the guy a small nod, silently telling him it's okay. Dom's the only person I trust to touch my shit. I'm waiting for him to ask me for advice like he usually does, but we both work in silence for several minutes.

"Whoa. No questions tonight? No advice seeking?" I return the records to their sleeves. "What the hell, man?"

Smiling, Dom unplugs a wire from the dual turntables. "Naw, not tonight, bro. Everything's cool."

"Yeah?" I snatch the wire from him. "Then why the hell are you here with me? I got this. Go to your girl."

"Denise wants to talk to her friends outside. Girl stuff." Dom places the turntables in the padded case as I finish coiling the wire.

I roll my tongue against my cheek. Dom shouldn't be hanging around me all the time anymore.

"Guess what?" Dom continues. "I aced my engineering finals."

I raise my eyebrows, but I'm not surprised. Of us three brothers, Dom was always the brainy one. "No shit? Good job, li'l bro. Are you gonna take summer classes?"

"Naw. I'm gonna get some extra hours at work. I could use the money."

"I hear that." I place the dual turntable in its case. "What's Denise doing for the summer?"

Dom hefts up the album-filled milk crate. I tote the rest. "She's going back home to visit her folks for two weeks."

"And she didn't invite you to come along?"

"She did, but I turned it down."

I blink. "What? You're not going with her? What the fuck is wrong with you, Dom?"

He hardens his gaze. "What the fuck is wrong with *you*? It's her family, man. And I'm gonna respect that she should have some privacy with them."

God, does he really not have a clue? "Yeah, but you need to meet them. You and Denise have been going out for what, three months, now? Her parents deserve to meet the guy who saved their daughter from almost getting raped."

Dom cringes then shakes his head. "No. I don't want her reminded of that shit."

"Look, li'l bro. If you expect to make this work between you and Denise, then you should at least meet her folks. You need to get on good terms with them." I start walking off the stage toward the back door, not giving him a chance to respond.

"You think it's that easy?" Dom calls. "What do I say if her parents grill me about *my* folks, huh?"

"They'd be more concerned about you than our parents," I say flatly. I kick open the back door and head down the few steps that lead into an alley, where my black hatchback sports car is parked.

"I need to give her some space. Anyway, it'll only be two weeks, and she'll be back for the rest of the summer."

"I thought you said she's from Seattle?"

"She is, but her parents live in Olympia now."

I pop open the hatch and start organizing my equipment in the cargo space. "Did you two talk about this?"

"Yeah, we did," Dom replies, handing over the equipment piece by piece. "She understands where I'm coming from. Besides, her dad is apparently the type who gives every guy she brings home the third degree."

"Well, you can't keep running from that. If you intend to spend a long time with Denise, well . . . you need to talk eventually."

"Yeah. Just not now."

My stuff all packed in, I slam the hatchback shut. "Whatever, man." I climb into the driver's seat, shut the door, and start the engine. I roll the window down.

Dom leans into the open window. "You doing anything tomorrow?"

I swipe the screen of the music player that's built into my dash and load up the playlist of house beats. "I'm probably gonna hit up the courts in the morning."

"All right."

"Why? What's up?"

He sighs. "What the hell am I gonna do for two whole weeks without Denise?"

I roll my eyes and put the car in reverse. "You'll figure it out. Just don't whine and bitch to me about it. Now, go back to your girl."

Dom smiles and pushes back from the car. "Later, man."

"Later." I back out of the alley and squeal the tires as I take off into the downtown night.

CHAPTER 3

SATURDAY MORNING, I HEAD TO THE COURTS AT DENNY Park around nine. A bunch of my buddies are playing a three-on-three game. I do some quick stretches at the edge of the court as I watch.

The matchup is absolutely ridiculous: Josh, Hector, and David versus Ty, Andre, and Carter.

Josh is nearly seven feet tall and has an insane vertical leap. Not to mention, he can block shots like nothing with his massive hands. He's definitely pro material if I ever saw it. Hector's the oldest of all of us and built like a bull. Nothing gets past his brick wall of a body, and those who try end up getting knocked on their asses. David's got fast hands and even faster feet. He can out-dribble anyone who challenges him. He taught me a bunch of dribbling tricks that have helped up my game.

Andre and Ty play like the average streetballer, sometimes sloppy with their skills. Carter's the rookie of our group. He's pretty damn good for a kid fresh out of high school, but he still has a lot to learn. Their side can't compete against Josh, Hector, and David, who practically steamroll over them, stealing the ball, blocking shots, and performing amazing dunks right in their faces.

Did they even manage to get any points on them?

"Booyah! Twenty-one!" David shouts, pumping his fists up in victory. His T-shirt is soaked in sweat. "You rookies got shut-the-fuck out!"

Well, that answers *that* question.

Ty trudges off the court and collapses on the grass, panting.

"That was an ass whipping of all ass whippings," Carter mutters, heading to the water fountain.

Finished stretching, I get up and bounce on the balls of my feet. "Yo, I got next."

My buddies look at me and grin.

"Thank God, Kev's here!" Andre shouts.

"'Sup, Kev!" Hector says, approaching. I'm pretty built, but standing next to him makes me feel like a stick.

We bump fists. "'Sup."

"You came just in time, man!" David calls as he waits his turn at the water fountain. "Maybe you can help your boys redeem themselves."

I laugh. "*My* boys? What're you trying to say?"

David grins and drinks some water.

Josh towels the sweat off his face as he stands next to me. He dwarfs me by a few inches. "They need help. Bad. You in?"

"I'm in," I say as I fist-bump him. "I like a challenge. Let's do this."

Hector tosses me the ball. I get a feel of its hardness and dribble it a few times, testing its bounce, and then take a practice shot. "Andre? Carter? You ready?" I ask.

My teammates nod and join me.

David takes off his soaked shirt and tosses it onto the grass. "Now let's see just how good you are, *Kevitron*."

I frown. "Hey, what did I tell you about that?" I know he's joking, but I'm dead serious about not mixing work with pleasure.

David waves it off. "Just kidding, man. Let's play."

"Half-court or full?" I ask.

"Half." He smiles smugly. "I'll even let you have the ball first."

"How sweet," I say, moving to the half-court line.

David steps in front of me. No surprise—he's gonna be all over me. I'll show him just how much his student has surpassed the master. Hector and Andre stand under the basket, and Josh and Carter are off to the side near the key.

I bounce the ball to David. "Check."

He bounces it back to me, and I pause a moment, as though I'm about to pass it off to Carter but, instead, dribble around David's right. He stays on me like glue, hands flailing everywhere, making it damn near impossible to see the rest of my scrambling teammates. If David wants to go one-on-

one, I'll give it to him. I bend low, dribbling between my legs, as I assess the distance from him to the basket. There's no way I'm gonna get around Hector without taking a serious hit. David's hands reach toward me, attempting to steal the ball. I give him a smirk, perform a crossover dribble, and spin to his left, finding a clear path around near the free-throw line. In the corner of my eye, I spot Carter maneuvering around Josh toward the side three-point line.

"Here! Here!" Carter yells, his arms up.

I dribble some more, seeing David coming toward me fast from my other peripheral line of sight. I pass the ball to Carter just as David whooshes past me.

"Shoot!" I yell.

But Carter hesitates, and it's just enough time for Josh to come in. Double-teamed, Carter starts to panic.

"Shit!" Carter yells as he starts backing closer and closer to the out-of-bounds line. He lobs the ball over Josh and David's heads. Everyone scrambles toward it as it comes down, and Josh easily catches it with one of his puma jumps. He dribbles it to the top of the key then does a quick pass to David, and they switch places.

"My turn," David jeers. "Now I'll show *you* how it's done."

He puts the moves on me. His lightning hands and feet make me dizzy trying to keep up. As I reach in for a steal, he spins and passes it toward Hector, who's under the net. Hector's poised to catch the ball when Andre runs past with the steal. I hustle toward the basket. Hector grunts and stretches his arms out over poor Andre like a goliath. David's on my heels.

"Gimme the rock!" I yell, not stopping.

Andre passes me the ball, just as Hector's about to maul him. I drive to the basket, glimpsing Carter holding off Josh and leaving me with a narrow, but clear, path to go in for the layup. The ball banks off the backboard and into the net. I slow my run and smirk at David. "I'm sorry, what was that you wanted to show me?"

David grumbles.

"Holy shit!" Ty says from the sideline. "Did you guys just actually *score* on them?"

"I know, right?" Andre says.

Hector grunts. "Lucky break, that's all that was."

We end up losing, 21–19. But it's definitely the closest score Andre and Carter have ever seen playing against them. I scored fifteen of those nineteen points. I really hate being a ball-hog, but these rookies need a *lot* more practice.

My whole body is slick with sweat. Exhausted, I lean over the water fountain, letting the cold water shoot up onto my face before taking a long, refreshing drink.

"Good game, man," Josh says when I finish. He pats me on the back.

I wipe my mouth with the back of my hand. "You too."

"You got mad skills, Kev!" Ty says, ogling me as if I'm some celebrity.

I grin. "Thanks. But I'm no Fresco Davis. I've got a long way to go."

"Are you kidding? Fresco can dunk with his fucking eyes closed. Did you see him in that one game against Houston last year?"

"Totally sick. But that's why he's a pro all-star."

Andre, Hector, Carter, and David join us at the fountain.

"You ever consider playing for UDub again?" Hector asks as he waits his turn.

My smile disappears. "I dunno, man. I've been out of college for two years. I don't think I'm eligible to play anymore."

David drenches his face with water. "What're you talking about, Kev? You're a fucking natural! They'd have to make an exception for you with those skills! Now, as for me, I'm planning on going to the D-league tryouts in New York next month."

"D-league?" I whistle. "That's pro, right?"

"Pretty much."

I thumb at Josh. "Take him with you. He'd make a team no problem with that sick vertical of his."

"I wish I could go, but I can't afford the trip," Josh says.

"They still won't let you back on the Huskies?" I ask.

Josh shakes his head. "Not with that academic probation bullshit. I knew I should've changed majors when I had the chance."

I ask Hector, "What about you, man? Gonna try out for D-League?"

"Nah." Hector shrugs. "Too old."

"Thirty-one's too old?"

"These days, probably. The league likes you fresh young guys. You're getting up there, too, Kev, so you better do it while you can."

"Whatever, man. I'm only twenty-four. Anyway, there's no way I can just up and go to New York right now."

"Then don't," David says. "Play for UDub, catch the eye of some scout, and off you go."

I shake my head and roll my eyes. But the thought of finishing school still nags at me. I know I should do it, and I don't know why I continue putting it off since, as Dom keeps reminding me, *it's only seven credits.* I might as well get that over with.

"I'll think about it," I reply.

Chapter 4

I fucking hate doing laundry. Dirty clothes, piled high from me putting it off day after day, week after week, tower beside the washing machine. After I smashed a huge cockroach that was hiding under a pair of shorts, I figured it was time I finally got around to doing laundry. While the clothes are going, I hop in the shower and relax after another heart-pumping workout at the courts this morning.

The water pelts my back as my mind wanders. Who am I kidding? I miss the game, my old teammates, the excitement and energy in the arena when the Huskies won the national championship.

Fuck it. I'll do it.

Today's Wednesday. I'll go to summer tryouts next week. Maybe Coach Langley will let me try out, who knows? And I still have to register for fall classes. But if I'm going to do something big like go back to school, then maybe Dom can drag his ass down to Renton to see Mama. Fair is fair, after all.

I get out the shower, dry off, wrap the towel around my waist, and pad to my room. Sorting through my clean and semi-clean clothes, I toss one of my hoodies over the back of my desk chair. Something white peeks out from the front pocket. It's soft against my fingers as I grab it.

Just a little square napkin.

I'm not sure where it came from—which club, what girl. I don't remember the last time I wore this hoodie. As I'm about to crumple the napkin, I stop and look at it. There's a phone number written in Dom's handwriting, and then it comes to me.

Trinity. I smile. Dom gave this to me at Chauncey's Bar one night, trying to hook me up with Trinity. I don't know why I've put off calling her. Maybe because of the way things ended with Justine—that thieving bitch. I've been hesitant to get involved with another girl again.

But Trinity is a special case. She's got me curious, though I barely know a damn thing about her, only that she's Denise's best friend. Trinity must be interested in me, too. I mean, she's always checking me out at the club, and the way we exchange discreet, flirty glimpses with each other makes me wonder. Maybe it's about time I give her a chance and see what she's all about. She's beautiful. *Big* and beautiful, just the way I like my women.

I take one last look at the napkin, sprawl out on my bed, and dial her number. She picks up on the third ring.

"Hello?"

I relish the sound of that voice. I damn sure hope it's hers. "Hi. May I speak to Trinity?"

There's a small pause. "Speaking." Her voice sounds a little more wary than before.

My smile broadens. "Hey, Trinity. It's Kevin."

Another pause. "Kevin who?"

"Kevin Anderson. Dominick's brother."

"Wait. *That* Kevin? As in Kevitron? *The* DJ Kevitron?"

I make a sour face. "Yeah."

She gasps. "Oh my God. Oh my God! It's DJ Kevitron!"

I hiss through my teeth. "Yeah."

"This is such a surprise. I mean . . . I'm a huge fan!"

"Yeah, so are thousands of other girls," I say flatly. "But I wasn't calling to talk to a fan. I was calling to talk to Trinity."

She laughs lightly. *God*, that laugh. That voice. There's a hint of playfulness in that voice that I find so fucking sexy. "Well, that's me. Seriously, you were the last person I thought would ever call me. Wait—how did you get my number?"

"Dom gave it to me a while back. I get girls' numbers all the time. I can never keep up with them."

"Oh." Her tone deflates.

Shit. That came out wrong. "Sorry, I didn't mean it like that. I do get a lot of girls' numbers, but I'm not interested in them."

"So why are you calling me?"

The playful tone in her voice is replaced with tension, and it makes me swallow a lump in my throat. *Did my answer come out wrong again? Damn, I'm really fucking this up.* "I'm calling you because I'm interested. In *you*. I wanna get to know you. Dom thinks we should hook up."

"So you're really just doing a favor for your brother?"

I blink. "No! I mean, no. I called on my own." I rub the back of my head as I gather my thoughts. "There's this one girl who's caught my eye for a while now."

"Oh?"

My smile slowly returns. "Yeah. She comes to almost all my gigs. Big and beautiful with shoulder-length hair. Dresses so amazing, showing off those gorgeous curves, because she can."

"Oh . . . "

"I wanna see that girl again. Maybe tomorrow?"

"Thursday?"

"Yeah. It can be a lunch date," I say.

"Oh, damn. A date? With *DJ Kevitron*?"

I cringe. "No, a date with Kevin. Does this girl I'm interested in like barbecue?"

"She's *always* down for barbecue." The playfulness in her voice returns, to my enjoyment.

"Great. Tell her to meet me at Al's Grill around one tomorrow, okay?"

"Sounds good."

"Great. See you tomorrow, then."

"Later, Kevitron!"

"Kevin," I say, but she has already hung up.

Tossing the phone aside, I stare up at the ceiling. *Damn it. What am I getting myself into? How the hell do the* real *celebrities do it?*

Rain hisses outside. I guess I picked the right time to do laundry. I head to the laundry room to transfer the first batch of clothes to the dryer, and I start up the second batch in the washing machine. Afterward, I raid the fridge for some leftover Chinese and half a sub. I always get so damn hungry after playing b-ball.

As I'm nuking a plate of lo mein noodles, my phone goes off in the bedroom. I hustle to grab it just in time. Checking the lit-up screen, I exhale. *Uncle Adam.* "Yo, Unc."

"Kevin, is this a good time to call?" he asks in a concerned tone.

The microwave beeps, and I make my way back to the kitchen. "Yeah, man. What's up?"

"Your mother's birthday is coming up in a month."

My throat tightens. "Yeah."

"I want to do something special for her fiftieth. Surprise her, you know?"

"What did you have in mind?"

"Well, I've been talking to her on and off about it all year. Seeing what she might like. You know what she said? 'I just want to see my babies again. I just want my family back.'"

I clench my jaw.

"It would mean the world to her if the three of you came home for her birthday," he continues. "Can you do that? For her?"

Sure—*I* don't have a problem seeing her. But Dom still does. And Michael . . . I don't even want to be in the same room with that son of a bitch. "I dunno, Unc."

"That's why I called now, so you have plenty of time to think about it. I'm going to call Dominick and Michael Jr. and let them know, too."

"Wait. Let me talk to Dom."

"You sure?"

"Yeah, man. He still gets upset about all that shit."

Uncle Adam sighs. "Yeah, I bet he does. I'm sorry, I just—I wanted to do something special for your mother, you know? She deserves this more than anything."

My blood boils the more I think about Mama's pain. I lean against the kitchen counter and stare down at the floor. "Yeah, I know. But this isn't gonna be easy, getting the three of us back like that."

"I know. And I know how you feel about Michael."

I exhale through my nose. Just the mention of his name strikes a bad chord with me. "That fucking coward should've joined Pops," I mutter through clenched teeth.

"Kevin! Jesus Christ, don't say that. He's your brother."

"No, Unc. A real brother wouldn't have run out on his family like that."

"Look. I know how you feel about him, but you can't change the past. You need to forgive him at some point." I can sense the frustration in his voice.

"Forgive him? *Forgive him*?" I push off from the counter. "I'll never forgive that coward!"

"Kevin . . . "

"Can *you* forgive *your* brother for what he did to your own damn *nephew*?" I yell into the phone.

"That's different, Kevin—"

"Tell me how the fuck it's different!"

"What my brother did to Dominick—and to you—was *absolutely* unforgivable. But to compare *that* to Michael Jr. running out on the family? I don't think so. I agree that Michael Jr. shouldn't have abandoned you all. But when faced with shit, we all deal differently. You don't know his story or his motives, Kevin. None of us do. Stop looking at this through a child's eyes, and see it now for what it is."

Maybe he has a point, but I'm too damn pissed to think straight. I yank the plate from the microwave and set it firmly on the table next to my wrapped-up sub. "Look, Unc, I dunno if Mama will get her wish. I'll be there, and I'll try to get Dom there, too, but that's all I can do. If she can't be happy with two out of three, well, she's SOL."

"Right. Well, I'll talk to Michael myself, then."

"Whatever, man." I slide into my chair and hover over my food. My stomach growls, but I don't even want to eat anymore.

"Kevin," Unc says a little more calmly. "You're a good kid. And I love you."

I close my eyes, holding back my tears. "Love you too, Unc," I say with a choked-up voice.

"I'm trying to do what I can to mend things with our family. Bear with me, okay?"

"Trust me, you've done more than that piece-of-shit brother of yours ever did."

He sighs.

"Hey, Unc—thanks for taking care of Mama. I mean it."

"You're welcome. She deserves to be happy, fifty and beyond. That's why I think we should—"

"Yeah," I say.

"All right. I'll let you go. Keep me posted, okay?"

"I will, Unc."

The phone beeps as he ends the call, but I keep holding it to my ear as I stare idly at the plate of cooled lo mein.

I spend the rest of the rainy afternoon sprawled out on the floor in a T-shirt and boxers, sorting through the massive collection of vinyls stored on my shelves and in crates. I'm choosing songs I plan on mixing for tomorrow night's gig. Most of the college students headed out of town for the summer break, so business in the clubs and bars around town has slowed down. It's been almost a week since summer vacation officially started, and my gigs have been cut from three nights a week down to one or sometimes none at all. I don't sweat it too much, though. Sometimes I get called to radio stations, or I get gigs out of town. Either way, I've built enough of a nest egg to hold me over for several months when work's scarce.

A motorcycle rumbles outside, and I look up from my vinyl stack. *Dom?* I spring up.

Peering through the blinds of my window, I spot my brother's red sport bike parked outside. There's a knock at the door. I slip on a pair of basketball shorts from the clean laundry pile and make my way to the door. Flinging it open,

I grin at my brother, who's dressed from head to toe in a soaked black rain suit. He carries his red, full-face helmet under one arm.

"What's up, man?" I say. We do our secret handshake.

"Hey." Dom wipes his feet then trudges inside.

Oh yeah, it's Wednesday. I roll my eyes. "Nuh-uh. Don't come in here with your 'girl problems' shit. I warned you before about that. And why the hell are you riding in the rain? You know how dangerous that is?"

Dom frowns at me then turns and unbuttons his rain-suit top. "I got caught in it when I left work. Jesus Christ, Kev. This is Seattle. I know how to ride in the rain."

I watch as rainwater drips from his suit. "Damn it, go hang that shit up in the bathroom or something."

He rolls his eyes and disappears into the bathroom.

I return to my room. "So am I gonna expect to see you hanging out here every night for the next two weeks?" I call as I sprawl back on the floor and resume sorting through the albums.

"Maybe." It sounds like he's in the kitchen now. "Got a problem with that?"

"Yup." I hear the sound of a can opening at my doorway, and I glance over my shoulder.

"Too bad," Dom says. He's out of his rain suit and wearing his blue, button-down mechanic work shirt and jeans.

I smirk. "Let me guess: roommate's girlfriend is spending the night again?"

He frowns then takes a gulp of beer. "Yeah, and they're always loud as hell."

"Damn, sucks to be you." I chuckle and sift through more albums.

"I miss Denise already."

"Hey," I warn.

He sighs and sits down in a spot next to the laundry pile on the bed. "You got a gig tonight?"

"Tomorrow. At Rayne. You coming?"

"Maybe." He takes another sip. "Denise told me that Trinity told her she has a date with DJ Kevitron tomorrow. That true?"

I want to smile, but it's difficult. "Yeah, something like that. Gonna meet her for lunch. Check her out, y'know?"

"That's cool, man. I was wondering when you were going to call her. I thought you threw her number away or something."

"Nope." I pull an album from the shelf and place it in a milk crate.

"That's good, bro. I'm glad you decided to give her a chance."

"Ehh . . . "

"What does *that* mean?"

"I'm just Kevitron to her. I don't think she wants to get to know the guy behind the deejay."

"Don't say that, man. Give her a chance." He finishes his beer.

"I will. Just one more chance because she's hot." I smile at that. Dom laughs.

The crate full, I slide it next to my mixer and turntable cases then get up. "I'm kinda glad you're here anyway, li'l bro." I approach the bed, grab the giant pile of clean laundry, and toss the heap on the floor. I sprawl out on the bed next to Dom, my back resting against the wall. Rubbing my hand over my face, I go over Uncle Adam's call in my mind. "We need to talk."

"What's going on?" Dom asks.

"Uncle Adam called earlier. Mama's birthday is coming up."

He swallows. "Yeah, so?"

"It's the big five-o. Uncle Adam wants us there. *All* of us. It's all she wants for her birthday."

Dom stares at his empty beer can and frowns. "I can't do that. I can't go back there."

"C'mon, man. It's been ten years."

"Yeah, and those ten years still hurt. I still hear Pops's voice in my head every now and then. I see that blue house. Just when I think it's over, I get reminded again."

"I know how hard it is, man. It's hard for me, too. But isn't it about time you faced those demons head-on? Look how far you've come after what happened with Denise. You handled your shit just fine. Mama really wants to see you."

"Did you see her lately?" Dom asks me.

"Yeah, last month. I stopped in to say hello. Uncle Adam was there, too."

"How are they doing?"

"Mama's good." I purposefully avoid mentioning her injury. Dom doesn't need anything else to worry about. "She seems better. Happier. Uncle Adam stops by every now and then to check up on her. He takes real good care of her."

"That's good to hear."

I harden my expression, preparing to guilt-trip him. "She wonders why you don't call her anymore. I think she misses you the most since you're the youngest and all."

"Fuck that. She probably still feels guilty. I don't need her bullshit. I don't need anyone's bullshit."

"She's not bullshitting you, Dom. She really does miss you. Mama and I talked for a while."

He raises his eyebrows. "About me? Seriously, Kev?" He springs off the bed, glaring at me. "Don't talk to her about me anymore. She needs to get over me—get over the damn past and move on with her life."

"And you need to do the same. She's still our mother, no matter what, and she wants to see you. She wants to see all of us. Now stop with this baby shit, and see things for what they are."

"Fuck this. I'm going back to my place." He leaves the room.

I slip off the bed and rush to the front door, blocking it. Dom comes out of the bathroom, his rain suit draped over one arm.

I fold my arms over my chest. "You're not leaving, li'l bro."

He narrows his eyes. "Get out of my way."

"I'm going by Mama's house this weekend. Are you gonna come with me?"

"What? Hell no, I'm not going!"

"Then I'm not moving."

"Fine. I'll go out through the back." Dom spins on his heels and heads toward the kitchen. I barrel past him, nearly knocking him down, and then stand guard in front of the kitchen door.

"Get the fuck out the way, Kevin!" Dom yells.

"Nope." I stay rigid.

Gritting his teeth, Dom slams his rain suit down and grabs my arms, attempting to pull me away. He's strong, but I manage to stand firm. I sense those demons riling him.

"Move, damn it! *Move!*" His eyes are getting glassy.

"Stop fighting me, man," I say calmly. "This little temper tantrum you're pulling is making you look like a pussy."

"Fuck you!"

"Do I need to get Denise on the phone?"

"Leave her out of this!" The dam breaks, and his fist comes at my face wildly.

I dodge and grab his arm, then spin him around until his back is against me. I hate having to do this. It makes me feel like a jerk to have him in such a vulnerable position.

"Stop!" Dom cries.

"I will stop once you stop fighting me," I say. "Listen to reason, man."

"Fuck you. Fuck you!" He struggles in my grasp.

I hold his arm up behind him in an armlock. For now, I'm only inflicting pain—and lots of it. But if I raise it up a few inches more, his shoulder will come out of its socket. Michael taught me this move when we were kids. I was his guinea pig whenever he needed a partner to practice his self-defense moves on.

I didn't think I'd actually be using that same move on Dom, but he's given me no choice.

Dom yells in pain, but he stops struggling, at least.

Well, damn. That move actually works.

"Are you done?" I say, keeping my grip firm.

Dom doesn't reply and exhales hard through his nose. I feel his body relax.

I release him. "Seriously, man. This is not healthy. And I damn sure hope you're not this angry around Denise." *He better not be, for his sake.*

"Denise is the only thing keeping me sane right now. I don't need anything else."

"Listen to yourself, man. This is a sickness. You *need* to see Mama."

He doesn't answer.

Time for plan B. "Okay, fine. How about a drink, then? Chauncey's. I'll even be Miss Dee Dee."

Dom's scowl lifts. "A drink?"

"Yup." I have an idea for another way to persuade him to go see Mama this weekend. But the plan will require a little luck. And lots and lots of alcohol.

"Fine. When do you wanna go?"

"Now." It's not even eight yet, but I don't care. We'll drink early because I've got a lot to say.

Chapter 5

At eight o'clock, Chauncey's Bar is busy with local patrons and a few college students who didn't leave for the summer break. Usually when I go out, I dress incognito to keep the fans away, but with the majority of my fans being college-aged kids, I don't have to worry so much about that now.

Dom and I take a seat at our usual places at the end of the bar, and Olivia, the cute bartender we know all too well, comes over. She's cool to be around but not really the type of girl I'm attracted to.

"Hey, you two," she says, wiping off the bar top. "The usual?"

"Yup," I say. "I'm driving, so go light on me, eh?"

"You got it." She winks, turns on her long, thin legs, and goes to the liquor shelf.

Dom sits with his folded arms resting on the bar, gazing off into space. He's been quiet since we left my place. I know he's probably still mad, but I don't care.

Olivia passes Dom a rum 'n Coke and pours me three shots of vodka. It's way below my limit, but I need to be sober enough to drive.

I down my first shot in a single gulp then wince, feeling the burning, hard liquor ease down my throat. "Okay, so here's the deal, li'l bro. Basketball tryouts at UDub start next week, and I've decided to go."

Dom puts his glass to his lips, looks over at me, and then lowers it. "You serious?"

"Yup." I nod then tip back my second shot. It doesn't burn my throat as bad this time.

"Holy shit, Kev. That's great! It's about time. Wait. That means you're gonna have to—"

"—enroll for fall classes," I say, finishing my brother's thought. "I'm hoping Coach Langley will let me back on the team. We'll see."

"Man! If he doesn't take you back, he's an idiot! You were the Huskies' all-star player!"

I run my finger around the brim of one of the empty shot glasses. "Well, if I don't make the team, I won't sweat it."

"Oh, c'mon, Kev. Aside from the deejaying, basketball is practically your life." Dom stares into his glass. "I know you still regret giving up your scholarship."

I glare at him. "I don't regret shit. You were way more important to me than some stupid scholarship."

"But still, that was a full ride. A once-in-a-lifetime opportunity. I appreciate what you did, but I never wanted you to give up your dreams for me, man."

"I was not about to leave you in that house with Mama and all that guilt—or whatever it was—built up between you two."

Dom nods absentmindedly and gulps his drink. He taps his finger on the counter, signaling Olivia to fill him another.

"Enough time has passed," I say. "The ball's in your court now, li'l bro. It's up to you to clear up this shit with Mama. She loves you, Dom. What happened wasn't her fault, but she's still blaming herself. You forget that she was a victim, too. We all were. You can't change the past, but you can stop it from fucking with your future. That's why you gotta forgive her, man. Go see her. Talk it out."

Dom chugs drink number two. "I can't go back there, man."

I spin the filled glass of my third and final shot. "You can and you will. Know why? Because if you don't, I'll forget about playing ball and going back to school." It's an empty threat, because I really *do* want to go back and play, so I damn sure hope Dom doesn't spot my bullshit. I just want him to reconsider his choice.

"Whatever, man. That's stupid."

"As stupid as you not forgiving Mama after all these years?" I swallow a lump in my throat at the irony, recalling my earlier phone conversation with Uncle Adam.

Looking exasperated, he rubs his hand across his buzz cut as Olivia sets down drink number three for him. That reminds me, I need to get a haircut soon. "No, stupid for thinking I'd believe you were being serious, dumbass."

I down the final shot. *Damn it. How do I make him understand?*

"This is your future we're talking about here," Dom explains. "You're not gonna give all that up on account of my stubbornness."

I smirk. "Yeah, you *are* a stubborn ass."

He tries to fight down a smile. "Seriously, Kev. You're the one that's being stubborn if you give all this up again because of me."

"So you won't agree to go to Mama's with me this weekend?"

He doesn't answer right away and drinks some more, albeit more slowly. I'm hoping the buzz has hit him already. Usually, three is his limit. When it comes to drinking, he's lighter than a featherweight.

"Not even as a favor to your brother?" I say, watching him wrestle with his thoughts.

"I guess I do owe you."

I raise my eyebrows. "More than you fucking know."

His mouth opens then closes. He hangs his head, closes his eyes, and sighs. "Fine, Kev. Fine. I'll go," he murmurs.

I do a silent victory shout in my head. "Great. I'll come by your place Friday night when you get off work. You better be ready."

"I told you I'd go! Geez!" Dom chugs the rest of his drink and orders another. *Sweet Jesus*—he's going to be wasted early.

My chest feels a little lighter. *Thank you, God.* Just the two of us will be visiting this weekend, but I'm wondering how things will go down for Mama's birthday if Michael comes.

Michael.

My heart drops to my stomach, and I grit my teeth, the urge to thrash my older brother rising. I realize I'll have to face him at some point. *I can handle this shit.* If Dom can face his demons, then so can I, and *damn it*, it'll be a fucking breeze.

Dom is conked out in the passenger's seat by the time we return to my place. I try waking his ass up, but he's down for the count. I unbuckle his seatbelt, pull him out of the car, and heft him over my shoulder in a fireman's carry. Compared to me, he weighs next to nothing, but then again, he's not built like I am.

I unlock the front door, kick it open, and flip on the living-room lights. I lay my brother down on the couch, take off his shoes, and stick a pillow beneath his head. He's going to have one hell of a hangover tomorrow. I turn off the lights and go to my room.

Setting my phone on the desk, I notice the green notification light blinking. Three missed calls—two from Uncle Adam, one from Trinity. I smile at Trinity's name, but decide to call Unc first.

"Hello?" It's strange that he sounds exhausted at only ten at night. He's usually a night owl.

"Hey, Unc." I climb on the bed and kick off my shoes.

"Kevin!" His voice perks up. "How're you doing, son?"

"Good, man. Had a long talk with Dom earlier. We're gonna come down there this weekend."

"Really? That's great! Your mother will be very happy."

"Yeah, I figured if she wants Dom to come for her birthday, then he needs to clear up the shit with her now."

"That's a good idea."

I lie back in bed and stare up at the ceiling. "You called earlier?"

"Yeah. I wanted to let you know that I spoke to Michael today."

I clench my jaw at the name.

"He's down in Miami right now," Unc continues when I don't reply.

"Funny, he called me from New York a couple months ago."

"Yeah, and he was in Chicago just last week."

Still running. "So he's not coming, I take it?" I force out a halfhearted chuckle. "It figures. That coward's gonna stay as far away from us as possible. Good fucking riddance."

"Kevin." Unc's tone sharpens. "You didn't let me finish. He's been fighting."

I arch an eyebrow. "Fighting?"

"Yeah, fighting for money, it sounds like."

"Holy shit." I sit up in bed. "Like that illegal underground kind of fighting?"

"I don't know the details, Kevin. But apparently he's been doing this for a while. I had no idea."

"Did he tell you?"

"No. Your cousin Xavier said he saw a raw video of Michael fighting on a website. 'Extreme Blood and Bone Fighting,' the caption said."

"Damn, what the hell kind of website is that?"

"Some sort of gambling one, it sounds like. People bet on matches."

My mouth opens, but I'm speechless. Michael was big on the weight training and martial arts when he was younger, but fighting for money doesn't seem like something he'd be into. I mean, he was a coward. How the hell could he be fighting now? "Why are you telling me this, Unc?"

"Because you have a right to know. He's your brother. I'm worried that he's gone off the deep end and won't turn back."

"Well, not like you or I can do anything about it. He's a man. That's his own choice."

"But it's not the right choice."

"You may not know the whole story, Unc." I purse my lips. I can't believe I'm defending that bastard.

He sighs. "I don't want to hear about him on the news one day. I don't want to find out he's in jail or dead—I don't need that. You and Dominick don't need that. And your mother *definitely* doesn't need that."

"So what are you gonna do? Go to Miami and kidnap him?"

"No. I'm not going anywhere. He needs to make his own decisions. But I'm hoping if we talk to him, perhaps he might be convinced to get out of that life."

I blink. "Wait, who's 'we'?"

"Kevin, I—"

"Were you were expecting *me* to talk to him? Are you shitting me, Unc?" I give an empty laugh. I can't believe the poison that's dripping through the earpiece. I'm so ready to destroy this phone.

"Damn it, Kevin! Will you just listen?"

"No, *you* listen!" I growl. "Michael's become just like his father. A coward and a punk. And I will *not* waste my breath on that piece of shit! Michael's *your* problem, so *you* deal with it!"

"Jesus, Kevin, please! Just lis—"

I end the call and toss the phone aside. I sit on the edge of the bed and rub my hands over my face. *Fuck him. Fuck it all.* And just like that, memories of *that night* flood my mind.

I'm fourteen. I run out my room as I hear Dom screaming. I discover Pops in the breakfast nook, on his knees with his pants down, having his way with my baby brother. Screaming in a rage, I run at Pops and try to pry him off Dom, but Pops is too strong.

He seizes me by the neck, cutting off my windpipe. I can't breathe. I fight back as hard as I can, and then he grabs a box cutter from one of the kitchen drawers. He swings that box-cutter at me like a madman. Cuts me deep.

I smell blood. This is it. I'm going to die right here. And I can't save my brother.

Pops flings me against the wall, and I feel a sharp pain in the back of my head. I suddenly black out.

It's dark.

I'm alone.

I'm dead.

Death is scary.

But then I wake up in a hospital bed.

I gasp and lift my hands from my face. My palms are wet from tears.

Chapter 6

I DON'T KNOW HOW I WAS ABLE TO SLEEP LAST NIGHT, MUCH less sleep in till eleven the next morning. I must've cried myself to sleep. I hate crying. I did enough of that as a kid.

I slide out of bed and drag myself to the bathroom to take a piss. Then I drench my face in cold water to wash away the dry, crusted remnants of tears. I suddenly realize that Dom's rain suit is gone. Leaving the bathroom, I head to the living room. Dom's gone. The pillow I'd given him is still on the couch. I peer out the window and notice his bike is gone, too.

Well, damn. He didn't even say goodbye. Not that I give a shit.

I head to the kitchen and swing open the fridge. I always crave milk in the morning. I grab the carton, only to discover it's empty. I'm pretty certain it was half-full last night, because I *never* keep an empty carton of milk in the fridge.

And neither does Dom. Damn our habits.

"Son of a—*Dom!*" I growl, tossing the carton in the garbage. I can't be too mad at him because he's coming with me to Mama's. But after last night's call with Uncle Adam, I suddenly don't want to go. I don't want to hear Unc scolding me all weekend.

I end up making toast, two hard-boiled eggs, and a protein shake. I'm nowhere near the chef Dom is. The only time I ever touch a stove is to make something that involves boiling water, because that's all I really know how to do.

I sprawl out on my bed and check my phone. Dom left a text around nine this morning.

Yo, felt sober enough 2 ride, so headed home. Thx 4 letting me crash @ ur place.

I text him back, trying to fight down a smile:

u drank all my milk, punk!

To my surprise, he texts back moments later:

So go drag ur lazy ass 2 the store and get some more, bitch!

I let out a small chuckle, and I don't reply. Instead, I search my Missed Calls list for Trinity's name. I owe her a call.

She picks up on the third ring. "Hello?"

I lie back in bed and close my eyes, enjoying the sound of her voice. "Hey, it's Kevin. What's up?"

"Kevin?" She pauses, mumbles something under her breath, then says, "Oh . . . oh! Kevitron!"

I open my eyes and frown. "It's Kevin. Kevitron's just a stage name."

"Sorry."

"I saw you called yesterday. Sorry for not getting back to you till now. I had to do some stuff with Dom."

"That's okay."

"Are we still on for lunch?" I ask.

"Yeah. I called to, um, see if you were still up for lunch, too."

By the way she says that, I have a feeling lunch wasn't the only thing she wanted to call about. "Yeah, I wouldn't miss it for nothing. Something else on your mind?"

"No, not really." She pauses. "Did anyone ever tell you that you have the perfect radio voice?"

I blink. That came way out of left field. I laugh out loud. "No, but I'm not surprised that I do. Do you like my voice?"

"I *love* your voice."

The way she says that in such a playful tone makes my body tingle all over. I fantasize about having my hands on that voluptuous body while she talks to me in that sexy voice. "I love your voice, too," I mutter, almost groaning from the tightness in my pants.

She giggles cutely. "Let's talk more at lunch today."

"Yeah . . ." I definitely need to get off this phone fast and take care of the ever-hardening issue in my pants.

"I can't wait to meet you, Kevitron!"

I clench my jaw as my arousal shrinks a little. "Kevin."

"I'm sorry. Kevin."

"Better. See you in two hours."

I pull up to the tiny hole-in-the-wall cafe that lies just over the Bay, west of the UDub campus. Al's Grill has some amazing ribs and barbecue sandwiches. Back in the day, when I was going to UDub, I used to come here for lunch. I was there so often that the employees treated me as if I were part of the family. These days, I'm not usually in the area of the university, so I don't come to Al's quite as often. Today, however, I am here on a date. And seeing the sign to Al's Grill makes me crave ribs. Lots and lots of ribs.

Getting out my car, I adjust my baseball cap and look around for Trinity, but she's nowhere to be found. I check the time on my phone. It's 1:04. When I raise my head, I notice a bus slowing to a stop farther down the road. A few people get off, and finally, I see her. She walks across the street wearing a black-and-purple shirt, dark denim jeans, and black-heeled sandals. As she closes the distance, I notice that her hair's styled differently than the last time I saw her in the club. It's long and wavy, down to her shoulders. It's the perfect style for her. I admire every inch of her gorgeous, full figure. Her jeans are tight around those amazing thick thighs.

"Kevitron!"

She sounds like she's only a few feet away, but my attention has zeroed in on her shirt and the way it stretches around that huge rack of hers. I can tell she's wearing a bra, but the peaks of her nipples are still visible through the shirt.

Damn, she's perky for a big girl. What I wouldn't give to have one of those nipples in my mouth.

"Kevitron? Are you okay?"

I tense. I'm hard right now, and I definitely don't want it to be obvious out here in public. I think of something else. *Anything.* Michael. My arousal quickly subsides, and a hint of rage bubbles inside me. At least that bastard is useful for something.

I blink once and look up at her face. "Hey. It's Kevin, remember?"

She smiles sheepishly. *Damn,* I love that smile. I'm going to do whatever I can to make her smile more. "Sorry—I'm nervous. I still can't believe I'm here. With you."

Really? Does she idolize me that much? I'm a nobody. Unfortunately, after today, I might have to break it off with this otherwise awesome girl if she can't get past her "Kevitron" thing. "It's okay," I say, opening the entrance door for her. "C'mon, let's go inside."

The place isn't busy. Rachel and Pete—Al's mother and son—greet me. I spot two people I don't recognize in the back of the restaurant. They're probably high-school or college kids working for the summer.

"Long time no see, Kevin," Rachel says, smiling.

I laugh. "It's not even been a month."

"Still, it always feels like something's missing without you here. We don't see you come around as often as you used to."

"Yeah, I know. I miss the ribs."

"Well, you're in luck, man!" Pete pipes up, stepping from behind the counter. "Thursday is all-you-can-eat ribs from twelve to three."

"Holy—!" I bite my tongue, taking care not to curse in front of Rachel. She's one of those old-school, hardcore, religious grandma-types who would scold me badly if I ever cursed—no matter if I'm an adult and here with a date. "When did you start doing all-you-can-eat ribs?"

"Last week. It's a new thing we're trying, to bring in more business," Pete explains.

"Oh, you'll definitely be booming now," I say. I see that Trinity is busy checking out the overhead menu. "You hungry for some ribs?"

She taps her chin. "Mmm. I think I'll just do the pulled-pork platter. Mac 'n cheese and baked beans for sides. And water to drink, please."

Pete scribbles on a pad of paper. "You got it, babe."

"Okay, more ribs for me, then," I say. "Load 'em up, Pete! And an extra-large lemonade."

Pete gives me a thumbs-up and returns to his spot behind the counter. Trinity and I find a place to sit, at a tiny table for two, and I pull out the chair for her.

Settling across from her, I stare, drinking up every bit of her, in case today really does turn out to be the last day we see each other.

She returns the gaze, batting her cute eyelashes and trying hard to hide her smile.

"Don't fight that beautiful smile, Trinity," I say softly.

Her eyes brighten, and I notice the smooth, mocha skin of her face turn a slight shade of red.

This girl seems amazing, but I just can't see the relationship working out. Not if she only sees me as Kevitron.

Our food arrives, and I put my thoughts on hold while I feed my growling stomach. I tear into the plate of three huge pork ribs as if I haven't eaten in weeks. Trinity steadily nibbles on her sandwich, being as neat as she can with it since the pulled pork is drenched in barbecue sauce. I like the way she eats—not dainty, but neat.

I finish my first plate in record time and signal Pete for round two. Within minutes, another plate is set in front of me, and I can't chow down any faster.

Trinity eyes my second helping and raises her eyebrows. "Wow! With an appetite like that, I'm surprised you're not as big as me." She laughs.

She jokes about her weight. Maybe it means she's not self-conscious about it. That's always a good sign, right? "I work out a lot, so my appetite is always through the roof," I say between bites. "Besides, I prefer you to be the big one." *Shit, I think that came out wrong.*

She scrunches her face. "What does that mean?"

I reluctantly set down my half-eaten rib and wipe my mouth and hands with a napkin. "It means . . . " I shift in my chair. I can't believe I'm revealing my kinks to this girl on the first date—if you'd even *call* this a date. "Ah," I mutter quietly. "I like big, beautiful girls. Like you." I look up to her. "*Especially* like you."

She bites her bottom lip, and that blush on her cheeks returns. "Seriously, Kevin?"

Wow, did she just call me "Kevin"? I nod and resume eating. The current subject of this conversation is getting all sorts of embarrassing right now.

"So you don't want me going on a diet?"

I stop eating again and blink at her. Did she really just ask that? *Hell no, I don't want you going on a diet!* "Whether I do or not doesn't matter. That's up to you. I mean, it's your body." *And a smoking-hot body, at that.*

"I want to know what Kevin thinks."

No, my ears are not deceiving me. She most definitely called me 'Kevin.' Maybe today won't be the last day after all. "Kevin thinks you're gorgeous. Sexy. And you don't seem self-conscious about your weight. Automatic turn-on."

Trinity covers her mouth and snickers. "Wow. Just, wow."

"I want to get to know you more, because you also seem like an intelligent girl beneath all that beauty." I finish my sixth rib and signal to Pete for round three. How I'm not full right now is beyond me.

She beams. "Thank you. This is so weird for me to say this, Kevin, but you're the first guy I've been with who doesn't have a problem with my weight." Trinity tucks a lock of hair behind her ear. She picks up her fork and begins eating her mac 'n cheese.

"Oh yeah?" Pete sets new rib plate in front of me. "Well those other guys suck, then."

"Yeah, they all wanted me to go on a diet, saying I was cute and all, but too fat. They seemed to only care about my body and not much else." She says this matter-of-factly. No emotions, no sadness. Nothing. It's as if she's immune to the insults. How many guys have treated her that way?

"First of all," I say, "you're definitely *not* too fat. And second, I like intelligence and personality in a woman. You seem smart, and you make me laugh and smile."

She grins. "Thank you."

"And I do care about your body, too. I care that you're happy with it."

"Honestly, I feel good the way I am. I try to maintain my weight and not overdo things. But I also don't want to be a stick with boobs like some of these guys seem to want."

It's my turn to laugh. "I don't want you to be a stick with boobs, either. I love your boobs, by the way."

"Oh my God, Kevin!" She blushes, looks around nervously, and giggles.

I love the way she says my name. I bet I can make her say my name more while I suck her tits and give her ass a good massage.

"Anyway," she says, snapping me out of my fantasy, "I appreciate your honesty. It really means a lot when someone can appreciate you for who you are and not who they want you to be."

I furrow my brow at the irony of that statement. "Oh? So, who do you think I am?"

She tilts her head. "I don't know who I *think* you are, but I *know* you are a deejay. The greatest deejay in Seattle. And a deejay who apparently likes ribs and big girls. Oh, and you play basketball, which I think is hot."

I smirk. I forgot Dom had told her about that a while back.

"What else do you do?" she asks.

"Aside from hanging out having lunch with sexy girls like you? Not much of anything. My life pretty much revolves around music and basketball these days."

"That's cool." She finishes her mac 'n cheese and starts on the beans.

I work on my last, and final, rib on the plate. I take a breath and feel the button of my jeans press against my gut. *Tight.* Wow, yeah, okay. So, I probably overdid it just a little.

"I'd love to watch you play basketball. Where do you play?" she asks.

"Here, there. Wherever I can get in on some pickup games."

"You go to college?"

"Nope." I pause. "Not currently, I should say. Had to take a couple of years off. I'm planning on enrolling for fall classes, though. I might try and get my spot back on the Huskies, too." I drop the bone onto the platter then sit back in my chair. Okay, so I *definitely* overdid it. But damn, was it good!

"Dominick once told me you were a legend at UDub," she says. "That's amazing! I wish I could've seen you."

"I was all right." I swill the rest of my lemonade. "How about you? Are you still in college?"

She nods. "Yeah, I'll be finishing my senior year next spring. Can't believe it's almost over."

"That's cool, Trinity. What's your major?"

"Education. After college, I want to work somewhere that helps pregnant teens."

"Wow, that's pretty deep. Any reason why you want to do that?"

Her smile falters a little. "I just feel like there's not enough being done to help young teen girls make better choices."

I nod. She looks like she wants to say more, but she doesn't, and I don't ask further.

Pete comes to the table with the bill. I slap money into his hand and tell him to keep the change. I give such crazy-ass tips here. He leaves us, beaming wide.

"Well, I'm a business major, but I don't know what I wanna do after college yet," I say. "I'm still kinda liking the deejay scene, though."

She stares, wide-eyed. "You're really going to deejay for the rest of your life?"

"Why not? I'll keep going for as long as my hands can keep spinning records. Music is something that'll never go away, and I'll never get tired of it." I grunt as I push myself out of the chair and stand up. *Holy shit.* I ate way too much. Why does it always feel worse when you stand? "Wanna go for a walk?"

"Okay." Trinity stands, and after waving goodbye to Pete and Rachel and swiping a toothpick from the front counter, I lead us outside.

The sky is overcast, but it doesn't look like rain—yet.

"Why don't you like being called Kevitron, anyway?" she asks as we start walking.

I adjust my ball cap. "Because only strangers call me that."

"So, I'm not a stranger to you?"

"You come to almost every one of my gigs. I'd say you're definitely not a stranger."

"I'm sorry if it bothers you that I call you Kevitron. I don't mean to do that. But I've known you as that name for so long."

"I know. It can be hard to break old habits. If you were a fan, I wouldn't care so much, but you seem like so much more than that."

Her eyebrows rise. "Oh? Then what am I?"

"A girl that I'd like to get to know a little more."

We walk around the block and talk some more about school, work, and life. College is a big thing for Trinity, because she'll be the first in her family to graduate. I need to get off my ass and get registered next week so I can graduate with her.

It's nearing four o'clock, and I need to head back home to get ready for tonight's gig.

"I have a gig tonight at Club Rayne," I say as we stand beside my car. "Would you like to—"

"I'd *love* to!" she answers in that sexy, playful voice.

My dick stiffens. *Geez*, the things this girl does to me with that voice alone. "Okay. Come around seven. I'll let you in backstage and give you a little tour or something."

"I'll be there."

I offer to drive Trinity back to her place, but she decides to take the bus instead. If she were a real fangirl, she would've jumped at the opportunity to get driven around by the "famous" DJ Kevitron. But her refusal makes me like her more and more.

I can't wait till tonight.

CHAPTER 7

I ARRIVE AT CLUB RAYNE AROUND SEVEN THAT NIGHT TO set up and do a sound check. The doors don't open until nine, which gives me plenty of time. My wireless headphones on, I start testing the mixers. The workers walk around, cleaning and getting the place ready. My phone vibrates in my pocket, and I lower the headphones around my neck. I pull out the phone and read the text.

Hey, I'm here.

I head backstage to the tiny multipurpose room, in which a single bulb hangs from the ceiling, barely providing enough light. There's an old couch against the wall and a card table with three metal folding chairs in the middle of the room. I push open the back door, and Trinity is there, all dressed up in a vicious purple hip-hugging dress with black fishnet stockings. The low neckline shows off just enough of her ample cleavage, and as before, the outline of her nipples is visible. *Holy shit*—she's definitely perky.

Her hair's done up this time, tied back in a bun with a few strands of her wavy hair grazing the sides of her lovely face. She wears makeup, but she really doesn't need to. Her skin is naturally smooth and unblemished.

I swallow and continue to ogle her, holding the door open.

She flashes an awesome, perfect smile that could brighten this fucking room better than any bulb. "Um . . . is it okay to come in?" she asks, fidgeting with her clutch purse.

I blink. *Oh, she's talking to me.* "Huh? Oh yeah, sorry." I move aside, keeping the door open for her. As I shut it, I admire her from behind. *My God, that ass.* Just the right size. Easy to grab. I envision my hands palming both of those cheeks. *Damn.* I want her.

She glances around the tiny room then turns to me. With her ass no longer in my sight, I focus on her face.

"Glad you came," I say, beaming.

"I can't believe I'm here right now. With you."

My smile lessens, and I narrow my eyes. "With who?"

She chuckles, tucking a lock of her stray hair behind her ear, then comes closer. "With Kevin. *Also known as* DJ Kev-itron." She presses her body against mine.

I'm sure she can feel my hardness right now, because I certainly can't hide it. "Listen. I'm Kevitron when I'm on the stage and Kevin when I'm not, okay? That's all you gotta re-member." I get a whiff of her scent—vanilla.

"Yeah, okay." She plays with the padded headphones around my neck.

I don't know why I find it so damn sexy. Hell, why am I even letting her touch my expensive-ass headphones? I will my hand to reach up and stop her, but it doesn't budge. My own body is betraying me.

"By the way, thanks for lunch today. I forgot to tell you that before."

"You're welcome." My eyes are glued to her purple-polished nails and the way she touches that equipment around my neck, and I think about those same hands touching the equipment in my pants.

"It fascinates me how you mix like that. I mean, you must have really good coordination."

"You gotta have good coordination in this job." I laugh.

"So, what do you listen to when you have these on?"

"I use them when I'm cuing up my next mix. I have to know what I'm playing first before I let the crowd hear it."

"Sounds like a lot of work."

"You learn to get used to it after a time."

"How long have you been at this?" she asks.

"Mmm . . . started when I was about thirteen after watching some videos. My uncle gave me his old turntable, and I bought a mixer from a yard sale. Figured out how to hook it all up to my parents' stereo system, and well, let's just say that it was an addiction after that."

"An addiction that turned you into a superstar." She beams.

"So it did. But beneath all the fame, I'm still Kevin."

"Yeah, I know." Her eyes glance down and then back up to my face.

I stare at her lips, wanting to taste them. I brush my hand across her cheek. She's warm. Her skin's so soft.

"Who do you prefer? Kevin, or the *other* guy?" I ask.

The corners of her mouth lift. "Is that a trick question?"

"Not really." My face hovers closer to hers.

"Why can't I have both?"

I smirk. "Because Kevin doesn't like to share."

"Then I don't have much of a choice, now, do I?"

"Damn right."

My lips part, and I lean in slowly to touch hers. I taste a hint of strawberries. She presses her lips to mine in a gentle kiss. She moans quietly and drops her purse on the floor. I let my hands explore her body, and she walks backward to the couch. I eagerly follow, not breaking the kiss. Hell, I have some time to spare. Besides, we're alone back here, and I don't usually have to worry about anyone bothering me before the show. She falls onto the cushions with a bounce, and I follow her. I kiss her face and down her neck, indulging on the warmth and softness of her body. I carefully set the headphones on the floor beside the couch, and my hands resume moving down her sides toward her amazing thighs. She slips off my baseball hat and runs her hands across my hair.

I kiss her cleavage and catch a whiff of more of that awesome vanilla scent. My mouth lingers there for a while.

She exhales and moans, and so do I.

"Kevin," she whispers.

I close my eyes. *God*, I love the way she calls my name. I let one hand travel between her thighs, groping that thick, soft skin. I hike the hem of her dress up a few inches.

Then, my phone chirps, breaking me from this fantasy. It sends me spiraling back into reality. "Shit."

She breathes raggedly. She's so horny right now. I can smell it. I can *feel* it. But in twenty minutes, the club's about to be packed.

"We'll finish this later," I whisper, peeling myself off her and standing. I take a few moments to work down my arousal. The damn phone made me get blue balls.

Trinity stands as well. She adjusts her dress, fixes her hair, and retrieves her purse. Then she pulls out a compact mirror and checks her makeup.

I wipe my hand across my mouth, hoping her lipstick hasn't gotten on me too much. She seems to notice my dilemma because she takes a tissue from her purse and approaches me with it, looking amused. "Here. Let me help you."

I stand still and let her wipe away the stray lipstick and makeup from my face and mouth. It's embarrassing and weird, but cute in its own way.

She holds up the little mirror. "How's that?"

Seeing that my face is clean once again, I nod. "Thanks." I retrieve the headphones and slip my ball cap on backwards. Then, I reach in my pocket and pull out a VIP ticket. "Show that to the bouncer out front. He'll let you in first, and you'll get free drinks."

She takes the ticket and beams. "Thanks!"

"No problem. Your friends here, too?"

"Just Alexis. Everyone else left for the summer."

I pull out another ticket. "Okay, give that one to her."

"Oh, wow! She's going to go crazy. She really loves you, Kevin."

I shake my head. "Naw, she loves Kevitron. She doesn't know Kevin. Not like you do."

Her face brightens. "Thank you, Kevin. You're amazing."

"I know." I laugh. "I'll call or text you when I get home, okay?"

The excitement on her face fades. "We can't talk after the show?"

"Can't. Sorry. I gotta go straight home after this and take care of some things."

"Oh. Okay." Her eyelids flutter downward, and she heads to the door.

Before she reaches the door handle, I spin her around and plant the longest, hardest, most passionate kiss on her lips, making sure she won't forget it. When I pull back, she smiles again, as I knew she would. She wipes the lipstick off me, this time with her thumb. It takes every ounce of my willpower to not suck on that digit.

Opening the door for her, I say, "See you soon."

Chapter 8

At seven the following evening, I pull up to the curb outside Dom's duplex and honk the horn. I'm feeling like utter shit, dreading going home right now. But a deal's a deal, and I hope this visit will give Dom closure with Mama. I've been on the phone all morning with Uncle Adam. I let him know what time we were coming today, and then we got into another argument.

I give the horn another long, firm honk when Dom doesn't come outside right away. *He'd better not be stalling in there.* I lift up the latch of the console and pull out a pack of gum. As I pop the minty stick in my mouth, Dom finally comes out the house, carrying a small duffel bag. He doesn't look too happy, but I don't give a fuck.

"'Sup, li'l bro," I say when he opens the door.

Dom settles into the passenger's seat and tosses the bag in the back next to mine. "Hey." He leans his head back into the headrest and reclines the seat a little. Then he closes his eyes.

"You ready for this?" I ask, watching him.

"Nope."

Smirking, I put the car in gear and crank up the music. "Too bad."

The thirty-minute drive to Renton seems like the longest drive ever. My throat tightens and I get butterflies in my stomach as we get closer. Then, as I snake through the quaint neighborhood, that little blue house surrounded by trees and azalea bushes comes into view near the bottom of the hill. I park behind Uncle Adam's SUV, in the driveway, and shut off the engine. Dom's eyes are still closed, and his head is lolling to one side.

I nudge my brother. "Wake your ass up."

He opens his eyes and glares at me. I stare right back at him. "Don't start with me, Dom. I'm not in the mood." I push open the driver-side door, grab my bag from the backseat, and slide out. The house's front door creaks open when I round the car, and Uncle Adam comes out and stands on the porch. He and I lock gazes. I'm the first to break the stare.

Dom doesn't open his door, so I yank it open for him. "Hurry up, man," I mutter.

Dom takes his sweet time getting out the car with his bag. He studies the house for several long moments then turns to me. "Hasn't changed much."

"Nope." I gesture for him to follow. As I walk up the front stoop, I stare through Uncle Adam's hard, but tired, expression. Without a word, he steps aside and lets me pass. I brush my shoulder against his and pass into the house. The smell of cooked beef overtakes my senses as I walk through the living room and set my bag on the couch.

"Hey, Uncle Adam," Dom says, and I turn around just in time to see the two of them hug.

"Dominick. You look great," Unc says.

"Thanks, you too. You still tinkering with old cars?"

Unc lets out a guffaw and slaps him on the back. "Hah! You know it."

Another sound greets me from the kitchen—the clanking of pots and pans. I smile and round the corner to see Mama—well, the back of her—at the stove. She's stirring something in a large pot. I creep up behind her and plant a kiss on her cheek. "Smells good, Mama."

She gasps and lets go of the wooden spoon, which hits the side of the pot. She widens her eyes at me. "Kevin? Oh, Kevin! Baby!" Her eyes brimming with tears, she gives me a big hug.

Closing my eyes, I wrap my arms around her in a warm embrace. She still smells like azaleas. "Guess what?" I whisper in her ear.

"Hmm?" She pulls back and looks at me.

I nod my head toward the living room, where Dom and Uncle Adam are standing. Dom's facing the breakfast nook, and I just know what he's thinking. I pull Mama out of the kitchen and to the living room.

She lets go of my hand. "Oh, Jesus. Oh, Jesus! Dominick!"

Unc steps back from Dom, who regards Mama impartially. I watch in silence.

Dom doesn't move. That expression of hurt becomes more and more evident. Even when she takes him up in her arms, he remains rigid. He doesn't show the least bit of affection in return. She kisses his cheeks, and he finally squirms to get away.

Tears of joy streak her face, and my eyes start to burn as well, just watching her. I wish Dom could see how much she loves him.

"Dominick, please, let's talk," Mama says.

Dominick's eyes flicker toward the breakfast nook again. Then he turns his head. "Damn it, I can't do this, Mama, I can't," he says through clenched teeth.

I pinch the bridge of my nose then step forward. "Let me talk to him first."

Mama purses her lips and nods. Uncle Adam moves closer to her and rubs her back comfortingly.

I hook my arm around my brother's shoulder and lead him away from the living room, toward his old room.

He stops at the doorway and exhales. I give him a light shove forward. He stumbles into the room, and I follow. I shut the door behind me and lean against it. I won't let him run anymore.

Dom just stands there, staring at his desk, which is still covered with motorcycle magazines, just as it was last time I was here. I grab the back of his shoulders and turn him to his bed. "Sit."

He does so and looks at me—or rather, *through* me.

I clench my fists. "Dom, you need to move on from this shit. You can't let it keep getting to you. Just remember, the more it bothers you, the more it satisfies Pops. You want that? You want him to win? Because he will if you don't cut this shit out now and talk to Mama."

Dom bites his bottom lip. His eyes glaze over. "This was a bad idea, Kev. I can't do this. I'm not ready to do this."

"You can do it, and you are ready. You hear me? I didn't drag your sorry ass all the way here just for you to give up on me now. I didn't give up on *you* that night."

He examines the carpet. "You never gave up on me. I feel like such an ass, making you give up half your life to take care of me."

"Look, we're not going through this again. You didn't *make me* do shit. It was my choice." I tighten my fists. I want to punch something. Maybe knock some sense into Dom's thick skull.

Dom buries his face in his hands. "I'm fucked up, Kev. I'm really fucked up."

"No, but you're a coward if you let this get to you." I open my hands and give him a firm slap in the back of his head. He lurches forward with a start. "You're gonna go out there and talk to Mama. I don't care how or where, but you're gonna do it. Right now. She loves you, man. How many times do I have to say it?"

Glaring, he rubs the back of his head and swiftly stands, confronting me. I puff out my chest and stare him down, daring him to take a swing at me.

Finally, he breaks away and marches out of the room, slamming the door behind him. I hear his and Mama's voices beyond, and I sigh.

As I leave Dom's room, I consider going to the kitchen to get some grub but decide against it. Mama and Dom are talking in there—in the breakfast nook, no less. So I go to my room.

I lie in my bed, listening to the muffled sounds of their voices, but have no idea what they are talking about. Suddenly, there's a knock at the door.

"Yeah?"

"Kevin, it's me."

I hiss and roll over onto my stomach. "Not in the mood, Unc."

I hear the door open anyway and look over my shoulder. Unc shuts the door behind him and stands there.

"Are you deaf?" I say.

"No, but *you* seem to be." He folds his burly arms over his chest.

"I don't wanna talk about it."

"How fair is it for Dominick to be forced to face his demons, but you don't, hm?"

"Get the fuck out my room."

Unc stays put. "I'm not going anywhere until we talk. We *will* put this behind us somehow."

"Not where Michael's involved."

"Jesus, Kevin! Listen to yourself. You're so blinded by this *rage* that you won't listen to reason."

I sit up in bed. "I see no *reason* to talk about this. Michael made his choice, and I made mine."

He rubs his hand over his face. "Kevin. You *need* to talk to Michael. You've been the most stable of your brothers. Dominick listens to you. And I'm sure—no, certain—Michael will, too, if you gave him a chance."

"And what the hell am I supposed to say to him, huh? I haven't talked to him in, what? Ten years?"

"Yes, about that long. Don't you think enough time has passed now? He is part of this family whether you like it or not."

I scowl. Why am I the "stable" one? "He's fighting in that illegal underground shit. He's not gonna listen to me. He'll just keep on doing what he's doing now."

"Yes, I agree that he's strayed off that good path, but he's certainly not forgotten about you. You are the first person he asks about whenever he calls."

I feel a small twist in my gut as I think about all the times he's called me and I ignored it. Sitting at the edge of the bed, my elbows resting on my knees, I keep my eyes on the floor as I wrestle with my thoughts. I guess I could try. Worst-case scenario, he tells me to go fuck off.

Unc walks to me and takes his cellphone out of his pocket. "Need his number?"

I shake my head. "Naw, I got it."

"Okay." He pats me on the shoulder then heads back to the door. "I'm going to go check on those two."

I bite my bottom lip. Unc's right, I guess. It's selfish of me to drag Dom out here, and I've got issues of my own to deal with. I keep running like a scared bitch. *Well, no more.* "Hey, Unc," I say as he opens the door.

"Mmm?"

I run my hands over my hair and exhale a long sigh. "Thanks."

Chapter 9

WHATEVER DOM AND MAMA TALKED ABOUT MUST'VE worked, because when I get up Saturday morning, I find them both in the kitchen, cooking breakfast. It's such a relief to see the two of them together like that, smiling. Uncle Adam has gone out to run some errands in town for Mama, and he won't be back until the afternoon. Thank God I won't have to worry about him pressuring me about Michael for a few hours.

For now, it's just us. And I'm nervous as hell.

I'm nervous because I didn't call Michael last night after all. I was too chicken shit. I tell myself I'll call him today, before Unc gets home.

I crash on the living room couch and flip on the TV. It's already tuned into the religious channel—the only channel, besides the news, that Mama watches—so I switch to sports.

I sink back with my feet propped up on the coffee table. Breakfast smells good: bacon, eggs, sausage, grits, toast . . .

"Kevin! Get your feet off that furniture!" Mama scolds.

Cringing, I instantly swing my legs around and plant my feet on the floor. "Sorry."

"Don't get too comfortable, bro. Breakfast is ready," Dom calls.

"Great!" I pop up from the couch and wander to the breakfast nook, where the table is set with empty plates, glasses, and a few covered dishes. Mama comes out the kitchen, carrying a basket of fluffy, steaming-hot biscuits. Dom follows with a covered pot.

I retrieve the milk and OJ from the fridge and take a seat at the table. After Pops died, Michael left, and Uncle Adam started coming over more, Mama bought a smaller dinette set—one for four people instead of six. She couldn't take seeing those two empty chairs every night whenever we'd sit down to eat.

But even now, as the three of us are seated, an empty chair lingers, and Mama frowns at it.

"Everything looks and smells good," I pipe up, trying to lighten the mood. "Who made what?"

"I made the potatoes and eggs," Dom says. "And you better eat some, too."

"Why? Did you put poison in 'em?" I laugh. Of course, I'm gonna eat them. Dom's a fucking savant when it comes to cooking. Seriously. All those days as a kid, spending time in the kitchen with Mama, have paid off.

We fix our plates. I pile mine with some—*lots*—of everything.

"What time do you boys have to leave tomorrow?" Mama asks.

Dom keeps eating, so I speak up. "Well, I wanna hit up the courts in the morning, so maybe around nine thirty or so."

She nods thoughtfully. "I was hoping the two of you could come to church with me."

I bite my bottom lip and exchange glances with Dom.

"But service starts at eleven, so . . . " she continues.

"Why don't we do it another time?" I suggest.

Her eyes dull. "All right. Well, then, I guess we need to make every moment last from now until you leave. I just wish Michael was here."

I feel my stomach clench, but I hide my discomfort by shoving a hefty bite of eggs and grits into my mouth.

"Have you talked to him recently, Kevin? He asked about you last time he called."

Dom looks sidelong at me, remaining silent.

"Naw, I haven't talked to him yet. But I will." I play with my food.

"Okay. I really want my family back, you know? To see the three of you together again would mean all the world to me."

I almost drop my fork. My hands are getting clammy, so I wipe them on my shorts.

"I want to let you both know that your uncle Adam has been taking very good care of me. He is a true blessing."

"I'm glad, Mama," Dom finally says. "You look happier now."

"Because I am," she says.

I finish my breakfast, push my plate aside, and chug down my glass of milk. I wipe the mustache off with the back of my hand.

"Kevin, please use a napkin," Mama says to me sternly, pointing to the napkin by my plate.

I manage to fight the urge to roll my eyes—thank God—and use the napkin.

Dom snickers, and I shoot him a glare.

"I've started a little garden outside and bought some new plants from the farmer's market last Thursday, but I haven't had a chance to plant them. Will you two help me?"

I really should help her, but I still have to call Michael. "Dom, why don't you help her? I need to make some phone calls."

He nods, frowning. "Fine."

There's still a hint of joy in Mama's eyes. Maybe she knows what I'm about to do.

After breakfast, I help my mother and brother clear the table and wash the dishes. It's strange the way the three of us are doing things together like this. It's like we've never done it before. And yet, I can remember many a day Dom and I as kids would help Mama wash, dry, and put away the dishes.

I retreat to my room, shutting the door, and collapse on my bed. I scroll down my list of phone contacts and stop at Michael Jr.'s name. It stares back at me. I can't believe I'm doing this. But it's for Mama, not me. At least, that's how I think of it. I guide my thumb to the Dial button and wait.

One ring. My heart starts pounding. Why am I so scared?

Two rings. My mouth goes dry, and I fidget with the bed-covers. *Stop being a pussy, Kevin. You can do this. Are you scared of him? Hell no.* I'm not scared.

Three rings. I shift around on the bed and drum my fingers on the night table.

Four rings. He's not going to pick up. He probably knows it's me. He's probably paying me back for all the times I ignored his calls. Fair is fair, after all.

Five rings. As I pull the phone from my ear, I hear a click and a rustling sound.

"Hello? Hello?" the male voice calls, sounding a little harried.

I take a deep breath and bring the phone back to my ear. I open my mouth, but no sound comes out. *Why am I doing this?*

"Hello?" the voice says again. It's definitely Michael. His tone is sincere, but there's a roughness. He sounds like someone from the streets. He might as well have been, having run away from home when he was fifteen.

"Mike." I choke up.

"K? Is that you, Little Brother?"

I fight down a smile. "Not so little anymore, but yeah." It seems like only yesterday that he left.

There's a brief pause, then he says, "Holy—! I can't believe you actually called. You realize I've been trying to reach you all this time, right?"

"Yeah." I shut my eyes. The last time he called was last month.

"So, you've been ignoring me?" He doesn't sound pissed, but rather, hurt. "Are you still upset?"

Leaning over, I rest my hand over my forehead. "Yeah."

"But it's been ten years."

"Yeah."

There's another moment of silence. "I ask Uncle Adam about you every time I call. He says you're doing good."

"Yeah." My inability to say more than that unnerves me, and I can only imagine what it's doing to Michael.

"Hey, I have to go in a bit. Got a big fight in a few hours downtown. We need to catch up on things, seriously."

"Yeah." I chew my bottom lip. "You still in Miami?"

"Yup, till Sunday. Then I head to Detroit. Trying to get something on the West Coast again, but Dante, my trainer, said I'm still not ready for that yet."

"What kind of fighting do you do?"

"Eh . . . underground shit, but mainstream media calls it 'mixed martial arts.'"

"Illegal?" I ask.

"It puts a roof over my head, clothes on my back, and food in my belly."

Well, that answers *that* question.

"I doubt you'd understand or even give two shits about what I'm doing, K," he continues.

"Maybe I don't understand what you're doing, but that's your business. You're right, though, I don't give two shits."

There's another voice in the background. It's a female. I can only make out bits and pieces of what she's saying. Something about a bra.

"Look under the bed," I hear him mutter away from the phone.

Well, damn.

"Hey, I gotta go now," he says to me.

"I bet you do." I smirk.

I hear a faint chuckle on his end. "It was good finally hearing from you again, man. So, does this mean you're not going to ignore my calls anymore?"

I shrug, even though he can't see it. "I dunno."

"Fair enough. See you later, K."

"Later." I toss the phone to the floor then lie back in bed and stare at the ceiling. My mind is numb, swarming with thoughts. Strangely, there's no anger rising inside me. Only sadness. And regret.

Regret that I hadn't done this sooner.

CHAPTER 10

Sunday morning after breakfast, Dom and I leave Mama's house. It's a little bittersweet when the four of us gather on the front porch. Mama has tears in her eyes. Uncle Adam stands rigid as he watches us hug and say our last goodbyes.

"Be careful on the interstate, Kevin," Mama says. "Too many people are in a hurry to go nowhere."

I kiss her cheek and smile. "I will, Mama. You take care, too, okay?"

She nods and turns to Dom. "Baby boy, please call me sometime. I miss you."

He frowns and nods curtly. "I will."

"I'll make sure he does," I interject.

Dom gives me the stink eye, and I stare him down till he gives up and turns his attention to Uncle Adam.

Unc steps forward and gives him a big hug. "Take care, son. It was good seeing you again."

Dom pats him on the back as he's embraced. "You, too. Keep tinkering."

"You know it."

Dom turns and heads for my car.

"Bye, Unc," I say, hugging the big man.

He slaps me on the back. "Goodbye, Kevin. Take care of your little brother, okay?" He leans forward and whispers in my ear, "Thank you for calling him."

I pull away and nod, not wanting to think about Michael. There's nothing more to be said, so with one last kiss for Mama, I grab my duffel bag and get in the car. Mama and Unc remain on the porch, watching us as we drive off.

"That wasn't so bad, now, was it?" I ask my brother, breaking the awkward silence as I pull onto the interstate and head north.

Dom has his head turned away from me, looking out the window at the passing landscape.

"Did you two make up?" I ask again.

"We talked," Dom replies.

"And?" I glance over to him.

Dom snaps his head to me, glaring. "What the hell does it matter to you? I told you, we talked."

"It means a lot to me, actually. I wanna know if you finally laid this shit to rest. Made up and all that. I don't want it bothering you anymore."

His tone softer, he says, "She told me how much she changed her life. She cried—*we* cried."

I remain silent and listen.

"Ironically, we talked about all this in the breakfast nook." Dom hisses. "I can't believe we actually ate breakfast and dinner in there."

"It doesn't hurt as much anymore," I say. "I mean, the memory's still there, but I don't let it get to me. I think the more you face your demons, the weaker those demons get." I crack a small smile. "You know I'm proud of you, right? I'm proud that you finally grew a pair and did this. And I'm happy as fuck for Mama."

"Thanks. It's getting a little easier now. It wasn't as bad as my nightmares had made it out to be."

"Heh. Yeah. Funny, ain't it?" I fall silent for a moment as I gather my thoughts. *I need to tell him.* "I faced some demons of my own this weekend, too."

"What'd you do?" He sounds more serious now.

I lick my lips, which had begun to go dry from the nervous thought. "I talked to Michael Jr."

"You what?"

"I had to, if I'm gonna have any chance of getting the three of us together for Mama's birthday."

Dom shakes his head in disbelief. "Wait. Back up. Michael's gonna be there, too? What the hell, man?"

"I don't know if he'll be there, but I'm trying. It's Mama's one and only birthday wish to have the three of us together again."

Dom is quiet, but I can feel his tension.

"I felt the same way, li'l bro," I continue. "I think I still do. But I've convinced myself that this is for Mama, not me. I don't give a fuck about what he's doing." But as much as I really don't, something still bugs me in the back of my mind.

"So, what did Michael say?"

I switch lanes to pass a slower semi. "Not too much. He sounded busy with a girl. He mentioned something about a fight he had to get ready for."

"Fight?"

"Yeah, he does that illegal underground shit. He apparently gets paid, though."

"Damn."

"Yup." I veer off toward the exit to Montlake.

"So, what happened between you two? I mean, did you guys make up or something?"

I raise my eyebrows. "Hell no. We didn't make up. We didn't talk long, anyway. I don't even know why I wasted my time."

"Well, the fact you actually called him after all these years seems pretty big to me. Kind of like me finally talking to Mama."

"Yeah."

Dom turns toward the window, and we drive in silence for a moment. "Maybe you were right about me seeing Denise's parents," he finally says. "I should do that."

"You should." I grin. "And of course I was right. I'm your big brother. I'm always right."

He laughs. "How did the date go with Trinity on Thursday? I just realized I never asked you about it."

My mood shifts from dark and depressing to stimulating. I've been thinking nonstop about Thursday night—I woke up with morning wood on Friday. Just hearing Trinity's name fills my nose with the scent of vanilla. "That girl is beyond amazing. Tastes like fucking candy."

"You kissed her on the first date?" Dom sounds surprised.

"It was slightly more than just kissing, li'l bro." I smirk.

"How the hell did you manage that?"

"Skill. And it does help a little to be a smoking-hot deejay."

Dom just snorts.

"Seriously, though. I really like her. I wish I'd called her that night when you first gave me her number."

"Damn right. I'm your little brother. You're supposed to listen to me."

It's my turn to laugh. "Yeah, yeah."

"I bet she's obsessed with you. She's probably gonna be a handful."

"Eh, not really. I've already made it clear to her that I want her to like the man behind the deejay. I think she's learning."

"I see. Well, that's good she's not like some of those crazy groupies who stalk you at the club," Dom says.

"Fuck no, she's not that crazy. I mean, she sorta stalks me, but in a cute way. I'd never get with a real fangirl, though. I might as well just be the next flavor of the week for them. Fangirls remind me too much of Justine."

He snorts. "Oh God, Justine was bat-shit crazy."

"That's less than an understatement," I say flatly.

"Anyway, be careful with Trinity, okay? She's been burned many times."

"Yeah, I know. She told me. I'll treat her like gold unless she gives me a reason not to."

I pull up along the curb in front of Dom's house. He grabs his bag from the backseat and opens the door. "Thanks for the ride, bro."

"No prob. Thanks for keeping me company."

We do our secret handshake, he gets out the car, and I drive off.

As I head for Cascade Playground downtown, my phone buzzes. I stop at a red light and check the screen. It's Trinity.

I'm here :-)

I grin. I told Trinity where my friends and I would be playing today, and I hoped I'd get to see her there when I got back. It's only been two days, and I already miss that girl. I can still smell her vanilla scent, taste the strawberries on her lips, feel the softness of her ass and thighs in my hands, and hear her say my name.

Everyone and their mother seems to be at this park today. I manage to squeeze my little hatchback in a parallel spot.

After jumping out of the car and hustling past the kid-infested playground area, I head toward a group of guys at the single basketball court tucked in the corner. The game's already in progress, and they've drawn a small crowd—mostly girls—who sit and watch from the stone benches nearby. Among the crowd, sitting next to a guy with a tablet computer, is Trinity. She's wearing a dark-blue and purple shirt. She notices me and beams, standing up. We meet each other halfway and hug.

I inhale vanilla. "Hey."

"Hi, Kevin," she says excitedly. It's awesome that she's calling me "Kevin" effortlessly now. "I've missed you."

"Missed you, too. Glad you could come out."

"You think I would miss this?" She gestures toward the game in progress.

"All right. Well, get comfortable." I ease myself away from her and turn just in time to see Josh leap up and make a dunk in Carter's face. The crowd goes wild. From the way things are going, it looks like it's David, Hector, and Carter versus Josh, Andre, and a kid I've never met before. But damn, the new kid is good. At least the game is somewhat fair this time.

"Yo, I got next!" I yell. Though my friends don't acknowledge me, I know they can hear me. I get it. They're in the zone. It must be a close game. I stretch and get ready while I watch David's team make the final three points needed to win the game. There's much female cheering afterward.

The guys break up and rest. The new kid passes me the ball. "Hey, what's up? I'm James," he says, nodding.

I return the nod. The kid looks no older than seventeen. "'Sup. I'm Kevin. Good game out there, by the way."

"Thanks. I'm hoping I'll be able to play for UDub next year."

"If you're good enough, the scouts'll find you. You still in high school?"

"Yup. Senior." He begins heading toward the water fountain with the others. "Nice meeting you, man."

While I wait, I mess around and shoot some free throws. I sink them in one after another, nothing but net. I was the Huskies' top free-throw shooter at ninety-one percent. As I sink them in now, I feel like I still have it. I miss playing on the team. I can't wait till Monday.

"Show off," David says. He suddenly slaps me on the back as I'm about to release the ball, and I falter. The ball hits the rim but then spins around it and sinks through the net. *Holy shit, I was lucky.*

"Damn! No pressure, man!" Carter says, approaching. "Did you even miss one?"

I shrug. "I dunno. I was just messing around."

"Nope, he didn't miss a single one," Andre says. "You've definitely *not* lost your touch, Kev."

I smile crookedly. Flattery is nice, but now I'm ready to play.

I team up with Andre and Hector, while David, Carter, and Josh form their team. James sits on the sideline with Ty.

"Check." David goes to the top of the key and bounces the ball to me. As I bounce it back to him, I glimpse toward the benches at Trinity, who watches, intrigued.

Forty-five minutes later, our team emerges victorious, 21–14. My legs ache, having played extra hard today. Tomorrow is the day for tryouts, and I need to make a damn good impression. I take a large gulp of water from the fountain and head to the benches. Most of the crowd had long since dissipated, with only a few female admirers lingering. But I don't pay them any mind. My eyes are drawn to one person.

Trinity rises from her bench and rushes to me. The guy that was sitting near her, with the tablet computer, is now talking with James on the sideline.

"So? Did I dazzle you enough?" I want to hug her, but I'm dripping with sweat.

"Oh my gosh, Kevin! That was amazing!"

I throw my head back and laugh.

David slaps me on the back. "Good game, man."

I return his gesture more formally with our special handshake.

David nods at Trinity. "You his girl?"

I clench my jaw. I don't know what we are right now, so I keep quiet and let her decide what we are.

Trinity blushes. "Ah . . . we're just friends, that's all."

Friends. I can deal with that.

David looks at the two of us dubiously. "Mhmmm." He turns back to me. "Hey, good luck at tryouts tomorrow. Let us all know how it goes."

I nod. "Thanks, man. I will."

My friends leave, and Trinity and I do the same. It's early evening, and I offer to drive her home. She doesn't refuse this time.

"Excuse me!" a man calls behind us.

We're only footsteps from my car, and I stop and turn around. A man wearing a white polo shirt and khaki pants runs up to us. He's carrying a tablet. It's the same guy who was sitting near Trinity and talking to James.

"Do you have a moment, young man?" he asks.

Trinity and I exchange glances. Then, with my arm wrapped protectively around her waist, I turn to the stranger. He's clean shaven and appears to be in his late thirties or early forties. I notice the small, purple-and-gold UDub "W" logo over his heart.

"What do you need?" I ask.

"Kevin, was it?" He extends his hand. "My name is Patrick Lowe, men's athletics recruiting and communications intern at UDub. I just wanted to tell you how impressed I was with your performance out there."

My hand falls away from Trinity's waist, and I shake his hand. My mouth opens, but no sound comes out. *A recruiter? Here? Now?*

"You're in the right place, Mr. Lowe," Trinity pipes up. "Kevin, didn't you say you used to play for the Huskies?"

I blink. "I . . ."

Patrick's eyes widen. "That true?" He fumbles with his tablet. "What's your last name? Did you graduate already?"

So many questions. I exhale and try to gather my thoughts. "Anderson. My last name's Anderson. And no, I didn't graduate yet. I had to take a couple years off. I do want to try and play again, though. I plan on registering for fall classes and going to tryouts tomorrow."

Patrick nods absentmindedly, but his eyes are focused on the tablet. "Kevin . . . " His mouth falls open. "Kevin Jerard Anderson? Three-time all-star point guard and shooting champion?"

Damn, he's got a database on me? Oh yeah, he's an athletics recruiter. Of course he does. "Yep, that's me."

"I've heard all about you. You're quite a legend at the school." Patrick shuts off his tablet. "I came out here to watch young James, but damn, now it looks like I might have *two* prospects." He fishes in his pocket for a business card. "Here's my card. I'm going to be at the Intramural Activities building tomorrow, with the other coaches, for the tryouts. We're starting promptly at nine in the morning in Gym E. After you're done taking care of your class-registration business, please come by and see me."

I take the card, read it, and nod. *IMA Building, Gym E.* "Will do. Thanks."

Patrick smiles. It's only now I notice he has a small gap between his front teeth. "No—thank *you*! I hope to see you tomorrow. You two have a good night." He strides off past us with a pep in his step.

Trinity ogles me. "You're not just an all-star, you're a *three-time* all-star!"

I frown at her. "It's just a title."

"But you're not an ordinary guy, Kevin. You're a famous deejay *and* a famous basketball player. What are the odds of that?"

"I'm just a man." I start walking toward the car.

She follows, and I open the door for her. "You're an extraordinary man." She gets in the car.

I close the door and hop in the driver's side. I put the key in the ignition but don't start it up. Facing Trinity, I stare deep into her eyes. "Trinity, look at me. What do you see?"

She arches an eyebrow. "What do you mean?"

I continue staring, unblinking. "What. Do. You. *See*?"

"I see a great guy in front of me. A handsome, talented, great guy."

I purse my lips then tear my gaze from her and lean my head back against the headrest. "Do you like me?" I don't know why I just asked such a stupid question.

"What? Of course. We're friends, right?"

My nerves are getting tense. "Do you *really* like me? Or just like what I do?"

She pauses. "I like both. Your talents are what make you who you are. I like what you do. It fascinates me."

I'm not sure if that's the answer I wanted to hear.

"What are you trying to get at?"

"I wanna make sure the girl I pour my heart out to isn't just another mindless fangirl."

Her gaze hardens at that, and she doesn't reply.

I stare back at her coolly and start up the engine. She gets out the car.

Startled, I shut off the engine and get out, as well. She's already walking down the street. "Where are you going?" I yell.

"Taking the bus," she replies without turning around. She walks with firmness in her step. She's angry.

Damn it. I fucked up.

CHAPTER 11

I WAKE UP MONDAY MORNING AND REALIZE I'VE OVERSLEPT. I had a rough night, anxious about tryouts, class, Trinity.

Fuck me.

I arrive on campus around ten thirty and head for the registrar's office. I'm not waiting long before I'm helped and given tons of paperwork to fill out. Afterward, I choose my classes. I figure if I'm to be eligible to play ball for an entire season, I'll have to stretch my classes for the fall and spring semesters. So I choose two of the three remaining investing, finance, and marketing classes I need to complete my business degree. When I finally finish, it's after one in the afternoon, and I wonder if I've completely missed tryouts. I drive over to the IMA building anyway and hustle inside. There are plenty of people doing fitness training and other activities. As I near Gym E, I hear the echoing sounds of basketballs and voices. I skid to a halt at the doorway and peer out into the busy gym of players. They work on dribbling and passing drills while the five coaches walk around, pointing and barking orders. My eyes are glued to Coach Langley. He hasn't changed much in two years. He has a greyish-brown receding hairline, a hard, stern, wrinkled face, and green eyes that carry a look of determination. His purple polo shirt is tucked into his khaki pants, as always, and he even wears those same white tennis shoes.

I smile. Coach Langley has the heart of a winner. He instilled it in all of us. He knew the game better than anyone, and I recall a rumor a while back about him playing pro in his younger years. I wouldn't be surprised if that rumor were true.

I spot Patrick sitting in a padded folding chair parked with several others on the sideline on the other side of the court. He steadily types away on his tablet, occasionally looking up at the goings-on in the gym. He doesn't seem to notice me.

My heart pounds as I walk inside, my steps heavy. One of the assistant coaches makes eye contact with me then returns his attention to a player who dribbles around a set of small orange cones. The memories of my workout drills become vivid as I observe. Some of the players are pretty good at handling the ball, while others are downright laughable. I recognize only two people from my playing days, Ronnie and Maurice, specifically. They were freshman benchwarmers back then. Now they're two of the best players on the court.

I wander over to some bleachers that are pulled out and occupied by a few spectators. I sit on the bottom bleachers and lean forward, my hands clasped and my elbows resting on my knees. Adrenaline rushes through my brain as I recount past games. But beyond all that reminiscing, I keep hearing a voice. *Her* voice. *I see a great guy in front of me. A handsome, talented, great guy.*

I cringe. Why couldn't she just see "Kevin"? *You're not an ordinary guy, Kevin.*

A whistle suddenly blows, breaking me from my thoughts. At center court, all the players and coaches have gathered around Coach Langley.

"Good job, everyone. Tomorrow, we'll be working on defensive techniques, so get rested up and be back promptly at 9:00 a.m. No exceptions."

"Yes, sir!" the players say.

The players and spectators leave, and I stand. Langley and the other coaches head to the row of chairs with Patrick. I hustle across the court toward them, brushing past the other players, who look too exhausted to acknowledge me.

"Hey, coach!" I call, waving.

The coaches turn around. All of them, including Langley, stare wide-eyed at me.

Patrick pops up from the chair. "Kevin! You made it!"

"A little too late, it seems." I give them all an apologetic smile. "Sorry, about that."

"No, no, that's fine," Patrick says.

Langley fumbles with his clipboard. "Anderson? What the hell—you're back?"

I nod. "Sure am, Coach. For one last go-around if you'll let me."

There's a hesitant expression in his eyes. "Like you even need to ask. This is amazing! The young all-star is back!" Langley gestures to the three new coaches. "These are our intern coaches, Mark Perry, Julius Hernandez, and Randall McMillan."

I shake hands with the three coaches. "Hello."

"I remember you at the regional championship game against Stanford," Randall says. "You were just a freshman and ended up single-handedly outscoring their best senior players, combined, by a 22-point average. I've never seen anything like it."

My smile widens. I remember that game, too. The Huskies had an undefeated season. I surprised myself by being the lowly freshman who could stand up against those hardcore seniors.

Your talents are what make you who you are. I blink as Trinity's voice returns. Maybe she knows me better than I do. My mind is in a haze as I try to process the rest of what the coaches are saying. At this point, all I notice are lips moving.

Then, Coach Langley slaps me on the back, and I'm shaken from my thoughts. "Of course, he wouldn't object to showing you all a bit of his skill."

Wait . . . what?

"I doubt he's gotten rusty. Not when he's got *that* kind of natural talent under his belt, eh?" Langley grins at me.

I shake my head, trying to clear my mind. "Oh, uh, right. Sure." *What did I just agree to?*

"Great! We have some time to spare. Anderson, pick up a ball and dazzle us like you used to." Langley nudges me forward toward the basketball rack.

Shit. The anxiety fills my mind and body, making all of my bones go numb. And I can't get Trinity's voice out my head. *You're amazing, Kevin.*

I take a deep breath then pluck a ball from the rack. I bounce it a few times and head down court. "What do you want me to do first, Coach?" I yell.

Langley points to the orange cones. "Dribbling. You still remember the drill?"

I nod. "Sure do." I take off, maneuvering around the small obstacle cones, spinning, faking, and showing off my quick footwork and ball-handling skills. But even as I'm working hard to get in the zone, I can't. It's an effort that puts more strain on my mind than it should. Maybe it's because I can't stop thinking about Trinity and the way she looked at me last night. The way I totally made an ass of myself in front of her.

Damn it all!

I trip over a cone as I perform a backspin, and nearly lose control of the ball. Butterflies fill my stomach. *They saw that. I know it.*

I round the last set of cones, and I focus my mind on the in-between-dribbling obstacle, but again, my mind drifts, this time to Thursday night at the club. When Trinity and I kissed and fooled around backstage. What I wouldn't give to have that moment back with her again.

She's not a fangirl. She's really serious about me. She didn't deserve what I said to her last night.

My body lurches forward. My foot gets caught on a cone and slides with an ear-piercing squeak against the polished wood floor. The ball slips from my hand, and I fall hard, face-first. Blackness.

I roll on my back, open my eyes, and find myself staring up at the group of coaches huddled around me. All appear concerned, but I can see a hint of disappointment in Coach Langley's face. I sigh.

"You all right?" Patrick asks, extending his hand.

I gingerly take it and stand. My forehead hurts. "Yeah, I'm fine."

Langley pats me on the back. The disappointment on his face lifts. "Hey, you're nervous. I get it. It's been a while. Take a deep breath. Why don't we look at your free throw shooting? Last I checked you were, what? Ninety-one percent?"

"About that much," I say, grinning proudly. Free throws. I can do that without making a total ass of myself.

The coaches back away, and I grab the ball.

"Shoot ten," Langley instructs. "Then we'll call it a day."

I nod and head to the free-throw line. I stare at the basket long and hard, trying to focus, but again, it's hard. Damn emotions. I try to ignore them and shoot anyway.

The first two shots go in with a clean swish.

I wonder what Trinity is doing right now. I should call her and apologize. No, I should talk to her in person.

Shots three and four ding off the rim. *Shit.*

Will she even give me the time of day? She was mistreated by other guys, and I was no better after what I said to her last night. How could I do that to an awesome girl like her?

Shot five—airball. *Airball? Really?*

I'm fucking up my chances big time, all because I can't get my head straight. *You gotta concentrate, Kevin.*

Shots six and seven miss as well.

I have to make things right with her. Somehow. I need to be Kevin. Kevin would never pull that shit. He's an all-star basketball player—and the best damn deejay in Seattle. *A handsome, talented, great guy.* Yeah, that too.

Shots eight, nine, and ten swish through the net with ease.

I remain at the free-throw line, my shoulders slumped, head hung low. The sounds of the lone bouncing ball echo throughout the gym until it bounces to a stop and rolls against the padded wall.

Someone clears his throat after what seems like an eternity of awkward silence. I don't even want to turn around to face the coaches. I might as well walk out right now. There's no way I'll play for the Huskies this year after that shitty performance.

"Anderson?"

Hearing the disappointment in Langley's voice, I shut my eyes. Then, I take a deep breath, open them again, and slowly spin around. The coaches stare at me with a variety of expressions in their eyes.

"Sorry, Coach. That totally sucked. I don't know what happened."

Langley purses his lips.

"It's nerves," Patrick pipes. "That's all. Today just wasn't your day. Tomorrow, you'll be back to your old self, just like I saw you yesterday."

His words are comforting, but it's not enough to take the sting away from my mind, knowing I totally let Coach Langley down. I never let Langley down in all the time I played for him. I've never seen him more disappointed in me than he is today. There's no excuse. I *have* to get my shit together. Fast.

"Hmm. Yeah, maybe you're right," Langley says. "It's been, what? Two years? You just need to get your groove again, and you'll be fine." He pats me on the back. "Okay, that's all for today. I expect to see you back here at 9:00 a.m. sharp."

"Yes, sir," I say, nodding. I leave the gym and find that it's raining outside. I hurry to my car, not caring that I get completely wet in the process, and collapse into the driver's seat with a huge sigh, mentally swearing about today's fuckups. And yet, despite it all, I feel a little hope ignite in my gut.

That night, I call Dom. He sounds half-asleep when he picks up.

"It's not even eight o'clock yet. What the hell are you doing sleeping this early?" I ask.

"Hey, I had five cars to work on today," he mutters. "Get off my back about it. Now what's up?"

"I need a favor." I sort through the box of new mix vinyls I got in the mail today from a company over in the UK. That store is one of the few places I love getting my music and deejay equipment from.

Dom makes an obnoxious yawn.

"Can you, uh . . . ask Denise something for me?" I ask.

"Denise?" His voice gets a little more chipper. "What is it?"

"I, uh . . . need you to ask her what kind of flowers Trinity likes."

There's a moment of awkward silence. Then Dom says, "Wait. What?"

"It's a little complicated, bro. But I need to know."

"You're getting Trinity flowers?"

"Yeah, I have to." My hand falls away from the box, and I stare blankly at the new albums.

"No, you don't, 'cause you've never given a girl flowers before."

"Yeah, well, I've never cared about a girl as much as I care about Trinity, so I need to do this."

"You sound desperate."

I huff. "I'm not."

"Yeah, you are. What happened?"

"Damn it, Dom, are you gonna do this for me or not?"

"Not till you tell me what you did."

I blink. "What *I* did? What makes you think I did anything?"

"You sound like you did something. You can't hide that shit from me. You're a terrible liar."

"So are you. And Denise can attest to that."

"Damn it. Fine. I'm a terrible liar. Happy?"

I fight down a smile. We're alike in so many ways that we might as well have been twins. "Yeah, damn it. I finally got you to admit to something."

"Good. Now, tell me what you did to Trinity."

I roll my eyes. "If you must know, I fucked up. Happy?"

"Not really. What did you do to go from 'more than kissing' to 'needing flowers'?"

I shove the box of vinyls away and rest my back against the side of the bed. "I let a good thing slip away from me. Now I have to get her back, because I can't stop thinking about her, and it's affecting my performance on the court."

"The court? Oh! How did tryouts go today?"

"Shitty. I'll be lucky if Coach Langley lets me be a benchwarmer this year."

"Damn, bro."

"Yeah. I didn't realize how much she really meant to me until that shit happened at the gym. I want her back. I *need* her back." I sigh deeply. "So are you gonna help me, or what?"

"Fine, I'll ask Denise tomorrow."

"Thanks, man! I owe you one. I got a gig tomorrow night at Club Elektra. Am I gonna see you there?"

"Not this time, bro. I'm packing up and heading to Olympia for the rest of the week. Larry said I have ten days' worth of vacation accumulated this year, so what better way to use some of it?"

"Olympia? You mean you're . . . ?"

"Yup. I can't say I'm excited about meeting her parents, but it's a step in the right direction, eh?"

A big step. He's grown up so much in just these past few months, doing things I never thought he'd have the courage to do.

That's a lot more than I can say for myself.

Chapter 12

DAY TWO OF TRYOUTS IS A LITTLE BETTER, BUT NOT BY much. I don't fall or lose the ball this time, but I also can't make straight passes or a driving lay-up for the life of me. I feel like a kid again, just learning the game. It's as if a part of me—the talented part—is practically missing. Coach Langley can see it all over my face. It's not as if I can hide how emotionally fucked up I am. How in the hell could a girl do this to me? I'm too crazy about her to ignore her.

Three o'clock rolls around, and I leave practice with the rest of the players, not stopping to speak. I just want to go home. But not before stopping at the florist to order a bouquet of purple orchids.

Home and showered, I drop onto the bed and relax. I have a few hours before I head out to the club. I check my phone for missed calls and notice one from Michael. I clench my jaw. Seeing his name still frustrates me, but the anger I once had for him seems to have gone away since the night I talked to him.

I call his number, and he answers immediately.

"I was wondering if that last talk we had was too good to be true," he says.

I exhale through my nose and close my eyes. His voice is sincere, but I can detect a hint of worry in it. "Naw, I was out all day."

"I see. Well, I'm glad you called back."

"What are you up to?" I listen for sounds in the background, but there are none. Perhaps he's alone this time.

"I'm up in Detroit now. Got a couple fights this week. Should be interesting. Read up on one of my opponents online. He just got out of jail two months ago for aggravated assault. The guy's got anger issues. But I'm gonna humble him."

I swallow. Listening to this gives me butterflies. I still can't get over the fact that Michael is fighting. Does he really find that kind of thing fun? "Damn. Well, how did your last fight in Miami go?"

"Awesome. Felled the guy in the second round with a scissor takedown. Almost broke his kneecap. It was great."

Holy shit. "Great because you almost broke his kneecap?"

"No, great because I won. You've no idea the shit I have to go through in this game, Little Brother."

I scrunch my brow. "What shit?"

"When you're six-one, one-fifty in a room full of guys who are six-five, two hundred and beyond, you don't get much respect. Those guys look at me and think I can't fight.

I'm not beefy, but I can easily bench three-fifty. I feel strong, but I obviously don't look it. It sucks ass."

I always remembered him being the scrawny kid with the goofy tortoise-shell glasses who could lift a damn semi. He was a freak of nature if I ever saw one. "Well," I say, "isn't it a good thing that your opponents underestimate you?"

"Heh, yeah, it is. I just really hate being treated like a pussy all the time."

Yet you ran out on the family like a scared pussy. I scowl as bad memories come to the forefront. "Is that why you fight?"

"Huh? What do you mean?"

"Because of the way people treat you? Is that why you're fighting? To prove a point?"

There's a moment of silence. "I'm fighting 'cause it's good money."

"Do you like it?" I say.

"It's got its ups and downs. There are days I don't feel like fighting and days I need to relieve the stress. Fighting is definitely a great stress reliever."

"Oh."

"Why do you ask?"

I trace patterns on the comforter with my finger. "Uncle Adam's worried about you."

He gives a fake laugh. "Of course he is. But I choose to do this."

"He doesn't want you getting hurt or killed or arrested or whatever from doing this underground shit."

"I'm already well aware of the risks. But like I said, I choose to do this."

"I'm not trying to change your mind, man. Do whatever the hell you want. I'm just saying . . ."

"I appreciate the concern." His voice gets slightly edgy.

I take a deep breath, trying to calm my nerves. "Look, Mama's birthday is in a few months, and what she wants more than anything is to see you, me, and Dom together again."

"Yeah, Uncle Adam mentioned something about that. I didn't think any of you guys wanted to see my face around there anymore."

Part of me doesn't, and part of me does. "It's for Mama."

"Right, well, I'll have to see what's going on. Summertime is when I usually have the most fights scheduled. And the last thing I need is to back out of a fight because it's my mom's birthday. I will never hear the end of that shit for as long as I live."

"Do whatever you want, man. I'm just letting you know."

"Thanks. How's li'l D?"

"Good. He aced his finals, so he's on his way to his junior year in the fall."

"I'm glad he's still at it," Michael says.

"Yeah, I'm proud of him."

There's another moment of silence, and then he says, "Hey, I know he's still upset with me and all, so, uh . . . tell him I asked about him, okay? And also tell him that I miss him. And that I'm sorry."

Something twists in my gut. He's definitely for real. So serious. "Yeah, man. I'll tell him."

We talk a while longer about life and random stuff. I glance at the clock when I hang up and realize it's after seven.

Shit. I have to get to the club.

As I get ready, I think about my call with Michael. At one point, I didn't want to get off the phone with him. It actually felt good to talk to him again. It was as if we were trying to make up for so many years of lost time in just forty-five minutes of phone conversation. And the fact that he might consider coming to see Mama for her birthday is a good sign.

Maybe she'll get her wish after all.

It doesn't take me long to get set up at the club, and I have about forty-five minutes till the doors open at nine. I try calling Trinity to see if she's coming, but she doesn't answer her phone. So, I text her. My heart pounds anxiously at the thought that I might see her tonight. God, I hope I do. But if she doesn't come, I'll understand. I deserve it.

My phone buzzes with a text, and I quickly check the screen for Trinity's reply, smiling in anticipation.

y should I come see some egotistical @$$ who hates his fans?

I nearly drop the phone. *Holy shit.* Furious doesn't begin to describe what she's probably feeling right now. My mouth goes dry, and I lick my lips and send a reply.

im sorry trinity.

I wait for her to respond . . .

And wait some more . . .

And wait some more . . .

Five minutes go by, so I text her again.

i miss u.

Still no reply.

With only ten more minutes till show time, I send her a final text—probably the longest text I've ever sent some-one—and hope to God she sees it.

U've been on my mind since that nite @ the park. I fucked up. i let a good thing slip away, and I want 2 try & get it back. if u get this message, then I hope 2morrow that we can meet @ Al's again around 4. It's where we had our first 'non-date date' & where i hope we can start over. -K

Nearing the three-hundred-character limit, this text is as personal as it gets. I *never* sign texts, but this one is signed. Because this message is straight from my heart.

Chapter 13

Day three of tryouts was the best day so far. We did a lot of three-on-three scrimmaging, and that was when I got my groove back, dazzling the coaches with my style. But it was more than that. It was the thought of possibly seeing Trinity today and surprising her with the flowers I'd picked up from the florist after practice. Now, as I sit at a red light, I think about the box of fresh orchids sitting in the backseat. I hope Trinity will give me one of her amazing smiles when she sees them.

That's *if* she even shows up.

I'm taking a big gamble, hoping that she saw my text from last night. What can I say? I'm a helpless fool. I've never been this uptight over a girl before. If Dom saw me now, he'd ride my ass about it. But fortunately, Dom's too busy dealing with his own girl to worry about me.

I park a few blocks from Al's and hop out the car, flower box tucked under my arm. I scan the streets as I walk toward the restaurant, but I don't see Trinity. Inside, it's busy, but the table we sat at before is empty, so I make my way there. I set the box of flowers on the empty chair before sitting.

Pete comes to my table, beaming. His white apron is stained with barbecue sauce in some places. "Hey, Kevin. What's up?"

Leaning my elbows on the table, I look toward the window then back to Pete. "Hey, man. Just waiting on someone."

"Oh." He looks at the flower box. "Your girlfriend from the other day?"

I swallow. *Girlfriend.* What I wouldn't give to be able to say that about her. "Naw, she's just a friend."

A hint of a smirk lines his face. "Right. Well, you want something while you're waiting? Sorry, the 'all-you-can-eat-ribs' special is not till tomorrow."

Despite my nervousness, I'm hungry as fuck from working my ass off at tryouts. I want to wait until she gets here—*if* she gets here. But it's after four, and she's not here, so who knows if she's coming at all? "That's fine. Let me get the three-rib dinner with a side of fries. And an extra-large lemonade."

Pete scribbles on his tiny notepad. "You got it."

"Hey, take your time back there." I immediately regret those words as I feel my stomach grumble in protest.

"I get it, man. Wanna wait for your girl. I'll go get your lemonade."

He leaves, and I return my attention to the window. I stare long and hard at the people walking past, hoping one of them will be her.

My phone buzzes, and I swipe it out of my pocket. My excitement is dampened. The text is just from my good friend and "sorta-manager," Russell, who sets up my gigs. I have another one at a club downtown on Friday night. I'm glad to see that I got more work during the summer.

Pete returns with my lemonade, and I guzzle about half of it.

As I'm busy responding to the text, I feel another presence nearby. After hitting Send, I look up, and Trinity is standing behind the chair across from me, her hands resting on the back. She wears a purple shirt with a neckline that dips just far enough to show a little cleavage and hip-hugger jeans that define those sexy, thick thighs.

God, how I missed her luscious, curvaceous body.

I scramble out of my seat. "Trinity! You came!"

She smiles, but it's not as bright as I've seen it before. She's still unsure about me. I totally get it. And I'm not going to fuck up again.

"Hi, Kevin," she says, giving a little wave. "Sorry I'm late. The bus ran past schedule." She looks at the box in the chair. "Is this seat being saved?"

"Yeah, for you." I set the box on the table and pull the chair out for her. "Those are for you, too."

She sits and peeks into the box. Her expression brightens ever so slightly. "Flowers. Purple orchids. How did you . . . ?"

She shakes her head, trying to fight down that smile. "Denise! So *that's* why she asked me that weird question."

"Hope you're not upset about that," I say, returning to my seat. "But those flowers are from the bottom of my heart. I swear."

She slides the box aside and looks at me intently. "No, I'm not upset about that. It's a sweet gesture."

She's not upset about that, but she's still upset. It's still in her voice. I reach across the table for her hand, letting my fingers brush hers. "Trinity, I'm sorry. I'm so sorry about what I said to you the other day. I swear I didn't mean it. You have every right to be mad. I fucked up." I pause and glance toward Rachel behind the counter, but she's too busy with a customer to hear me. "I *messed* up, and I swear I will do my best to not let that happen again."

Trinity purses her lips and examines my hand on hers but doesn't reply.

"I like you, Trinity," I continue. "A lot. You are constantly on my mind. During tryouts, the more I stressed about you never wanting to see me again, the worse I performed, but the more I hoped that perhaps you'd give me a second chance, the better I performed. In fact, today has been the best day of them all. My coach was really impressed."

Redness graces her cheeks, and she clasps her fingers with mine. "That's great, Kevin. Does this mean you're going to be on the team?"

"Well, Coach hasn't said anything about that yet, but I think it'll be a no-brainer."

"I'm really happy for you."

"Thanks. And hey . . . I'm really sorry about being such a dick—uh, a *bad guy*—about the whole 'Kevin' thing." With a quick peek over my shoulder, I notice Rachel wiping down a table nearby. She doesn't appear to have heard me.

Trinity scrunches her brow. "What are you looking at?"

"Ah . . . " I whip my head back around. "Rachel doesn't like people cursing in here. If you do it, she'll publicly embarrass you."

Trinity smiles, amused. "Oh, one of *those* ladies, eh? I once had a grandma like that. Hardcore old-school southern church lady, she was."

"Yep, that's pretty much Rachel." I stare at Trinity's face again, gathering my thoughts. "Anyway, about the 'Kevin' thing. I don't know why it bothered me so much. I guess I was afraid you would treat me differently because you know who I am. And I didn't want that. I wanted a genuine girl who saw me for me. But you've been nothing but genuine, probably the only genuine girl I've ever met."

"I told you before, Kevin. Your talents are what make you who you are. That's what I like about you."

I smile. "Yeah. I remember. That's why I want to start over. You can call me Kevitron, Kevin, or whatever you want. I won't be mad. I don't ever want to be mad at you, Trinity. That's just not my style. I like you. I really wanna make something work between us."

The redness on her cheeks brightens, as does her expression. "Apology accepted."

It's as if a great weight is suddenly lifted from my chest. I can breathe again. "Thank you. God, you're amazing, Trinity."

She pulls her hand away. "All right. Stop making me blush so much, and let's get some food."

I laugh. "You don't have to tell me twice."

At tryouts on Thursday, I bring Trinity along to watch. I dazzle everyone with my skills, and during the scrimmages, the players practically fight over having me on their team. It's a great feeling, just like the old days.

Trinity is ecstatic for me. She chats away at some of the other spectators in the bleachers, and I can hear her excited, sweet voice over all the noise.

"Yeah, isn't it? Did you know that he was the Huskies' all-star two years ago? Yup, you're right. Oh, of course! No doubt, he'll go pro after he graduates."

Coach Langley blows his whistle to signal that today's tryouts are over. We all gather around him and the other coaches at center court.

"All right, guys," Langley begins. "First of all, I want to congratulate you all for making it this far. You've all played hard, many of you showing some extraordinary abilities, but only twelve of you will make it on the Huskies' roster. We will have the final results posted on the bulletin board in the lobby by two o'clock tomorrow afternoon, so stop by and check then."

"Yes, sir!" the rest of us respond.

My heart thrums in my chest, and I have no idea why. I can't possibly be sweating not making the team after the way the coaches all looked stunned at my performance.

The huddle breaks up, and the players head for the exit, while the coaches gather at the sideline. I turn to the bleachers and go to Trinity, who's already making her way down with the rest of the spectators.

We meet halfway and hug. "Kevin! That was amazing!"

"Thanks," I say, staring at her lips. What I wouldn't give to taste her right now.

"There's someone who wants to meet you." She takes my hand and leads me to a lone middle-aged man in the bleachers. He's wearing a navy button-down shirt and brown slacks. Smiling, he gazes at me with slate-grey eyes.

"Kevin, this is Ben Madison," she says.

Ben extends his hand. "Kevin Anderson? It's a pleasure to meet you."

I shake his hand. "Hello."

"I represent the Madison-Roberts Sports Agency here in Seattle."

Trinity's jaw drops open. "A sports agent!"

"That's right, young lady."

"You didn't tell me that!"

Ben chuckles. "You didn't ask."

I do a double take. As if things couldn't get any better.

"I was here checking out some of the prospects, and Trinity told me all about you."

"Good things, I hope." I laugh nervously.

"Oh yes," Ben says. "We're always on the lookout for exceptional young talent that we can represent. And based on what I just saw out there minutes ago, you, young man, are absolutely phenomenal. Better than some of the professional players I have seen. You have a bright future ahead of you in the pro leagues if that is the route you wish to take."

I can't stop grinning. "Definitely, sir. And thank you. I'm hoping to go far."

"Oh, you will." He studies me. "*Now* I recognize you. You have a very long list of accomplishments." He wrinkles his brow. "And you're still in school?"

I purse my lips. "Yeah, I had to take a couple years off."

"Oh, that's unfortunate—for UDub, that is. But extremely fortunate for you."

What does he mean by that?

He pulls out a business card from his pocket. "If you don't mind, I'd like to schedule an appointment with you to talk about this more in depth. Here's my card. Please call me when you get a chance, so we can arrange a time to meet."

I take the card and glance at it before pocketing it. "Thanks, I will."

"No, thank *you*." He turns to Trinity. "And thank you, young lady, for the talk."

She beams. "Anytime, sir."

He leaves, and I scrunch my brow at her. "You mean this was all your doing?"

"Not really. I mean, I was bragging to him about you, and he said he wanted to talk to you. I had no idea he was a sports agent. This is great, Kevin!"

I pull her to me and give her a kiss on the lips, too quick for her to protest. "Hang on."

I leave her standing there, looking stunned.

"Coach! Coach!" I yell across the court, rushing to the group. I wave the business card in the air.

The coaches turn around. Langley's face is pale.

"You won't believe what just happened!"

Langley turns to the other coaches and dismisses them. "I will talk to you all later," he says then turns to me.

I feel a sudden uneasy feeling in my stomach as he looks at me—or rather, *through* me. "What's up, Anderson?"

I try to smile, but it's hard with that bothered expression on his face. "Uh, I just got approached by a sports agent."

His eyes widen. "You serious?"

"Dead serious, Coach. His name is Ben Madison." I flip out the card.

He scans it a moment. "Ah, yes. Ben. Very reputable guy."

"He says I have a bright future in the pro leagues."

"Oh, yes. You'd be in good hands if you end up signing with him. You'll probably be the top pick in the drafts, no problem." He purses his lips.

"What's wrong, Coach?"

He sighs. "Look, I don't know how to break this to you, but . . . " His eyes shift left and right, as if checking for eaves-droppers. But we are alone, with the exception of Trinity, who sits across the court, fiddling with her phone.

My throat tightens. Maybe I *didn't* make the team after all. I had such a piss-poor showing the first day of practice.

It's haunted me all week. But I take a deep breath, hold my head up high, and listen for what comes next.

"First of all, I want you to know that this has nothing to do with your skill level. You are a phenomenal player. The very best player of this entire group. However, unfortunately, your four-year tenure is up, and I'm unable to let you on the team."

The blow feels even worse than I anticipated. "Wait. I don't understand, Coach. I'm not allowed to play?"

He shakes his head sadly. "Not college level. Athletes are only allowed four consecutive years to play in their college careers. After that, that's it. You dropped out two years ago. You would've been eligible for one more season if you'd stuck around, but, well . . . I respect the fact that you had some family issues to deal with. Life's a bitch like that."

My shoulders slump. This is what I get for dropping out of school so I can care for my brother. But I can't blame him for this. No, I *won't* blame him. It was my choice to do what I did.

"Hey." Langley puts his hand on my shoulder. "Rules are rules. If I had my way, you'd best believe I'd take you back in a heartbeat. But as it is, I can't." There's a brief twitch in his eye.

"You knew about this already, didn't you?" I ask.

He pauses and looks down. "I did . . . and I'm sorry."

"What the hell, Coach? Why did you make me waste my time over this? And I was all nervous and shit. All for nothing!"

"Anderson, it wasn't for nothing. You got yourself a sports agent out of all this. That's the next step after college. You should check into whatever he's offering."

"It was only coincidence that Ben happened to be here."

"Would you rather him *not* have been here?" he asks.

I get flustered trying to argue with him because something good *did* come out of all this. I still feel like an ass, but I also feel a little hopeful. "You think I should sign with him?"

"Talk to him and see what he has to offer, first. You have all year to decide what you want to do. Don't be too quick to sign papers. The glamor of the pro leagues is not always guaranteed."

I nod. "Thanks for the advice."

Coach scratches the back of his head. "I'll tell you the real reason why I . . . did what I did . . . "

I raise my eyebrows.

"Since it had been so long since you last played, I wanted to make sure your skills were still on par before I talked to you about a certain offer."

"What offer?"

"I want to offer you the opportunity to volunteer some of your time and help your would-be teammates at practice. They were amazed at your skills at tryouts, as I knew they would be. I think having someone like you around is just what they'll need to stay motivated to play hard."

That offer sounds surprisingly appealing. "Would I really be allowed to do that?"

"Of course. You're not on the roster or anything. You're just helping the players practice. But I think you'll make practices much more engaging for the guys."

I beam. "I think I'd like that. I'll do it."

"Great! The first day of practice will begin in October. I'll tell Patrick to e-mail you in a week with the details."

I'm smiling so much, my cheeks hurt. Maybe things aren't so bad after all. "Thanks, Coach."

"All right, go home and get some rest. You earned it. See you this fall."

Chapter 14

After spending a few hours on the phone telling my friends—as well as Dom, Uncle Adam, Mama, and even Michael—about the agent and Coach Langley's offer, I collapse in my bed. The excitement and adrenaline have long since worn off, and I'm exhausted.

Trinity, sitting at the desk, gives me a pitying look. It's her first time at my place. It's a miracle that she was willing to come over here at all, and she only did it on the condition that I behave. As much as I want to touch her, hold her, and kiss her, I restrain those urges. I want her to trust me.

"I should go," Trinity says, standing.

"Already?" I don't move from my spot on the bed.

She rolls her eyes. "It's ten thirty. And you look tired."

I don't bother arguing. Besides, I can't force her to stay if she doesn't want to.

She smirks. "What? You intended to keep me here?"

I smirk back. "Yes, but since you're off-limits tonight, it would be fucking torture to have you stick around. And yes, I'm tired, but never of you."

She laughs.

"I'll take you home."

"Oh, you don't have to do that. I'll just take the bus."

"Hey, if it means I can spend a little more time with you, then damn it, I'm driving you home." I roll out of bed and search for my sneakers.

"Oh, all right, if you insist," she says.

The streets are pretty much empty this late on a Thursday night. I drive through town and pull into her apartment complex, which is not far from campus.

Trinity sighs in the darkness of the car. Her face is lit a shade of green from the illumination of the dashboard.

"What's wrong?" I shut off the engine.

"You have a lot going on with basketball, deejaying, and soon, classes. You're going to be really busy."

I suddenly feel a lump in my throat. I don't like the way this is starting off. "Yeah, so?"

"Maybe we shouldn't let things get too close between us right now and just stay as friends. I mean, we'll barely be seeing each other once the fall semester starts."

I slam the back of my head against the headrest. "Damn it, Trinity. But I like you."

She smiles. "I like you, too, Kevin. I really do. But it won't be much of a relationship once the season starts, and I barely see you because you're either volunteering at practice or playing a pickup game somewhere or working at the club, or—"

And with that, I silence her by leaning over and pressing my lips into hers. Hard. Fuck behaving. I missed her taste. Her warmth. I stroke her cheek then draw my hand down upon hers. "Listen, don't think for a second I'm not gonna find some way to see you or talk to you every day, because I will. That's a promise."

I pull back, and she looks at me, stunned. She doesn't move her hand away, though.

"Sorry, Trinity. I just . . . I want it to work. I want *us* to work. I know we can. Let's not worry about what might happen and just concentrate on what's happening right now." I clasp my fingers with hers. "I never wanna let you go again."

Her face softens. "Maybe we can try. But if things start getting distant between us, then we need to stop, okay?"

A fair enough deal, I guess, but I sure as hell don't intend to let it get that far. "Fine. Now kiss me."

As she leans in to do so, I meet her halfway with my lips, and we engage in a hard, needy kiss. My body goes rigid with excitement. I run my fingers through her wavy hair, and she strokes her smooth fingers along the side of my jaw. Just the feel of those fingers grazing my skin sends electrifying pangs of pleasure right to my groin.

She moans against my lips. I attempt to scoot closer to her, but I'm barred by the damn armrest and console between us.

She pulls away. "Okay, now I really have to go," she says with a laugh.

"What? You didn't like it?"

"I *loved* it. But I promised Alexis I'd call her tonight when I got home."

"Mhmm."

Smiling, she bats me playfully on the bicep. "It's true! I swear!"

"Well, just remember we still have some unfinished business to take care of." I smirk.

She hurries out of the car, and I glimpse an embarrassed grin. "Good*night* Kevin."

"What are you doing tomorrow?" I ask.

"I'm getting my hair done."

As if you can get any more beautiful. "You gonna make it to Club Trendz tomorrow night?"

Her eyes light up. "Definitely!"

"Okay. I better see you there, or else I'm gonna find you . . . and we'll finish that unfinished business we started." I laugh.

She giggles and spins around. "God! Okay, Kevin. Goodnight."

I make sure she gets into her apartment safely before driving off. Her vanilla smell still lingers in the car, and it makes my mind go crazy.

Friday morning, I call Mr. Madison, and he tells me to come down to the office immediately. The trip downtown takes mere minutes, and as excited as I am about the whole thing, I do keep Coach Langley's advice in the back of my mind. *Don't sign anything.* Walking through the revolving glass doors of a pristine sky-rise office building, I scan the immaculate lobby and see a lone security guard sitting at a computer in the midst of tiny surveillance monitors. He looks up at me as I approach.

Thank God I decided to dress up a little more today. But even the button-down shirt and slacks make me feel underdressed for this location. It's definitely a suit-and-tie kind of place if I ever saw one.

"Yes, may I help you?" the guard says.

"Hello, sir. I'm looking for the Madison-Roberts Sports Agency."

The guard scans a list that I can't see from this angle, and he nods. "Floor twenty-nine." He points to the four elevators beyond the desk.

"Thanks."

As I'm about to walk over there, he taps on a clipboard sitting atop the desk. "You need to sign in first, please," he says.

I scribble my information and then head for the elevators. Punching the elevator button, I immediately feel butterflies in my stomach. Then my phone buzzes, startling me, and I whip it out.

It's a text from Trinity.

Good luck today! <3

I smile, and all the nervousness subsides.

i think i need to kiss u for good luck. can u stop by real quick?

She replies:

lol you're crazy.

One of the elevators rings and opens, and several people dressed in business suits pour out. They glance at me then continue on their way. I slip inside and punch the button to floor twenty-nine.

Just hear him out, I keep telling myself, rubbing my sweaty hands together. *Don't sign anything.*

The doors slide open, and I exit into yet another elaborate level with white marble floors and fancy wood furniture. I peer at the board with the list of businesses and locate the agency. I follow the signs with slow, heavy steps. As I round a corner and see the letters on the frosted glass window, my heart skips a beat. I swallow a lump in my throat and open the door. A quirky, red-haired receptionist sits at a large oak desk in one corner, a phone receiver cradled at her ear as she steadily types on a keyboard and talks advanced business lingo that I'll probably learn this fall. She catches my eye and says brightly, "Good morning, sir—please have a seat, and I'll be right with you," then returns to her phone call. I glimpse beyond the desk at a lighted, shallow hallway with a few closed doors. I plop down on the brown leather couch in the opposite corner to the receptionist's desk. Inhaling the authentic leather smell, I'm reminded of the amount of money that was probably put into this place. This agency is most definitely banking—they're making six figures, easily. And they want me. *God,* what would I do with that much money?

I had this on again, off again idea about opening my own nightclub, which is one of the main reasons why I am a business major. I thought it'd be cool to invite my deejay buddies from around the country and across the world to promote their music and whatnot. But the idea was so huge and would require a massive monetary investment, which I didn't have—and would probably never have, for that matter—so I didn't pursue it.

But now I'm thinking too far ahead. Assuming I even *make* it to the pros, I probably won't see any eye-popping figures for a long time.

The receptionist hangs up and peers over the desk at me. "I apologize, sir. How may I help you today?"

I stand and return to the desk. "Hi, my name is Kevin Anderson. I have an appointment with Mr. Madison."

For a moment, she simply looks me up and down as if she's checking me out. The caked-on makeup she wears makes me think she's hiding her age and is, in fact, much older than she seemed at first. The age is in her eyes, which the makeup can't conceal. "Mr. Anderson? Oh yes, he's been expecting you." She fumbles with the buttons on her phone and punches a number. "Mr. Madison? Mr. Kevin Anderson is here to see you." She hangs up the phone and smiles at me, revealing lipstick-smeared teeth. "Go right on in, sir."

As I head down the hallway, one of the doors swings open. Ben appears, grinning broadly, dressed in a sharp, grey business suit. "Kevin! Great to see you." He beckons me inside.

"Hello, Mr. Madison."

He waves his hand dismissively. "Please, call me Ben."

Ben's office is bright from the morning sun that filters through the massive glass window overlooking Downtown Seattle. This place smells fresh and new. New carpet, new leather, new wood, new paint. Hanging on the cream-colored walls are framed posters of popular pro sports stars I've idolized since I was a kid. There's even a picture of Fresco Davis doing his signature dunk. Had Ben represented these guys? I would fucking die if he had.

He gestures to the two plush chairs in front of his large cherrywood desk. "Please, have a seat."

I sit down. Carefully. The chair is so soft and comfortable that I sink a good three inches. I can totally use one of these for my apartment. But the chair does little to ease my nervousness. I scoot to the edge and repeatedly clasp and unclasp my hands.

"I trust you found your way up here okay?" Ben asks in a calm voice. He must realize I'm nervous.

"Yeah, it was pretty straightforward."

"Good, good." He studies a flat-screen monitor that sits on his desk. "I was just looking up some of your past accomplishments from when you played your first three years. Very amazing stuff here, Kevin. You averaged a triple-double in points, steals, and assists in thirty of the thirty-three games played during your sophomore year. MVP all three years. As a freshman, you were number two in the nation in scoring. It's amazing you're not playing pro now."

I beam as he reads off just a few of my many basketball accomplishments. "Thank you, sir."

He tears his gaze from the monitor and looks at me. "Now, my only concern is the two years you took off after your junior year. You pretty much disappeared from the headlines, as did your legacy from the Huskies. They had one of their worst seasons this year."

I bite my bottom lip. "Yeah, I, uh . . . had some family issues to take care of." *Dom.* But that was personal shit I didn't want to talk about. I hope he doesn't ask.

He nods, much to my relief. "I see. Well, you are aware that you are ineligible to play on the college level at this point, right?"

"Yeah, my coach told me that. But he said I can volunteer my time and help out at practice sometimes."

"Oh yes, that's fine—good on your part, actually. Professional sports associations do like seeing their athletes give back to their community. Now, as for you, I'd like to go over a few things."

The "few" things take close to an hour to discuss and are mainly about what he does, what his clients get out of it, and the whole process of getting drafted and playing in the pros. It pretty much matches the drafts I've seen on TV, only there's a lot more going on behind the scenes that I never knew about. *Wow, this shit is more involved than I thought.*

"So at this point, this is what I can guarantee you as your agent: even though you're no longer eligible to play college basketball, you're eligible for next year's draft. Because I'm sure every team around the country is going to want you. I can make sure you are on next year's roster."

Don't sign anything. Just hear him out. It's all too tempting, but I need some time to think about it. "Is this going to affect my going back to school?"

"Of course not. In fact, if you are able to graduate by next spring, that would be perfect."

That's definitely doable. "How long do I have to decide about whether or not I want to go forward with this?"

"The entry deadline for the drafts is in April, so anytime before then would be ideal. The sooner the better, really."

I nod. "So what—if I work with you—will you need from me?"

He chuckles and sits back in his chair. "The only thing I will need from you is your ability to maintain those untouchable skills, and most importantly, to stay healthy. Injuries can—and sometimes will—make or break a deal. They might even jeopardize your chances of getting drafted. That's the reality of it."

"Yeah." It's been a miracle that with all my intense game playing over the years, the only injury I ever sustained was a jammed finger.

We talk a little while longer, and then I take my leave. It's noon by the time I step out of the building into the mild, overcast downtown. My head's still spinning as I text Trinity and Dom about my day. This has got to be some sort of dream. Or maybe this is that long-awaited reward I'd wished for as a kid.

Either way, I like it.

Friday night, Trendz is packed solid. It doesn't matter if it's summer vacation or not. It's a sold-out crowd every time I have a gig here. With all the new music I've got, I'm mixing up a storm. I'm going to make sure this is one of my best college days, one that I'll remember for a long time. The beats flow, echoing the ridiculously awesome mood I'm in. I get lost in the music, swapping vinyls with flair and mixing in song after song, riling the crowd even more. Everyone's lost in the ambience of the thrumming beat. The lights strobe a colorful prism across the sea of dancing people. Then they land on my beautiful girl, Trinity, who hangs out near the stage with her friend Alexis. The girls dance together, taking turns stealing glances my way. Both of them look as if they just stepped off a model runway, their hair done all fancy and outfits to die for—especially Trinity's. Her curvalicious body beneath that purple, off-the-shoulder halter top and black pants is mesmerizing.

The hours that go by seem like a blur. Before I know it, it's two a.m. I guess it's true what they say: time flies when you're having fun. And *God*, was this the most fun night I ever had. After the last of the crowd heads out of the club, I start packing up my equipment. I instinctively search for Dom, as he always comes to help me, but then I realize he's in Olympia until Sunday. I can't believe how much I miss my baby brother.

But this is what I wanted, I keep telling myself. *This is what he needs.*

Loading up my car takes a little longer without Dom's help, but I get it done. As I slam the trunk, I spot two women—one big, one small—heading my way. I smile, already knowing which one is Trinity.

"Hey, you two," I say, as they step into a spot of illumination cast by a floodlight posted on the brick wall.

Trinity draws closer to me, arms outstretched, and consumes me in a bear hug. I sink into her warm, soft body like it's a pillow and moan. Her touch and her vanilla smell make all the blood in my body rush to my dick. She must feel my sudden hard-on pressing against her belly, because she makes the faintest of moans. *God*, I want to take her right now, right here, in the back of the club.

But the sound of Alexis clearing her throat behind us halts my fantasies, and Trinity and I reluctantly pull out of the embrace.

"Sorry to disturb you two, but, Trinity, do you need me to drive you home tonight?"

I bite my bottom lip. *Please say no. Please say no. Please say no.*

Trinity looks at me, and I hope to God she can see the look of want on my face.

"Do you mind if I ride with you, Kevin?" she asks in a voice so innocent it causes my dick to strain in my jeans.

"Hell no," I say breathlessly.

Trinity grins.

Alexis smirks, the black lipstick contrasting with her ghostly-white skin. "Okay, I'll leave you two lovebirds alone." She glances at Trinity. "You're a lucky bitch, you know that? Getting the hottest fucking deejay in Seattle."

"That's right, and I don't intend to share."

Trinity's response makes me squirm and clench my thighs as my dick starts to throb. *My God. Did she just say that?*

Alexis playfully pokes out her pierced lip and then waves as she leaves.

Alone, I wrap Trinity in my arms and pull her close. "Kiss me," I say, enjoying the plumpness of her body once more.

She laughs then kisses my lips with a small moan. I kiss her back again and again, each kiss more needy than the last. I kiss along her jawline and down her neck. She exhales then pulls away.

"Not here," she whispers. "Someone will see us."

I close the gap and kiss her some more. "So?"

"So? I don't want some creep watching us." She pulls away again and heads to the car.

Smirking, I take out my keys. "Are you saying you're ready to finish that unfinished business?"

She rolls her eyes and fights down a smile as she lowers herself into the passenger's seat. There's my answer.

CHAPTER 15

I CAN'T GET HOME FAST ENOUGH. I'M DEFINITELY SPEEDING, but I can't help that my dick is ready to rip through my pants every time I move my foot. Fortunately, the cops aren't out in full force tonight.

I practically pull Trinity out of the car when I get home, excited, as if I were about to open a Christmas gift. And *damn*, do I want to unwrap Trinity from those clothes right about now.

As soon as we're inside, our lips are on each other. I loop my arms around her waist and, without breaking from the kiss, lead her toward my room. She doesn't protest, doesn't try to pull away. In fact, she does quite the opposite. As soon as we're in my room, she starts tugging my shirt up. I take a breath, reluctantly breaking the kiss, and help her. The article gets tossed on the floor.

Her hands are on me, rubbing my chest, tracing one of my many tattoos on the left side. She looks over my chiseled physique and gives a satisfied smile. It's her first time seeing me with my shirt off, and I'm glad I'm able to make such a good impression. All my years of playing ball have definitely paid off.

"Like what you see?" I smirk.

"Oh, God, yes," she says breathlessly, running her hand along every muscle in my abs and chest. Her fingers follow the line of tattoos that goes from my pecs up to the left side of my neck. When she touches my neck—particularly *that spot* of my neck—I cringe. My erection shrinks. Because for a moment, I don't feel Trinity's hands touching my neck—I feel my father's. His big, calloused fingers choked me at that spot, and the scar from the box cutter is still there. Covering it with tattoos didn't take away the pain or the memories.

I swallow once and gently take hold of her hands, guiding them back to my chest. "I like them here."

There's curiosity in her eyes but only for a moment, because once her hands are back on my chest, that seductive expression returns.

My dick springs back to life.

Her lips return to mine, and I run my hands along her sides, down to her hips. My fingers sink into her softness. I love the contrast of her body against mine. I deepen the kiss, and I feel her tongue prod against my lips.

Oh, hell yes.

My tongue comes out to play with hers. Her taste is more addictive than candy. Our tongues tease each other, tangling, doing a sexy dance in our mouths. I slide my hands around her hips, inside the back of her pants, beneath her panties, and over her ass. Pressing her body harder against mine, I squeeze both cheeks, and she moans, breaking the kiss.

"God, you're so beautiful," I whisper with ragged breaths.

She looks at me with swollen lips and half-open eyes.

"I want you, Trinity."

She bites her bottom lip. *Damn*, she's so cute when she does that.

"Do you want me?" I ask.

Still saying nothing, she leans forward and kisses down my sternum, then over my abs. Lower. Lower. She reaches the button of my jeans and undoes it.

Well, there's my answer.

Running my hands through her hair, I watch her inch down the zipper, and I shrug my pants and boxers down to my ankles. I step out of them, and she looks back up at me, grinning wide.

"You're huge," she says, and I suddenly feel her hand close around my dick.

I can't control the loud moan that escapes me. My mind reels. Her hand fits around me perfectly. "Uhh . . . what are you gonna do with that?"

She gives it a playful squeeze then lets go. *That tease.*

"Undress me and find out," she replies with a smirk.

It takes a moment for my mind to return to reality, and when it does, I tug at her top, yanking it over her head, not caring in the least that it messes up her hair. She unhooks her black lace bra, and her tits spill out. There's powder under them. Sweet, vanilla-scented powder.

She bites her bottom lip, and my dick twitches. That gesture is so innocent, yet so sexy. She tosses the bra on the floor.

I pull down her pants and panties and then ogle every inch of her. She smells like sex-laced vanilla. And she's dripping wet between her thick thighs.

I kiss her deeply, inhaling her scent, my mind going wild. My hand grazes her belly and between her thighs, where I stroke her wet, waiting center.

She shivers and moans against my lips. "Kevin."

Oh, hell yes. I rub my fingers across her folds, letting them get coated in her juice. Teasing her with my fingers, I watch the changing expression on her face, the way she bites her bottom lip, the little sounds she makes. The strain in my groin becomes almost unbearable.

I withdraw my fingers from her and bring them to my lips. She watches me in a daze as I lick each of my coated fingers greedily.

"Oh God, Kevin." She blushes and looks away shyly.

I raise my eyebrows. "What? I like the way you taste."

Chuckling, she pulls me to the bed. "And what do I taste like?"

I follow her without protest. "Like vanilla. My favorite flavor."

Sprawling on the bed, I gaze at her, my erection practically resting over my abs. Her full body is like that of a goddess.

Every curve is perfect. Soft. Ample. And I want to be smothered in her body. I want to be smothered in *her.*

"I want to feel you inside me," she purrs, her ass in the air. My entire crotch area goes numb.

And I want to be inside you. Not taking my eyes off her, I reach for the drawer of the night table and yank it open. I grope around the miscellaneous items inside until I feel a square packet. But she reaches over and takes it from me.

I watch her, curious and cautious.

She crawls on top of me and sits, her wonderful ass pressing into my thighs. She tears open the packet with her teeth and pulls out the condom. Her hand returns to my dick, stroking and squeezing it in ways that make my body tremble. I close my eyes and enjoy her soothing touch. Every caress is like an electrifying jolt on my body. I'm going to come soon if she doesn't stop that.

"Your hands . . . feel so good on me," I murmur.

I feel the cool lubrication of the condom, and I open my eyes. She hovers over me on all fours then lowers her face to mine, our lips meeting in a deep, intimate kiss. Her body collapses onto mine, and I exhale through my nose. *My God, those curves.* I wind my arms around her and thrust my body up into her to tease her with my hardness. She moans and grinds her hips into me.

Breaking the kiss, I exhale again, this time through my mouth. My fingers get lost in her flesh as I grope her everywhere. I draw one of her tits to my mouth and suck greedily. My hips move and shift as my dick locates its target. My hands move down to her thighs then around her ass, where they cup her cheeks and steer her lower half to my throbbing manhood.

"Kevin . . . please," she whimpers in short breaths.

Oh, hell. Now she's begging. The throbbing sensation becomes more painful, and I press the head of my cock against her pussy, gently at first.

"Please!" she says a little louder.

Not giving it a second thought, I thrust into her hard and fast. She screams then breathes steadily. *Hell yes.* She feels absolutely perfect inside. My lips return to hers while we rock a slow, steady rhythm. She groans, and it makes my mouth vibrate. Faster, we move, and I'm lost in the moment. *This* moment with the most gorgeous girl I've ever met. She's too addictive to resist. Too amazing to ignore. Harder and faster, I move, not missing a beat. She moans with every inward push. I fantasize about her and me in the club together, under the swirling lights, making hot, beautiful love to the possessive beat of the music, her curves bouncing and my body getting lost in them.

I gasp, and my body shudders then tenses. A rush of hot energy flows through me, and I draw out a breath of pleasure. My fingers dig into her ass cheeks, as the dizzying sensation sweeps over me. She cries out.

I collapse beneath her, panting. She kisses my jawline and nips near the left side of my neck, but I redirect her to my lips. She rolls over and faces me, and we lie side by side. I kick the covers up and over us and then hold Trinity in my arms. She has her eyes closed, and she looks relaxed as she savors the afterglow. I kiss her forehead.

"Kevin," she murmurs.

"Hm?" I pull my lips away.

"Is it wrong for me to be falling for you right now?"

That question makes my heart flutter ten times over. "If it's wrong, then arrest me now."

<h1 style="text-align:center">Chapter 16</h1>

THE CROWD IS ELECTRIFIED TONIGHT DURING MY MIX session at Club Xscape. I'm one of three deejays performing at the Summer Bash event that the club puts on every year to draw in a little extra business during the slow days of summer. I have the last two hours of the night. Denise and Dom are here, and at the foot of the stage, next to Alexis, is my sexy girlfriend. It's been three weeks, and we finally made things official. I don't know why we waited so long. She knew, and I knew, that neither of us was going anywhere, despite the talk we had a month ago about my busy schedule coming up. She trusted that I wasn't going anywhere, and I'm still not, no matter what.

The colorful lights trace Trinity's purple halter top, and the black, flared pants that make her hips look two sizes smaller. But when she dances and sways to the beat, her full, curvy frame is revealed. My eyes are glued to my girl for the rest of the set. She ignites that fire in me that I release through my mixing. And the crowd can feel it, too. There's so much energy in this place, like a musical orgasm, and I don't want it to stop.

But my phone vibrates in my pocket, giving me the five-minute alarm for closing time. With a sigh, I end the current song, but I do it with a bang. The crowd cheers, and the emcee comes onstage and makes his announcements. It takes me several moments to regain my composure. Man, I was really lost in the music tonight. And to think that Mama wants me to quit deejaying.

This is my life. My sanity. I'll never give this up.

Before I know it, the club's emptied out, except for Dom, who hops onto the stage and begins breaking down my equipment.

"Wow, bro. That was one of the most amazing sessions I've ever heard you do!" Dom says.

Smiling, I turn off the turntables and set the records in their sleeves. "Thanks."

"You were really in it tonight. Have you ever thought about taking this deejay thing internationally?"

"I did once, but right now, I need to stay here and concentrate on school and basketball."

"So, is everything official yet? You gonna be playing in the pro leagues for sure now?"

"Naw, I didn't sign anything yet, but I plan to after this weekend."

This weekend, I need to focus, because tomorrow is Friday, and Dom and I are going home for Mama's birthday. Michael is even supposed to be there.

I can't believe Mama's going to get her wish.

We pack up my car, which is parked in the back, and I shut the hatch. Several footsteps approach us, and I turn around. Three female figures come our way, and I can't help grinning as my eyes rest on the fullest figure in the middle. Trinity rushes into my arms and kisses me deep. I inhale her vanilla scent, and my groin strains. *My God*, the things this girl does to me.

Next to me, Denise and Dom embrace and go into a mini-make-out session.

"You were amazing, Kevin!" Trinity says. "The best deejay of the three!"

"Yeah, I think everyone else agreed, too." Denise says, looking over her shoulder at us.

I chuckle and focus on Trinity a moment before my gaze slips over her shoulder to Alexis, who stands alone. *Damn, poor girl.* Watching her two best friends hook up with boyfriends must make for an awkward situation. She doesn't look the least bit upset, but that doesn't mean she isn't. I've been around enough girls to know how some of them think.

I gently pull out of Trinity's embrace and circle my arm around her waist. My hand rests upon her soft hip, and I resist the urge to grab her. "Hey, Alexis," I say. "Thanks for coming out tonight." I don't know why I feel guilty enough to say this. Maybe because I don't want her to feel as though she's being left out or I don't notice her. I mean, she's still a fan, and as much as I hate doing it, I have to keep them appeased.

Alexis smiles a crooked smile, her lip ring giving off a faint glint in the light. "No prob. You're a sexy beast up in that booth." She flicks a lock of purple hair away from her face. "Hey, you two," she says to Denise and Trinity. "Bite of Seattle starts at eleven tomorrow. If we're gonna get any of the good shit, we need to be there early, so I'll come around ten thirty to pick you guys up, okay?"

Bite of Seattle is one of the largest annual food festivals in the city. I've gone almost every year, usually as one of the many deejays that perform there, but I'll have to skip it this year, unfortunately. *Damn*, I would've really loved to go with Trinity.

Why does Mama's birthday have to fall on the same weekend as Bite of Seattle? This is going to be one of the longest weekends ever. Now I know how Dom felt when Denise went back to her parents' place for two weeks.

Trinity turns to Alexis. "Sure thing. I'll be ready."

"Denise? Did you hear me?" Alexis calls.

Denise and Dom are still leaned up against the side of my car, kissing like there's no tomorrow.

I roll my eyes. "Guys, take that shit home."

Dom breaks the kiss and looks sidelong at me. "Don't be jealous, man."

I snort. "Whatever."

Chuckling, Trinity peels my arm from around her. "Don't worry, Lex. I'll make sure Denise is ready."

"'Kay." She gives a little salute and turns. "See you guys later."

Dom pushes off the car and takes Denise's hand. "We're out, too."

I nod. "Be ready around nine tomorrow morning, bro."

"Yup." He and Denise leave.

I turn to Trinity beside me, only to find that she's gone around to the passenger-side door. We both slip into the car and buckle up. She's spending the night at my place tonight, and I'm going to take her home early tomorrow for the festival. I want to spend every last moment with her before I leave for the weekend.

"Alexis still single?" I ask not long after I drive off.

"Yeah, pretty much. Me, Denise, Cherie, and Bianca all tried hooking her up with some cute guys, but she wasn't interested."

I smirk. "Maybe she doesn't like guys?"

"No, she's into guys. There just aren't any she's found remotely interesting. She's so picky, I swear."

"I see." I nod. Not like I know anyone, anyway. I'll leave the matchmaking to Dom. He seems to be good at that.

We arrive at my place, and I practically kick open the front door. I pull Trinity inside, barely giving her a chance to pick up her small overnight bag. Our hands and lips are all over each other. Just as I'm tugging the strings on the back of her halter top, my phone vibrates in my back pocket. I yank it out and am about to hurl it across the living room, when I notice the number flashing on the screen.

Michael. I make a growling sound in my throat. Did he *have* to call at such an inconvenient time?

"Gonna answer that, or what?" Trinity murmurs with a heart-melting smile.

I sigh and reluctantly draw away from her. "Guess I have to." I press the Answer button on the screen.

She plants a kiss on my cheek then tiptoes to the bathroom. "I'll be in the shower," she whispers.

Damn it! What I wouldn't give to be in the shower with her. With a sigh, I press the phone to my ear and plop down on the couch. "'Sup, Mike."

"Oh, good—you're still awake."

"Yeah, but you kinda called at a bad time."

"Oh? 'Bout to tap some?"

I blink. "How the hell did you know that?"

"'Cause I've used that same line one too many times."

I can't imagine his cowardly ass getting any. "What do you need?" I ask.

"I just wanted to let you know that I got a flight scheduled for Saturday. That's when you guys are doing the surprise thing for Mama, right?"

"Yeah. But Dom and I are heading down there early Friday morning." A part of me is a little annoyed that he plans on coming at the last minute.

"Oh, I see." He sounds a little disappointed in this. "Sorry, man. I would come earlier, but I'm on my way back to New York now. Got another fight there—a pretty big fight—scheduled Friday night. My flight leaves from LaGuardia early Saturday morning."

I pause. "Wait, you're headed to New York? You realize what time it is?"

"Almost five in the morning. I know."

"Are you driving?"

"Dante is. We just left our hotel about an hour ago. I had a fight in Pittsburgh."

"How'd it go?" I ask.

"Great. Squared off with this near-seven-foot brawler dude, only to find out that even with all those muscles, he couldn't fight worth a shit. I took him literally off his feet with a back sweep and finished him with an arm bar that made him shit bricks."

"Did you break his arm?"

"Nah. But that guy probably wishes I had. His face is pretty fucked up. Broken nose, black eye . . . he'll probably be eating soup for a few days. But that's what he gets for underestimating me. Can you believe it? The odds were against me a hundred and fifty to one. I ended up winning one of the largest pots so far in my career."

"Wow," is all I can say.

I decide to direct the conversation elsewhere. "So, uh . . . about Mama's birthday stuff. You staying for the weekend?"

There's a brief pause. "I want to, K, but I can't. I gotta be back in New York by Sunday morning."

I roll my eyes. "So what the hell is the point in coming all the way out here if you're only gonna stay a few minutes—a few hours at most?" *Maybe he's still trying to run from this.*

"Hey, this is the best I can do, K. Take it or leave it." His voice is rigid.

I don't bother arguing anymore. "Whatever, man. This is for Mama, anyway."

"Right."

All goes silent again, other than the sound of Trinity's shower. I get a sudden queasy feeling in my stomach. Part of me is happy that he's coming, but the other part of me doesn't care to see his cowardly ass.

"Can you text me Mama's address when we get off the phone, so I'll be able to direct the taxi when I get there?" Michael suddenly asks, breaking the silence.

"Sure, whatever."

"Thanks. Well, I'll let you go. Take care, Little Brother."

"Yeah, you too."

We hang up, and I stare at his name on the screen until it dims and shuts off. I hear the shower still going, but that phone call has put me in too pissy a mood to join Trinity. I text the address to Michael and then head to my room, strip down to my boxers, and curl up in bed. Not waiting for Trinity tonight, I shut my eyes.

CHAPTER 17

The next morning, after I take Trinity home, I stop at Dom's place to pick him up. I honk the horn a few times, and minutes later, he's trudging out the front door, his duffel bag slung over one shoulder. He's carrying a large carton of milk in his hand. He tosses the bag into the backseat with mine, and as he slides into the passenger's seat, I swipe the milk carton from him.

"Sweet. I ran out this morning." I chug about half its contents. *God,* I love milk in the morning.

Dom grabs the carton back. "Damn it, Kev! Don't drink it all!" He peers through the spout and frowns.

"That's payback for drinking all of mine before." I put the car in gear and drive off.

The ride to Mama's house doesn't seem as long as it did last time, though somehow, I think it ought to. Soon, this family is going to be reunited, even if it's only for a minute.

And I don't even get the slightest feeling of butterflies in my stomach.

Dom, however, can't stop fidgeting. I know this isn't even about Mama as much as it is Michael Jr.

"You think he's really gonna come?" Dom asks, as though he can read my thoughts.

I snort. "Who knows? I won't be the least bit surprised if he doesn't, though." No, I wouldn't be surprised, but I'd be hurt. Our time apart has made me want to know Michael all over again. Maybe that was what we needed. But if he chickens out at the last minute, well, that would be typical Michael, and I'd be done trying.

Arriving at Mama's house, I park behind Uncle Adam's SUV. The front door flings open as soon as Dom and I unload. Uncle Adam comes outside, all smiles. "Hey, you two."

Dom follows me up the walkway, hefting his duffel bag.

"'Sup, Unc," I say, giving Uncle Adam a brief hug.

Dom engages in a stiff hug. "Hey."

"Glad you both made it." Unc turns to me. "Any word from Junior?"

I purse my lips. "Yeah, he called and said he'll be here tomorrow sometime."

"Oh." Unc's face falls.

"It sounds like he won't be staying for too long, anyway."

"I see. Well." Unc's face brightens again. "Go on in. Your mother's waiting."

Inside, Dom and I are greeted with the smell of breakfast cooking. Mama's in the kitchen, hard at work, and doesn't seem to notice us come in. The TV's tuned to the morning news, the anchorman's voice a stodgy buzz of background noise.

Mama flips some bacon sizzling in a frying pan. Uncle Adam comes up behind her and whispers something in her ear as he takes the spatula from her and tends to the bacon. She turns, and the wrinkles around her eyes crease as she beams at Dom and me standing in the kitchen doorway.

"Oh! Dominick! Kevin!" She rushes to us and hugs us tight, kissing both our cheeks.

"Hey, Mama. Happy birthday," I say, even though her birthday isn't until tomorrow.

"Happy birthday, Mama," Dom says.

"Thank you," she says softly. She pauses and cranes her neck around us to peer behind us. "Michael is here, too?"

I shake my head. "Naw, it's just us."

"Oh." Her smile fades a bit. "Well, I'm happy that you two are here, at least. Are you hungry? Breakfast is almost ready."

She'd have to be crazy to think Dom or I would refuse a free home-cooked meal. We not only agree, but Dom helps her in the kitchen while I set the table. Uncle Adam leaves the kitchen, grabbing our bags on his way out. He knows that this is our bonding time with Mama.

With breakfast ready and on the table, the four of us take our places. Mama says the blessing, and we pass around the food, with Dom and I piling our plates high as if this were the last meal of our lives.

Mama laughs. "Don't you boys eat where you live?"

I tear into a strip of bacon, while Dom gobbles a spoonful of buttery grits.

"Yeah, but the food's not as good as it is here," I reply.

"My girlfriend's a master chef," Dom says. "But she can't hold a candle to you."

"Flatterer," Mama says. "So when will I get to meet her?"

Dom stops eating. "I dunno. Maybe we can come down during Thanksgiving or Christmas break or something."

"That would be nice."

I smile at that, because just a few months ago, there was no way in hell that Dom would've wanted Denise to meet Mama. His emotional scars have healed much better than I thought they would.

"So, Kevin," Unc pipes. "Any news about that sports agent?"

I chow down on a forkful of scrambled eggs. "He's waiting for me to sign on the dotted line. I brought a copy of the contract and hoped you could help me decipher it first."

"Of course. You know I will."

"I want to give him my decision by Monday."

"Ohh, Kevin, honey, this is so exciting!" Mama says giddily. "My baby is going to be a professional basketball player!"

I laugh. "Well nothing's official yet. I have to get through school first."

"You're all squared away with that?" Unc asks.

I nod. "Yup. I only have three classes left. I'm slated to graduate in the spring."

"That's great to hear." Unc bites into a mini sausage link.

We finish breakfast and clean up, and while Dom and Uncle Adam talk inside, I help Mama with her outside gardening chores. I figure since Dom helped her last time, it's my turn. She looks so happy on her hands and knees, tending to her little flowers and vegetables. She's at peace—something I never thought I'd see again.

"Kevin, honey," she says, not looking up from her work. "Have you talked to Michael recently?"

Frowning, I pluck a few weeds and toss them into the small plastic bin between us. I can't tell her what he's been up to. It would devastate her. She'd be a nervous wreck. "Yeah, he called yesterday. He was on his way to New York."

"New York? What is he doing?"

I lick my dry lips. "Uh, I'm not sure what kind of work he does, but it requires him to travel a lot, it seems."

"I see. Well, those travel jobs tend to pay well. He must be doing well if he's got some business in New York."

"Yeah." I cringe. "Has he called you?"

"A few times, yes, but he hasn't really talked about his work or anything."

"Well, I wouldn't worry about it, Mama. He's holding his own." I pause and consider telling Mama about him coming tomorrow, but I don't want her to get her hopes up too soon.

By the time we finish outside, it's lunchtime. Dom helps Mama make sandwiches. Uncle Adam and I sit in the living room, poring over the twenty-page contract. He's read it over several times, pointing out certain key points. He's no lawyer, but being a business owner who has regularly dealt with third-party suppliers, he's had to sign a lot of contracts.

And really, it's the best I'm going to get. There's no way I'd be able to afford an actual lawyer.

"This all looks legit to me," Unc finally says, handing the contract back. "You're getting a really good percentage, signing with this agency. I don't see anything out of the ordinary in the fine print, either. This agency sounds very reputable."

I stare at the empty dotted lines of the signature page. "Yeah, that's what my coach said, too. But I wanted to make absolutely sure that was the case."

He pats me on the shoulder. "You've got a good thing here, son. A real good thing. But it's up to you if you want to sign."

I nod, and my eyes glaze over the paper once more. This all seems like a dream. No way would I have ever thought I'd be holding my future in my hands.

That night, I finally collapse in my bed after a long, exhausting, but productive day. Mama's happy, and that's all that matters. I'd been so caught up in family stuff, I didn't even get a chance to check my phone. When I do, I notice missed calls and texts from David, Carter, and Trinity, and twelve new emails.

I call Trinity first. It's only nine, so I know she's still up.

"Hey, Kevin," Trinity says in a cheery—but sexy—voice.

"Hey, where are you?" I murmur, laying my head back against the pillow.

"Over at Denise's hanging out with her and Alexis. How's it going there?"

I stare at the ceiling, envisioning Trinity on top of me. "It's okay. I miss you."

"I miss you, too." I hear girlish giggling in the background. Then Trinity speaks away from the phone in a muffled voice. "Oh my God! You guys are impossible!"

I smile, detecting the embarrassment in her voice. Something rustles. Perhaps she's going somewhere more private. I hope so.

"Sorry about that," Trinity says to me.

"It's okay. Did I call at a bad time?"

"No! Of course not. I was looking forward to talking to you today."

"Yeah, sorry I missed your call. I was doing family stuff all day."

"I understand," she says. "Was your mom surprised to see you and Dominick?"

"Yeah, she was. And she's happy, too. I'm glad."

"That's cool. You don't talk much about your family, other than Dominick. I'd love to meet your parents sometime."

I purse my lips. It's then that I realize I've never told Trinity about my past, or how broken my family was—and still sort of is. And the fact that she thinks I have two parents indicates that Denise never told her anything. Dom said he told Denise all about our family. To know that she kept that a secret means a lot. She really is a great girl, and I'm glad Dom is the one who got her.

But the more I think, the more I realize how selfish I've been to lead Trinity on like this and to keep her in the dark for so long. Things have been going so good for us this past month, and I didn't want to destroy that momentum.

"Hello?" Trinity says, and I stir from my thoughts.

"Sorry, I'm here," I say absentmindedly.

"So when can I come meet the rest of your family?"

"I don't know. Soon, maybe. Okay?"

There's a slight pause. "Okay."

I have to tell her at some point. But I don't want to destroy the good thing we have going here by telling her my shit, letting her in on my baggage. What would be the point?

Yet, why does this bother me so much right now? "Hey," I say, changing the subject. "Guess what I'm gonna do Monday?"

"A radio gig?" Trinity asks.

"Naw. I'm gonna sign that contract. I'll officially have myself an agent."

"Oh, that's great, Kevin! I'm so happy for you! Maybe Monday, we can go there together."

"I would *love* that." I shut my eyes, dreaming about her. "I wish you were here right now. I wanna hold you."

"I wish I was there, too. What time on Sunday are you coming back?"

"It'll probably be late afternoon. I think my mom's gonna want us to go to church with her in the morning. It's her birthday and all, so we're doing whatever she wants."

"That's really sweet of you, Kevin. Your mom is lucky to have you for a son."

I sigh. *If only you knew.* "Yeah."

"We're going to Bite of Seattle again tomorrow."

I frown. "How was it today?"

"It was great! We didn't get a chance to taste all the food since it got crowded fast. But there was plenty of music and entertainment. Lots of local bands and deejays."

I probably know some of the deejays who showed up there. It puts me in a sour mood. "That's cool. I'm glad you had a good time."

She laughs quietly. "I'd forgotten that you were in Renton, and I kept looking for you around the deejay area. You're, like, *always* at Bite of Seattle."

As if she can make me feel any guiltier.

"You know," she continues, "Bite of Seattle was where I first heard about you. I saw you up on stage playing some great music and pumping the crowd. Then, some random stranger said you were a local deejay, and gave me a flyer for an upcoming gig you were doing. And the rest is history."

The bitterness suddenly ebbs as I listen to her story. My heart thumps so hard, I feel as if it will beat right out of my chest. "Wow, that's awesome, Trinity. I can only wish I could've met you sooner."

"We were meant to meet when we did," she says. Then I hear Denise and Alexis's voices in the background, and Trinity sighs. "Hey, I gotta go. My friends need me."

I need you, too. "Want me to distract Denise by telling Dom to call her?"

She laughs. "No, don't do that. It's okay. You're sweet, Kevin. I love you."

I beam at those three words uttered from her mouth. "I love you, too."

We hang up, and I stare at the phone screen. I trace my hand over her name, and my heart pounds furiously for her.

Chapter 18

I wake up late the next morning and realize I've completely missed breakfast. *Damn.*

I'm trudging out of my room and toward the bathroom when I spot Dom hustling from the living room to the kitchen. The TV's on, tuned in to the classic-movie channel that Uncle Adam always watches. Dom sees me and waves then disappears around a corner. I know today is Mama's birthday, but what the hell's going on out there?

Finished with my business in the bathroom, I go out to investigate. Dom's in the kitchen, mixing something in a large bowl. A carton of eggs, strawberries, bags of flour, sugar, and other ingredients cover the kitchen counters.

I stand in the doorway until Dom notices me. "So the dead have arisen," he says with a smirk.

I snort. "Damn it, why didn't you wake me up for breakfast?"

"Since when is it *my* job to wake you up? Anyway"—he turns back to the bowl and continues in a murmur—"Mama said to let you sleep."

I scour the kitchen for leftovers and find a covered plate of bacon, eggs, potatoes, grits, and a biscuit sitting in the microwave. *Thank God they saved me some!*

Dom gives me an amused look when I discover the plate.

"Where's Mama and Unc?" I ask as I reheat the plate. "And what the hell are you making now?"

"They're outside in the garden," Dom replies. "And I'm making Mama's birthday cake."

I nod, impressed.

Dom fishes through the cabinets for the electric cake mixer. He pulls it out of one of the larger cupboards and uses it to thoroughly combine the bowl's lumpy, cream-colored contents. I watch him while I enjoy my piping-hot meal, which I top off with a tall glass of milk.

"Any word from Michael?" Dom asks when he finishes mixing.

I dump my empty plate in the sink. "Nope." My mind goes numb at the mention of Michael.

"Think he's coming at all?"

I shrug. "I dunno. And frankly, at this point, I don't give a fuck if he does or not. Mama has you and me."

He nods faintly and stares at the batter.

"Hey," I say, putting my hand on his shoulder. "Today's Mama's birthday. She deserves to be happy. Let's not bring her down with Michael's shit."

But it's hard for Dom to smile, I can tell. Maybe, somehow, he feels a little of what I feel: Hopeful.

Hopeful that we can all be a family once again.

It's almost two in the afternoon when I get a call from Michael. I don't feel like answering it, but I do anyway, just to see what he has to say this time. I go to my room and shut the door.

"'Sup, K." Just by the sound of his voice, I know something's wrong.

"Yo," I say in a neutral tone.

I can hear murmurs of crowds, and loudspeakers blaring every so often. He must still be at the airport. "So, uh, I've got some bad news, bro."

I roll my tongue around in my cheek. "What's up?"

He pauses a moment. "Yeah, so . . . my flight's been cancelled because of bad weather in Chicago, and all the other flights to Seattle today are booked solid. There won't be nothing available until tomorrow afternoon at the earliest."

"In other words, you're not coming," I say matter-of-factly.

"Sorry, li'l bro. You know I'd be there if I could."

"Actually, I don't. I don't know anything anymore. Haven't seen you in ten fucking years. Why don't you just admit the fact that you're still a coward and don't want to face the family you ran out on?"

"What? No, man, I swear I really wanted to come see the family. Believe me when I say that."

"I think everything leading up to today was bullshit. All these fucking excuses—*Bullshit!* Why the hell did you even call me?" I sit on the edge of the bed.

"K, I'm not making excuses. I feel terrible that I won't be able to make it. Tell everyone I'm sorry I can't be there."

"Tell them your damn self. I'm done. Don't call me ever again, you hear me?"

"Please don't do this, K."

"Stay away from me. Stay away from Dom. Stay away from Mama and Uncle Adam. Stay away from all of us. You had your chance. Go back to your illegal fighting. Have fun with that. Stay out of our lives. You're a fucking disease."

I end the call.

The rage in my blood makes the room spin. I lie back in bed and stare at the designs on the glass light of the ceiling fan.

Once a coward, always a coward.

Just for shits and giggles, I check the weather in Chicago on my phone. Sure enough, there are news alerts and warnings about severe weather, flooding, and power outages in and around the city.

My mouth goes dry. If I can be any more of an ass, I might as well just kill myself.

My mind isn't all there when we sing happy birthday to Mama and eat every last bite of her amazing cake that Dom made. In fact, I'm the first to head to my room. I shut the door. It's how I shut away the pain, because it took everything I had to not tell Mama—or anyone—about Michael. No one had said anything about him, but I knew he was on their minds.

Lying in bed, I toss the basketball up in a perfect free-throw form and catch it. Michael may have pissed me off, but my weekend isn't totally ruined. I still have something awesome to look forward to, come Monday.

My phone buzzes on the night table, and I reach over and check it. A text from Trinity.

> Miss u. hope ur day is going well. Tell ur mom happy bday for me.

I grin.

> miss u too. And i'll tell her. Hope ur having fun.

I stare longingly at her name, feeling the urge to call her, but she's probably still at Bite of Seattle with her friends and won't have time to talk.

She texts back:

> I am, but it's not the same without u here.

I sigh.

> ill be back tomorrow. I love u.

My heart thumps as I hit Send. Every time I tell her those three words, I feel a rush of warmth inside.

She texts back, not a minute later.

I love you, too. c u tomorrow! <3

A sudden knock at my door jolts me out of my reverie. Setting the phone aside, I sit up. "Yeah?"

"Kevin, it's me."

The concern in Mama's voice has me bolting out of bed and to the door. I don't even bother putting on a shirt. I fling the door open and gaze upon her small form. She still looks young for fifty and could probably pass for thirty with a little makeup. Studying her, I notice for the first time how thin she is—thinner than she probably should be. I blame it on the stress—on Pops. He destroyed her. I can only imagine how beautiful she must've been before she met him. Full of life, and all smiles. Kind of like Trinity.

She gazes at me with concerned almond eyes.

"Hey, Mama, what's wrong?"

She peers into my room then focuses back on me. "Can we talk?"

"Of course." I step aside to let her through. As she passes by, her azalea scent calms me.

She scans my nearly bare room and then sits on the edge of the bed. Pursing her lips, she pats a spot next to her.

Frowning, I walk to the bed and sit beside her. Not looking at her, I rest my elbows on my knees and fold and unfold my hands.

I can feel her staring at me, perhaps studying me. But I keep quiet. I'm not entirely sure what she wants to talk about, but I have a few hunches.

Suddenly, I feel her soft hand gliding across my neck—across *that* spot. Cringing, I instinctively grab her hand. She gasps, and I realize I grabbed her a little too hard. I swallow, look at her in a silent apology, and then let go.

"You got a new tattoo?" she murmurs.

My gaze flutters to my lap. "Naw, but I need to touch up the ink on some of them. The scars are starting to show again."

She reaches out to touch my neck again. This time, I don't stop her. But I close my eyes and tense up. Her fingers barely graze the same spot again before they fall away, and I hear sniffling. I open my eyes.

She has her face buried in her hands and is crying gently.

God, no. Not now.

"Please don't, Mama," I say, my voice choking up. "Not on your birthday."

And with that, she goes into an all-out sob. I embrace her, letting her tears fall onto my bare chest. I don't care at this point. The world's dead to me right now. Fuck basketball. Fuck life. The memories run so deep.

Mama's been holding this back for so long, and it's finally come to a head.

"Lord Jesus, I promised I wouldn't cry for my husband anymore," she whispers between sobs. "I promised I would be strong for you boys. I can't help but be reminded that our family is still broken."

Closing my eyes again, I kiss the top of her head and rest my chin there. Even her hair smells like azalea shampoo.

"Our family's not broken, Mama," I assure her, rubbing her back. "You've got Dom and me. And Uncle Adam."

"Yes." She cries some more and then pulls out of my embrace, rubbing her bloodshot eyes.

Frowning, I wipe her wet face with my palms. "Stop. Please. You can't keep doing this. It's going to kill you. That son of a bitch is going to kill you from his grave."

She sniffles and averts her eyes. "I'm trying to cope every day, Kevin. Lord knows, I'm trying. Some days are great. Others are like this. Your Uncle Adam has been a godsend, taking care of me. I appreciate it. But not even he can erase those memories."

"No one, can, Mama. But you gotta be strong. Why do you think I got these tattoos in the first place? Because I didn't want to wake up every morning, look in the mirror, and see those damned scars on my neck. Knowing what he did permanently damaged me—mentally and physically. You need to find a way to shut away that pain, or else it's gonna keep eating away at you little by little, like it's doing now."

"I had hoped for my birthday that I could have had all three of my boys together again. Even just for a moment. I just wanted my family back for a moment."

I swallow a bad taste in my mouth and focus on the floor. "Yeah."

"Kevin, look at me, please," she says in an almost pleading voice, as if she's about to cry again.

I snap my head to her. Her almond eyes are glassy. I stay silent.

"Did you talk to Michael today?"

I purse my lips. "Yeah, he called earlier."

"And?" she says expectantly.

"And?" I repeat, then my heart suddenly pounds. "He said he was sorry he couldn't be here for your birthday."

"Oh." She nods. "I guess work's been pretty demanding."

I frown. "Yeah."

"Well, I should be happy about that, right? I mean, he's got himself a good paying job that lets him travel everywhere. I should be grateful that he's living a better life. Praise the Lord he's not living on the streets or getting into trouble."

My heart drops. With that statement, I'm unable to tell her the truth. I'm not going to shatter those dreams she has of him. It would be like telling a kid that Santa Claus isn't real. I don't want to see her cry anymore. "Yeah, he enjoys what he does. He's happy."

"That's good. I'm glad." She gets up from the bed and starts for the door. "I'll leave you alone now."

"Mama," I call as she reaches for the handle.

She turns to me, a hint of a smile on her face. "What is it, baby?"

"Trinity says 'happy birthday.'"

Chapter 19

Sunday's church service drags on till two in the afternoon. Seriously, what does someone have to talk about for three fucking hours? Dom and I rush out of the building before we're bombarded by old church ladies and desperate single women who couldn't keep their eyes off us during service. Fortunately, Uncle Adam has gotten the hint and meets us outside with Mama in tow.

Leaning against the hood of my car, I loosen a button around the collar of my dark-green dress shirt. Dom does the same with his navy blue one.

"In a hurry, are we?" Unc says with a smirk.

I roll my eyes. "Seriously, man. Doesn't that preacher get cotton mouth or something? I don't even think college professors talk for that long nonstop."

Mama chuckles. "Reverend Richardson is very thorough." She kisses Dom and me on the cheek. "Thank you both for coming. It really meant a lot."

"You're welcome, Mama," Dom says.

"So when will I see you two again?" Mama asks.

Dom shrugs then looks to me.

"I dunno," I reply to her. "I'll call you, okay?"

She nods.

Dom kisses her cheek and gives Uncle Adam a hug.

"Bye, Dominick. I love you," she says in a quivering voice.

Dom hops in the car and settles into the passenger's seat.

I kiss and hug her. Our embrace is longer than I care for. She's hurting, and I have to be there for her, since Dom and Michael aren't going to do it. "Take care of yourself, okay? No more tears, Mama. I mean it."

"I know. I'll try," she says. "Please be careful driving on that interstate. Call me when you get back, okay?"

I nod a little. "I will."

Uncle Adam slaps me on the back as we hug. I notice a hint of concern in his eyes as we pull apart. Maybe Michael called him. I don't know. I don't care. Michael is his problem now. Not mine.

"Take care, son," Unc says.

"You, too." I hop in the driver's seat. I send a quick text to Trinity and then head out.

The ride to Montlake is short and quiet. I pull up to Dom's place and continue staring straight ahead, waiting for my brother to get out. After a few moments, when he doesn't so much as budge, I finally look at him. "You getting out or what?"

Dom flicks his eyes at me and purses his lips.

"What?" I say, starting to get annoyed.

"Michael called, didn't he?"

I blink several times, the question blindsiding me. How the hell did he know that? "Maybe."

"What did he say?" Dom asks, seeing right through my bullshit as usual.

I shut off the engine and lean my head back against the headrest. I run my hand up my face, over my hair. "Why the hell are you asking me this now?"

"Kev . . . "

I twist my mouth to the side and tap the steering wheel with a finger as I mull over my thoughts. "He called yesterday afternoon. Said his flight got cancelled in Chicago due to bad weather."

Dom arches an eyebrow. "Was it true?"

I run my finger along the steering wheel, brushing my thumb over the chrome logo in the center. "Yeah."

"Why did he call you instead of Mama?"

"I dunno. Maybe he was too scared that she'd be upset about it."

"She was more upset that he wasn't there."

I roll my eyes. "You think I don't know that? But I'm sure as hell am not gonna tell her what he's really been up to. For God's sake—she thinks he's got some great, honest, well-paying job. She has no idea he's doing this illegal shit."

"When are you gonna tell her, then?"

"Never. None of us are gonna tell her." I look at Dom sternly. "Uncle Adam said that she doesn't need the stress of worrying about Michael like that. And he's right. This is our secret. If Michael wants to tell her the truth, then that's on him. Not us."

Dom nods slowly then reaches into the backseat for his duffel bag. "Okay."

I start up the car again. "Get your ass out the car and go see your girl," I say with a smile, trying to lighten the mood.

Dom returns the smile and gets out. "See you around, bro," he says and shuts the door.

On my way to Trinity's place, I call Mama, letting her know Dom and I got back safely. My throat tightens every time I hear her voice.

Arriving at the one-story brick apartments, I hop out of the car and rush up the walkway to Trinity's door. She answers it only seconds after I knock, and she greets me in a pair of black sweatpants and a tank top that fits her snugly, showing off every ounce of her ample tits. Her wavy hair's pulled back from her face.

I lean in and kiss her luscious, full lips that taste like vanilla, just like the rest of her. "Hey," I whisper.

She pulls me against her soft body, and I melt. "Hi, Kevin. I missed you."

Her warmth causes a tingle and stiffness in my groin. I'm sure she can sense how much I want to do crazy things to her right now. But as she pulls away, taking her soothing heat with her, my arousal subsides.

She leads me inside. "I made some jambalaya. Want some?"

"Hell yes." This girl just spoke to my heart. Up until now, I've not had any of Trinity's cooking. Hell, I didn't even know whether or not she could cook. But I'd be a damned fool to reject a free meal from a sexy girl. As I step into the small apartment, I realize this is my first time here. Trinity always came over to my place, and I never wanted to pressure her into letting me come over. But today, finally, she seems cool with it. The apartment is furnished and decorated to a bare minimum. I don't expect much more for on-campus housing. Trinity's friend and roommate, Cherie, is still gone for the summer, so we have the whole apartment to ourselves.

On our way to the kitchen, I spot a laptop sitting among a slew of papers and books on the couch in the living room. The TV's tuned in to an R&B music video with the volume down low.

Trinity lets go of my hand when we reach the kitchen, and she pulls out a blue dinner plate from one of the cabinets. I lean against the doorframe, watching the back of her body as she walks to the stove in green socks with rainbows on them. She uncovers the lone pot sitting on the stove, and a plume of steam escapes as though she'd prepared the meal only minutes ago. I push off the doorframe and approach her. I circle my arms around her waist and push my hard dick against her round ass. I feel her body stiffen at my initial touch, but then she relaxes, and I rest my chin on her shoulder. I peer into the pot. Just the sight of the seasoned rice, cut-up sausage, chicken, and vegetables makes me salivate.

"That looks awesome," I murmur, watching her load the plate up by the spoonful.

"Hope you like it," she says, sticking a fork in the mountain. "It's a family recipe. My dad is from Louisiana."

I swipe the plate from her and lean against the counter with it. I shove a forkful of the Cajun goodness into my mouth, and I almost drop the plate. *Wow, this is good!* It's spicy as hell, but awesome.

Trinity looks at me expectantly. "So? Do you like it?"

"Like it? I love it!" I say between bites. I polish off the plate in minutes and ask for more. Trinity laughs and complies.

"Dom knows how to cook, too, but he has nothing on you," I say, enjoying my second helping. "You can tell him I said that, too."

Her smile turns coyer. "Yeah, Denise tells me how Dominick spoils her all the time, cooking for her and all that. Wish I had a man who did that for me."

I stop eating. "Trust me. You don't want me to cook."

"But it's such a sweet gesture. The food may not be any good, but it's the thought that counts, right?"

"Yeah, I guess." As I finish eating, I think of something I might be able to cook for her. Hard-boiled eggs. Yeah, I can do that—no problem. "So what were you doing before I came over?" I start for the sink to wash my empty plate, but she plucks the plate from my hands.

"Checking on all my scholarships," she replies, running the water. "I want to make sure there are no stipulations. And I wanted to see what day my monthly stipend will come once school starts back up."

I blink. "Whoa, you get a stipend? That's like the mother of all scholarships right there." Even with all my basketball talents, not even *I* earned a stipend with my scholarship.

"It's not a whole lot. I use a good chunk of it for rent, food, and bills."

"How did you manage to land *that* kind of scholarship?" I tote the jambalaya pot to the refrigerator. It's not fair that Trinity's doing all this work.

"I come from a low-income family. And I'm a first-gen student."

I close the fridge. "First-gen?"

"It means neither of my parents went to college." She shuts the water off and dries the plate.

"I would've thought one of your siblings would've gone to college."

She'd never really talked about her family much, only that she had two sisters and two brothers. And I never wanted to pressure her into talking about personal issues.

She walks past me, casting a glance as she returns the plate to the cabinet. "No, unfortunately. Both of my younger sisters dropped out of high school because they got pregnant. As for my brothers, the oldest is in prison, and the youngest went off somewhere and got married. We never heard from him again."

She says this nonchalantly, as if she's grown numb to the fact. I can only imagine how hard it must've been for all of them. "I'm sorry," is all I can say.

She shrugs then walks toward the living room. "It was their choice. But I still love them and all my baby nieces and nephews all the same."

"That sounds rough, Trinity. I'm sorry for prodding like that." I follow her to the living room.

She closes her laptop, stacks the strewn papers and sets them on the coffee table, and plops down on the couch. "Don't worry about it. You didn't know. But I'm not ashamed or anything. I mean, we all make our own choices. I chose to follow a different path than the rest of my siblings."

I sit beside her and drape my arm around her shoulders. She nestles into me, laying her head on my chest, and watches another music video playing on TV.

"You're the smartest of the bunch," I say. "So, I take it that's why you want to help young teen girls? Because of your sisters?"

She nods. "I don't want to see others make the same mistakes my sisters did." She looks at me. "So what about you? What's the story with you and Dominick?"

I purse my lips. I certainly don't want to spill my horrible past to her, but she did tell me about her family. Wouldn't it only be fair? "Eh, it's just us. Well, there's one other brother, but I don't like to talk about him."

She opens her eyes. "Why? What happened?"

I shift my gaze to the scantily clad women dancing on TV, but the images become a blur as I think about how to answer.

"Let's just say he ran out on the family and never came back."

"Oh. Sounds like Brandon—my brother that got married."

"Yeah." I swallow a lump that has formed in my throat.

"What about your parents?"

I stiffen at the question. "My parents are from New York, but they moved here not long after Dom was born. Pops was a block mason for a small construction company, and Mama was a stay-at-home mom who took care of my brothers and me."

"Sounds like you have a loving, hardworking family."

I exhale. If she only knew. "Naw, Trinity. It was anything but loving."

She lifts her head up from my shoulder and stares at me intently. Perhaps she sees the trouble in my eyes, or the way I'm constantly moistening my lips with my tongue. "You don't have to talk about it if you don't want," she says gently.

I rub my hand down her arm and sigh. "You've a right to know. If we're gonna make this relationship work, I mean, *really* work, then we need to learn and understand each other, right?"

She nods and lays her head back on my shoulder. "Yeah, you're right."

I take a deep breath. The TV's still muted, and my ears ring from the room's silence. "My father cut me and choked me until I blacked out. Next thing I knew, I was waking up in a hospital bed. I was fourteen."

She lifts her head from my shoulder again and stares at me, horrified and concerned. "That's terrible, Kevin. I'm so sorry." She places her palms on my cheeks then leans in and kisses my lips. "I'm sorry."

While I don't protest the kiss, the memories make my heart ache and my mind go numb. "There's no reason for you to be sorry. You didn't do anything. Anyway, Pops is dead now. Committed suicide because he knew he was guilty of raping my baby brother."

Her eyes widen at that, and she covers her mouth. "Are you serious? Your dad did that to Dominick?"

I nod once and stare at the floor. "Don't tell anyone this, okay? Not even Denise, even if Dom already told her."

"I promise."

I suddenly feel her warm fingers at my neck, and I suck in a breath, reaching up to stop her. I grab her hand, but not as forcefully as I did when Mama touched me there.

Trinity looks at me apologetically. "So, that explains these tattoos. Is that where your father cut you?"

"Yeah," I say, not letting go of her hand.

She places her other hand over mine. "It's okay, Kevin."

I'm not sure what she means by that, but I don't let her go. I'm still overly self-conscious about that area because it's a constant reminder of my past. "It's *not* okay."

She purses her lips. "I mean, it's okay to let go of the past."

"How the hell can I let go of something that's been practically branded on me?"

"You can start by not being afraid."

I fall silent.

"Will you let me touch it?"

I'm not sure if I should let her. Why is this so hard?

I inhale and breathe deeply through my nose as I slowly let go of her hand. I shut my eyes.

"Open your eyes," she says.

My heart pounds at that, but I do as she says. I feel her hands on that spot on my neck, and it feels like a thousand jolts in my body. Her touch, like Mama's, is soothing. But there's something more—much more.

Then I feel her lips on my neck.

She kisses that spot so tenderly, so lovingly, as if she means to erase the bad things imprinted there. The area is sensitive to her touch. The violent jolts of anger and sadness from childhood memories wash away. Her lips feel good on me there, and I involuntarily tilt my head to the side, fully exposing my neck to her. Her kisses turn into little sucks, and then she uses her tongue.

"It's okay. Don't be afraid anymore," she whispers in my ear. "Don't let the past take control of you."

She's right. I can't let the past control me. But that's what I keep doing, from Pops to Michael.

She lays me back on the couch, resting my head on the armrest, and straddles me. I stare up at her, at this big, beautiful angel, who is loving me like the perfect woman she is. I run my hands under her tank top and along her sides, groping her soft skin. She caresses my cheek then runs her fingers down both sides of my neck, and for the first time, I don't flinch.

Chapter 20

I'M UP EARLY MONDAY MORNING, AND I PUT ON THE BEST dress shirt and pants I own. I call Trinity before heading over to her place. She's just as excited as I am.

By nine thirty, I'm at Trinity's, and she's dressed in a work-casual pantsuit that makes her look sexier than she probably realizes. She can make any random outfit sexy.

Most of the morning rush-hour traffic has died down by now, and I pull up in front of the agency building ten minutes before the scheduled appointment. Trinity and I hurry through the ornate doors and take the elevator up to Ben's floor. When we enter the office, I notice a rough-looking girl, probably no older than me, sitting in the waiting area, leafing through a tech magazine. The redheaded receptionist smiles at us.

"Mr. Anderson?" Her eyes brighten as though she's seen a celebrity.

"That's me. I have a ten o'clock appointment with Mr. Madison."

"And I'm his girlfriend, just tagging along," Trinity says, interlocking her arm with mine.

The brightness in the redhead's eyes dims a little at this, and then she nods. "Please have a seat. He will be right with you."

We sit across from the lone girl, who lifts her hazel eyes from the magazine and stares at me and Trinity.

I nod to her. "'Sup."

The girl cracks a brief smile. Then her face goes rigid. "Mornin'," she says with a thick southern drawl. She flicks a lock of dirty-blonde hair from her face and returns to the magazine.

Pulling out my phone to pass the time, I check my e-mail. Russell had put me in for a gig tonight at Club Skyline, one of the newest clubs downtown. *Hell yes, I'll be there.* Work's been slow over the summer. I'll take what I can get.

I hear my name called and see Ben standing at the door leading to the small hallway of offices.

"Kevin! I hope you are as excited as I am today." He gestures for me to follow. "You're free to bring your lovely girlfriend, if you like."

I pop up from my chair and extend my hand to Trinity. She stands as well, and we follow Ben to his office. After shutting the door behind him, Ben gestures to the two chairs in front of his desk. I wait for Trinity to sit before seating myself.

"So, today's the big day, huh," he continues, sitting down. "The start of an exciting career for you. I'm honored to hopefully be able to represent you. All of my clients have done well for the duration of their contract tenures, but I've not had someone of your caliber in a very long time."

I beam. Trinity checks out the various pictures, awards, and other sports paraphernalia displayed on the walls and bookshelves.

"It's a dream come true, Mr. Madison," I say, returning my attention to him. "I've wanted this since I was a kid."

He opens an unseen drawer behind the desk and pulls out a stack of papers secured with a binder clip. He flips through the pages a moment. Then he lays the stack in front of me. "I will explain each page to you one by one before you sign."

It's a good two hours' worth of explanations. We go through the twenty-page contract point by point, detail by detail. I'm glad I had Uncle Adam look at this before me, because everything Mr. Madison says is on point with Uncle Adam's explanations. This contract is as legit as it gets. When we get to the blank dotted lines at the end of the twentieth page, Mr. Madison slides a fancy black pen across the desk to me and folds his hands, waiting patiently. Biting my bottom lip, I pick up the pen. I feel Trinity's hand on my shoulder, and she smiles at me when I look over.

"You got this," she mouths.

I grin back at her. I'm so glad she's supportive of me doing this. I take a deep breath, turn back to the paper, and scrawl my name across the dotted line.

That night, at Club Skyline, I bust out with some all-new material for an excited crowd that's filled the place to capacity. These kinds of nights are rare during summer break, but this is a new club, and a damn nice one at that. The two levels are lit up with ambient lights that give the entire place an atmosphere I've not seen nor felt in the other clubs around here. The owner is supposedly from LA and must be trying to get an LA vibe here, too.

From the stage, I stare out at the sea of people moving synchronously to the beat as multicolored lights beam and swirl across random faces. I haven't talked to Dom all day. I've no idea if he's here, but I don't bother scanning the hundreds of people in this dim, colorful place for him.

But Trinity? I spot her easily. She's in her usual spot at the foot of the stage, dressed in some sort of purple outfit, moving that voluptuous body to the thrumming beat. She's a purple beacon of beauty that my eyes—and my heart—are attuned to. Next to her is Alexis, who is chatting it up with some guy who looks too drunk to even be listening. Her short, purple hair emanates a glow when the overhead black lights hit it.

I'm mixing hard on the ones and twos, bobbing my body as I become caught up in the music. The crowd reacts with cheers, shouts, and whistles. I mix in another song, switching out vinyls on the fly. Then, as if awakening from a long dream, I stare out toward the crowd again and eye my beautiful woman. But this time, she's no longer dancing, and her back is turned to me. Not faltering from my mixing, I continue to watch while my hands steadily work the vinyls. She turns slightly, and a man's head appears at the side of her face. He could be my age, or maybe Dom's. He's clean-cut and wears a white, button-down shirt. He looks shorter than me, but I can't really tell from up here. He whispers something in Trinity's ear, and I notice his hands holding the sides of her bare arms. Smiling, he leans back, and Trinity's shoulders shake as though she's laughing. My eyes are glued to his hands, which are still touching her arms, and I frown. There's nothing I can do when I'm in the middle of a set, so I try my best to ignore it. The guy's probably an old friend. At least, that's what I'm trying to tell myself.

The screen of my phone sitting next to the mixer suddenly lights up, revealing the time—1:50. It's time to wrap this shit up. As the emcee comes up on stage to make announcements, I glance back in Trinity's direction. That guy is still with her, and they're still talking. Fortunately, he took his damn hands off her.

Still, I want to know who the hell he is.

Then it hits me. *Holy shit. I'm jealous.* I've *never* been jealous like this toward anyone before, not even my previous girlfriends. Maybe because I didn't care about them like I do Trinity.

I didn't love them like I do Trinity.

God. I can't do this. Act like a dick every time a random guy talks to her. I have to trust her. I'm sure she trusts me . . . right?

The crowd begins to shuffle toward the exit, and I soon realize that Dom's not here tonight to help me pack up. But that's okay. I need to be alone with my thoughts for a while. I watch Trinity leave with that guy, not even looking back at me on the way out the door.

What the fuck?

After packing up my car, I hop into the driver's seat, not even bothering to wait for Trinity to come meet me as she usually does. I hate the thoughts going through my head right now about her hooking up with that guy. I wonder how long they've known each other. I grit my teeth at the thought of them meeting up during Bite of Seattle while I was away for the weekend. *Why the hell am I so insecure about this? I need to trust her. There's nothing going on. He's probably just a friend.*

"Just a friend." I've heard that song enough times to know that to think he's just a friend is bullshit.

Scowling, I start up the engine and crank up some music. My mind is all sorts of fucked up right now.

But a tap on the glass shakes me out of my thoughts, and I roll the driver-side window down. Trinity leans over, smiling. I get a whiff of her enticing vanilla scent, and all the bad thoughts melt away.

"Hey, you didn't wait for me," she says.

I force a smile. "Well, you looked preoccupied, so I didn't want to bother you."

She raises her eyebrows. "You mean Terrell?" She chuckles. "He's a friend of the family and my philosophy tutor from last year."

I mirror her expression. "That all?"

Her gaze hardens, and she pushes back from the car. "Seriously, Kevin? What the hell do you think is going on between us, huh?"

Her tone has me tensing. I never wanted this to happen—*again*. I promised her it wouldn't. "Nothing. Sorry."

She purses her lips and shakes her head. "Right. I'll talk to you later. Bye, Kevin." She whirs and begins walking off.

I slap my forehead. *Damn it!* "Trinity, wait! Let me take you home."

She stops and glances over her shoulder. "I'll be fine, Kevin. The bus is still running."

"It's after two in the fucking morning. Please let me just take you home."

She turns all the way around and crosses her arms. I look at her pleadingly. She sucks her teeth and walks around to the passenger side. *Thank God.*

We drive to her place in complete silence. What is there to say at this point? I fucked up majorly by misjudging—mistrusting—her like that. I don't blame her for being royally pissed at me right now. I park by the curb and wait for her to get out. I stare at her longingly, wishing she'd kiss me and tell me she forgives me for being such an ass, but I know that's not happening. I hurt her again, and she's never going to let me live that down. She glances at me before opening the door.

"Thanks for the ride," she says quickly, getting out.

Before I can say anything, the door slams, and she's already heading up the walkway. I keep watching her until she's safely inside, and then I drive home.

I need to get my shit together. Fast.

I think the both of us just needed a little time to cool off. The next afternoon, not long after I return from the basketball courts, Trinity calls, and we talk for a while, laughing and talking about how stupid it was for me to ever doubt her like that. It *was* stupid of me, but I can't help but worry that I'll lose her to someone else. Besides, after what Denise's ex did to her, I'm paranoid that all these guys out here are nothing but assholes. And I'll be damned if I just sit back and let Trinity become another victim.

"Wanna hang out tonight?" I ask as we're winding down the call.

"Sorry, Kevin. I already promised Denise I'd go over to her place tonight."

I frown, but I understand. I can't keep her from having fun with her friends, nor would I want to. "Okay, that's cool. Tomorrow, then."

"Tomorrow's good." There's a hint of a smile in her voice. Everything's all right. For now.

Tonight's a perfect night for Chauncey's. As I'm about to text Dom, I receive a text from him.

Got a gig 2nite?

I grin at my brother's impeccable timing.

nope. Meet me @ chauncey's in 20.

He replies:

k. bout 2 clock out. c u then.

I take a quick shower, get dressed, and head out the door. It's almost seven by the time I arrive at Chauncey's, and I spot Dom's red sport bike parked out front. Heading inside, I find Dom at the bar, and he's saved a seat for me. He's already starting on his first rum 'n Coke. Thinking of my car parked out front, I sigh. I need to lay off the hard shit tonight.

"Starting without me, eh?" I say, sliding onto the stool.

Dom looks up from his drink. "I couldn't wait for you."

I roll my eyes and order a beer. Olivia pushes a filled, ice-cold mug my way.

"Your woman ditched you, too, huh?" I take a sip.

Dom snorts and downs the rest of his drink. He crunches on an ice cube. "How'd you know that?"

"That's what happens when you and I date two best friends."

"Seriously, Denise and her friends have the most *girls' night out* nights I've ever seen."

"You'd think they'd be sick of each other with the amount of time they spend doing hell knows whatever girls do."

"Probably talk about us," he says.

I guffaw. "Yeah."

Dom traces his finger around the brim of the glass. "Denise and I were talking about going to Mama's place for Thanksgiving."

"Hey, that's great, bro. I'm sure Mama would love to finally meet her." I take another sip.

He nods. "What about you? Gonna bring Trinity?"

"Thanksgiving is months away, man. I have no idea what's going to happen between now and then."

Dom wrinkles his brow. "Everything okay with you two?"

"Yeah, I guess." I stare blankly at the bar top. "I dunno."

"You dunno?"

I motion to Olivia for another drink. "I nearly fucked up again last night. No—I *did* fuck up again last night."

He studies me. "What did you do?"

A new mug of beer is slid my way. "I misjudged her. Mistrusted her. *Again.* I'm such an idiot."

"What?"

"I saw her with another guy at the club last night and nearly lost it. I can't believe I got jealous. I've never been jealous over a girl before. Not like that."

"Seriously, Kev? That's all? You're afraid of being jealous? Well, I've news for you—that's part of being human."

"I know that, Dom. But seriously, Trinity and I have been together for a little over a month, and I've never had any reason to not trust her. And now, as soon as I see her talk to a guy, I get all nervous and shit."

"How do you think I felt when I watched Denise and William together? And William bragging on me about how great she was every chance he got? You wanna talk about jealousy . . ."

"William was different. He was a first-class asshole."

"That's putting it mildly," Dom says.

"I don't want to think Trinity's moved on from me."

"Why do you think she would?"

I shrug. "Women are weird, bro."

He chuckles. "True that."

I take a modest sip and realize that Dom didn't order any more drinks after his first one. I'm glad he's playing it safe, especially since he's riding his bike tonight. "Trinity doubts our relationship. She's afraid about what will happen when the semester starts. She thinks I won't have time for her. I told her I will, but she doesn't believe me. And you know what sucks? A small part of me thinks she's right."

"Hey. You got a lot going on now. This is the start of your career. You're just now getting your shit together. You have to figure out what's more important."

"Trinity's more important," I say.

"But is Trinity gonna make you enough money to settle down? Have a good-paying job?"

"You sound like Mama."

Dom frowns. "Look, man. I know how much she means to you. But if she loves you, then she should understand where you're coming from. If she can't handle that, well . . . maybe she's not the one for you."

I bite my bottom lip. I can't imagine another girl having the same effect on me that Trinity has. "I'm not gonna give up on her. And I don't want her to give up on me. She's the best thing that's happened to me. After all, if it weren't for her, I wouldn't have met Ben Madison."

Dom pats me on the shoulder. "It'll all work out in the end, bro. It always does. Remember what you and Uncle Adam once told me? 'You have to keep moving through the dark tunnels of life, no matter what. Because at the end of that tunnel, you'll eventually find that light.' Maybe you should consider taking your own advice."

Shaking my head, I finish my drink. Really, I'd love to. Problem is, this tunnel is so dark I've no idea if I'm even going in the right direction.

Chapter 21

School's back in session for the fall semester, and once again, the UDub campus is full. Students old and new are still stuck in their summer-break mode, walking aimlessly with maps in their hands as they search for the buildings where their classes are located. As I walk to the School of Business building for my Finance class, I feel more like a first-class freshman than a senior. I can't believe it's been two years since I stepped foot on campus. What's weird, but not at all surprising, is the number of Kevitron fans I pass. Almost all of them make some sort of remark or compliment about my music. One girl asks me to autograph her music player. My deejay crowd definitely seems larger than my b-ball one this time around, and the fans are approaching me. This means I'm going to have a flock of annoying groupies to deal with all semester long. But I have to go along with it to keep up my reputation. To them, I'm DJ Kevitron in and out the club.

I enter the double doors leading into the grand lecture hall with stadium-style seating. I'm ten minutes early, and there are already a few people hanging out in the far back row on their tablets and phones. I consider sitting in the back, too. There was a time I would have done that, but today I decide on the front, instead. Fans won't annoy the hell out of me if I sit right in the professor's line of sight.

I set down my backpack, which I've used since my freshman year. It's dirty, ripped in some places, and one of the zippers is broken, but it still holds my school stuff just fine. I take off my ball cap, set it on the desk, and then run my hand over my hair. As I wait for the rest of the class to arrive, I check my phone. Trinity and Dom have texted me, both wishing me good luck on my first day. I text them back, wishing them the same.

Someone sits down in the swivel seat next to me, and I look up from my phone. A caramel-skinned girl wearing a dark-blue beret over thick, curly hair smiles at me then takes out a spiral-bound notebook and a pencil from her oversized, multicolored tote bag. She's cute and reminds me of one of those eclectic artist people. I glance behind me and notice nearly all the back seats are filled. I meet the gaze of one person, who hollers, "Oh shit! DJ Kevitron's in this class!" Suddenly there's much excited whispering throughout the class. Exhaling, I whip back around in my seat and slide down, attempting to hide my embarrassment.

The girl beside me raises her eyebrows. "DJ Kevitron? For real?"

I purse my lips. "Just Kevin right now."

"I'm Candice."

A man in slacks and a button-down shirt comes through the doors in a rush, carrying a briefcase, and makes his way to the podium. The class settles down. For two and a half hours, I'm left alone, and the class is more or less attentive to the lecture. When we're dismissed, I slip my hat back on, pulling the brim low, almost over my eyes. I grab my stuff and rush out the door before the rest of the class has a chance to bombard me. I have a few hours before my next class, so I send Trinity another text to see if she wants to grab some lunch. Leaning on the bike racks outside the building, I pocket the phone and hear Candice's voice behind me.

"Kevin!"

I turn toward the steps and glimpse her waving at me as she clutches the straps of her tote bag over her shoulder. I nod and give her a small wave back. I push off the bike racks, stuff my hands in my pockets, and continue on my way. I think this girl's trying to get close to me. I can't let that happen. I *won't* let it happen.

"Kevin, wait."

I halt. There's one thing about her that sets her apart from Trinity. She called me "Kevin"—not once, but twice—without a thought. I'm sure this girl only knows me as Kevitron, but the fact she's able to separate the two so easily intrigues me. I think that alone should earn her a moment of my time, at least.

Candice catches up with me and takes a moment to catch her breath. "Hey, you left before I had a chance to talk to you."

"Sorry, I'm meeting my girlfriend for lunch," I say hastily, hoping to defuse whatever's going on in that mind of hers.

Her expression dulls. "I just wanted to say that a bunch of us are forming a study group for this class, and I was wondering if you wanted to join."

I arch an eyebrow. "A study group? Already? Is this class really that hard?" From the syllabus we were given, it doesn't seem like it. And I'm pretty good at math—maybe not a whiz like Dom, but good enough to be able to pass this class.

She looks dumbfounded. "What? You mean you don't know the rumors about Dr. McKenney's classes? You'll be lucky to pass with a low C. His tests and random quizzes are brutal."

I bite my bottom lip. "It's just math stuff, right? I'm good with numbers."

Her eyes light up. "Really? Then please join our study group! Me and a few others have struggled in our math prereqs. We can use an extra brain."

If what she says is true, then this is going to be one long sucktacular semester. "If you knew all this about his class, then why did you sign up for it?"

"Because all the other ones were full. And Registration wouldn't allow any overrides. I'm supposed to graduate in the spring, so I didn't have much of a choice."

I sigh. "Right."

"So can you help us out, Kevin? Please?" She looks at me pleadingly, and my heart practically melts. Something about that kind of expression on a girl turns me to jelly.

"Fine. When are you guys gonna meet? And where?"

She beams. "Oh, thank you so much! And, um, I'm not sure yet. We're getting everyone's contact info, and we'll let the group know sometime this week. I'd like to meet in the library if there are rooms available."

I nod. "Okay, sounds good."

She takes out a small notepad and a pen, and hands them to me. "Can you write down your contact info for me, please?"

Keeping my eyes on her, I take the items. I'm about to write my phone number but then halt in mid-stroke. No fucking way am I giving this girl my number. I don't care how attractive she is—I'm not falling into that trap. I give her my e-mail address instead and hand it back to her. "Here you go."

She takes the items back, her face bright, but when she reads what I wrote, that enthusiasm in her eyes dims a little. "Thanks, Kevin. I'll add you to the e-mail loop when I get back to my dorm."

I wrinkle my brow. "Dorm? I thought you said you were a senior?"

"I am, but I couldn't find a suitable place close enough to campus, so I just opted for the on-campus dorms. I know a few other seniors who have stayed on campus all four years."

I nod thoughtfully.

"Anyway, thanks for joining the study group. I'll send you the info ASAP. See you next week."

She leaves, and as I watch her disappear into the crowd, my phone vibrates in my pocket.

A text from Trinity.

How does Al's Grill sound? :-)

I grin. As if she needs to ask.

With it being the first day of classes and the heart of lunch hour, Al's Grill is packed solid. Unable to find a place to sit, we opt to get our food to go and return to campus to eat. Our next class doesn't start for another hour. It's mere coincidence that my final class of the day starts the same time as Trinity's.

It's a sunny day for a change, with blue skies and a light summer breeze, so we head to Greig Garden. We find a wooden bench in a secluded spot beneath white birch trees and tall azalea bushes. I'd forgotten about these cool little gems that UDub has sprinkled throughout campus. I used to come out here to clear my head. That was back when I was a sophomore, and shit was starting to get rough for Dom back at home. It was here that I later made the decision to drop out of school—to sacrifice my scholarship and basketball career in order to take care of my brother.

And yet, here I am again. But this time, I'm picking up where I left off.

Trinity finishes a rib and wipes her hands with a napkin. "So? How did it go?"

I'm already on my second rib when she asks me this. "Well, I found out that I have one of Dr. McKinney's classes, which apparently is hard as fuck to get a good grade in. So the students are already forming a study group and asked me to join."

Trinity laughs. "McKinney? Oh yeah, I heard about him. I can't believe you picked his class."

"How the hell was I supposed to know? I just picked what was left. It's been two years since I've been in school."

"Well, it'll work out, I'm sure. So, did you join the study group?"

"Yeah. I didn't have a choice, really. I mean, if he's as bad as they say he is, I don't want to take any chances. My basketball career is riding on me finishing on time."

"I see." She uncovers her fork and starts on her side of mac 'n cheese. "Sounds like you'll be even busier this semester."

My throat tightens when she says that. "Hey. I'm not gonna be too busy for you, if that's what you're getting at."

She says nothing and eats quietly.

I sigh, and as I'm about to continue with my own lunch, my phone vibrates. It's a message from Russell, who has set me up with a radio gig next week and two club gigs this Friday and Saturday. *Hell yeah.* Work has finally picked up again. I text him in reply.

"So, how was your first day back?" I ask Trinity, trying to break the awkward silence.

She doesn't look up from her food. "Fine. I had a Special Topics class on teaching primary and secondary education. Pretty easy stuff, and my professor is really laid-back. My next class, though, Educational Administration, is supposed to be tough. The professor who's teaching it is new, and I've no idea what he or she is like. I skimmed the textbook, and it's ridiculous. I'm thinking I'm probably going to be looking for a study group or tutor very soon."

I shake my head. "Why is it that as soon as we're about to graduate, we get all the hard-ass classes?"

"All the more reason to stay focused." Sadness fills her eyes. "If I do end up getting some extra help in my class, I may have to cut back on my clubbing nights."

I frown. So it's okay for *her* to be busy, but not okay for me? At that moment, I remember a talk that Dom and I had a month ago. "Look, Trinity. I know how hard this is going to be for us, being busy and all with classes, but don't think for a moment that I don't consider you important." I take her hands in mine. "You are very important to me. And I love you."

She looks down at our hands. Then she raises her eyes to meet my gaze. "I understand you have a life, Kevin. Believe me, I do. I just . . . I'm afraid we're going to fall apart. Become more distant as our schedules get busier. I don't want to end up like Denise and William."

My body tenses at the mention of Denise's asshole ex, William. "Denise and William? What about them?"

She sighs. "Back in high school, they were a lot like us. They were very close and loved each other to death. But during junior year, William had to move to Chicago with his parents. William and Denise's relationship was never the same again. They tried to make the long-distance-relationship thing work, but as their schedules got busier and busier, they didn't have time for each other anymore. So they just stopped talking."

I bite my bottom lip. I never knew the whole story about William, but now a lot of what happened, and the way Dom acted, makes sense. "That won't be us, Trinity," I assure her. "For one thing, we don't have a long-distance relationship."

"It's going to seem like it with our schedules."

"We can't let our schedules dictate our lives. Let's pick a time and place to meet every day."

She shakes her head. "No, Kevin. Don't you see? I don't want our relationship to be 'penciled in' an available slot."

I give her hands a small squeeze. "I don't either, but this would only be temporary until the semester is over, right?"

Trinity's expression is skeptical. She pulls her hands back. "I guess."

She stands up and starts gathering napkins and empty food containers. I take the items from her and toss them in a nearby garbage can. As she picks up her backpack, I lay my hand on her arm. She looks sad, and I can see it in her eyes that she's doubting this. Doubting *us*. Doubting *me*.

I lean in and kiss her deeply because I'm sick and tired of seeing sadness and pain. I miss her beautiful smile.

She melts and kisses back, moaning softly against my lips.

I pull back and stroke the side of her cheek. "We're gonna make this work." Because *damn it*, I'm not going to lose her.

By Friday, I'm riding the high of surviving the first week of classes and the news of Ben entering me into next year's basketball drafts. According to him, my chances of becoming one of the top picks are high. *Man,* it's like a dream come true.

The club is especially hopping tonight. The first week of classes is over, and everyone is out to celebrate. Trinity's friends are all back from vacation, and they mingle in their usual spot by the stage in my line of sight, watching me and dancing to the music. I smile at Trinity, my eyes only on her. She gives me so much energy for deejaying. And yet, I can't get what we talked about earlier this week out of my head. It bugs the hell out of me. Does she really think this relationship won't work? I'm going to prove her wrong.

Dom's at the bar getting drinks for Denise and her friends like the gentleman he is. Or maybe it's just that Denise has my little brother wrapped around her finger. I wouldn't doubt that. The two of them are inseparable. It's almost sick—in a good way.

I wish Trinity and I could be that close. Sometimes I think we're not. Something is obviously missing in our relationship. Every time Trinity and I talk, it's as though a barrier forms between us. It feels like she's trying not to get close to me, as if she's thoroughly convinced of this relationship not working. How can she doubt me like that? I thought she liked me too much to worry about what happens.

The set is over, and the crowd begins to leave. Dom hops up onto the stage and helps me pack up like he usually does. "Great set, bro."

"Thanks, man." I unplug cords, wind them up, and stick them in a milk crate without making eye contact.

"Long day, eh?"

Shrugging, still not looking at him, I slip records into sleeves. I feel a touch on my bare arm, and freeze. The touch goes firm, and I look sideways.

"Kev, what's up?" Dom asks.

I scowl. "I dunno, man. I feel like I'm doing the right thing, but it's never enough, know what I'm saying?"

Dom blinks. "Something going on with you and Trinity?"

I shrug his hand off. "Maybe, but it doesn't have to. I bet she doesn't want to come over to my place again."

"Did you ask her?"

"Nope. I just know."

Dom rolls his eyes. "For fuck's sake, man. Talk to the damn girl!"

I shake my head. "What's the point?"

"What the hell's wrong with you?"

"It's complicated."

Dom purses his lips and finishes packing the last of the equipment. "Fine, whatever. But keep your drama to yourself, then."

I narrow my eyes at him. He's right. It's not his fault I can't keep my head straight. "Sorry, man. I'm feeling shitty right now. So much going on."

"Wanna talk about it?"

I pick up some milk crates and head for the back exit. "Yeah, maybe. But don't you and Denise have something going on tonight?"

"I'm sure Denise will understand if we postpone the rest of our night."

I manage a small smile. It's rather ironic that I'm the one coming to Dom for help and advice. It's usually the other way around. "Thanks."

We pack up the car, and I hop in the driver's seat.

"I'll swing by your place after I take Denise home," Dom says.

"You don't have to do that, but thanks, man."

I watch him leave, though I'm waiting to see if Trinity is going to come around back to meet me like she usually does. But several minutes go by and she doesn't, so I drive around the front of the building and search for her among the lingering club goers. I discover her, Alexis, and two more of their friends chatting with some guys. The guy Trinity is talking to is the same one from before.

The "tutor"—Terrell.

I clench my jaw at the sight. Rolling my window down, I pull up alongside the curb, where she has a clear line of sight to me. She notices me, grins, and after gesturing to Terrell to hold on, walks over to the lowered passenger-side window.

I want to smile back at her, but it's too hard, seeing what I'm seeing right now.

Terrell glances over at me from afar. Then his attention turns back to Alexis and the others.

"Hey, sorry I didn't come out back," Trinity says. "Terrell was here, and he was telling me about the tutoring services he's doing starting next week. Lord knows I'm going to need all the help I can get this semester."

"Yeah," I say in almost a whisper. My voice is practically choked up at this point. Nothing's probably going on between them, but the way I see Trinity smile when she's around that guy makes me uneasy.

Maybe she really *is* trying to move on from me. *God*, my insecurity has me fucked up.

Her brow wrinkles. "You okay?"

I suddenly realize just how pathetic I probably seem right now. "Huh? Yeah. You, uh, need a ride home?"

She gives me a sympathetic smile. "You look whipped. Why don't you go? I'll take the bus."

"I'm not whipped." I frown. "I would like to spend some time with you tonight."

"Okay." She leans back from the car, says something to Terrell and Alexis, and hops in the passenger's seat.

The ride to her place is quiet. About halfway there, she says, "It was a good set tonight, Kevin. I really enjoyed it."

"Thanks." I snap back to attention. "So, you doing anything tomorrow?"

"Laundry, grocery shopping, and homework, mainly," she replies rather quickly, as if to say, "I have no room for you." I get the hint, and I don't press the issue further.

"Okay. Well, call me whenever, I guess." I pull up to her place and wait for her to get out.

"Thanks for the ride," she says, then leans over and kisses me. On the cheek.

Fuck that. As she moves to get out, I grab her hand, stopping her. "Hey, give me a real kiss."

She looks back at me, somewhat hesitant, then presses her lips to mine. I taste her kiss, but I don't taste her love. She doesn't want this. I pull away. "Never mind. See you later."

She gets out of the car without hesitation, not even giving me a goodbye, and then slams the door. I watch her make her way up the walkway, ensuring she gets inside safely before driving off.

My hands clam up on the steering wheel, and my heart sinks to my gut. I don't like where this is headed. I don't like it at all.

Chapter 22

TONIGHT IS FRIDAY, TWO MONTHS INTO THE SEMESTER, AND that means Midnight Madness, one of the biggest events at UDub, because it marks the first official day of pre-season training for the Huskies' men's basketball team. TV cameras, local radio stations, and other media are spread out all around the arena's front exterior, where a long line of fans clad in purple and gold wait anxiously for the arena's doors to open.

Luckily for me, Coach Langley got me a VIP ticket to join the team in the locker room. A TV mounted on a wall near the exit is tuned to the live broadcast. This year, UDub is hosting as the West Coast school for the network's coast-to-coast televised coverage of Midnight Madness. UDub never got this kind of national recognition for the event back when I was playing. Usually UCLA or one of the other big schools down in Cali got that honor.

The cameras pan over the arena's exterior, over the many faces of the crowd, some—mostly kids—partaking in pre-event activities, while others wait on line. Thirty minutes before midnight, the visitors begin to shuffle into the arena.

Midnight Madness is about a three-hour event, and there are plans for a dunk contest, three-point shootout, and at the end, a freewheeling scrimmage. I called and texted Mama, Uncle Adam, and all my friends—including Trinity—to tune in to the event. This is my first time at Midnight Madness in two years. It's going to be absolute torture being a spectator instead of a player.

I stand with Patrick and the two assistant coaches and watch Coach Langley give the team a final pep talk. My attention is especially on Ronnie, my protégé, who was fresh out of high school when I met him two years ago and has since then taken my spot as the new point guard. I hope he has a future in the pro leagues after college. Ronnie's a senior now. I think he'll take the team far, especially if I can be there to help keep him and the rest of the team motivated, which is what Coach Langley is hoping will happen. Unfortunately, Maurice didn't make the team this year, so it's all up to Ronnie.

My eyes drift to the TV again. There's a crowd six thousand strong filling the arena. I suddenly feel butterflies in my stomach. It's the feeling I always got whenever I was getting ready to play. It's awesome that these guys got such a big turnout.

The team forms a huddle and starts chanting. My body buzzes with the energy in this place. I can't stop smiling. The assistant coaches join in, and so do I. We jump and chant and shout, just as I remember doing a few years ago. Finally, the team hustles out the door and through the long hallway that leads to the court. I follow behind the last coach, the adrenaline of the small jog making me more pumped. Memories of home games flood my mind. The sights, the experience, everything used to be amazing—like a dream.

The crowd cheers as the twelve players jog onto the court, six going to one end, and six going to the other. They start shooting around. I follow the coaches to the sideline and watch the multicolored lights strobe across the polished wood floor as hip-hop music starts blaring from the overhead speakers. Cheerleaders move and dance to the beat, and someone dressed in a husky dog costume runs around the court, gesturing for the fans to cheer louder.

I scan the arena and the six-thousand-plus crowd. There are still a bunch of empty seats, but the energy in this place feels like another home game.

I search for Dom and spot him and Denise sitting together on the visitors' courtside. At least they got good seats. Dom meets my gaze and waves. I smile and wave back. Of course, there's one person I've been really hoping to see here, but she conveniently had to miss the game in favor of staying home to do homework and study for midterms next week. I grit my teeth at the thought. Seriously? It's Friday fucking night. Who the hell does homework then? I don't understand that girl sometimes.

Our relationship has been getting shittier and shittier each day, each week, each month. I don't even know if I'd call it a relationship anymore. She's been using school as an excuse to put us on hold. I mean, I guess I can't be mad at that, right? She has her priorities straight. School is more important. But I do miss her like crazy.

She's been meeting Terrell the Tutor a lot, too. After about a month of that, I snuck around the library during one of his "sessions" and found her, him, and a few others together, working. None of them saw me, thank goodness. I felt horrible for doing that, but I needed a peace of mind to know that she and Terrell had nothing going on. I trusted Trinity, I really did, but the weird way she'd been acting around me kept fucking with my mind.

As for my study sessions, I'm glad I've been attending them, because half the class is failing. I'm just getting by with a high C average. The rumors about Dr. McKenney's class were obviously true.

There had been a point when Candice and some other girl in my study group tried getting close to me, and I defused that shit fast. Not long after that, I'd discovered Candice and Terrell on campus one afternoon, making out. It was hard not to laugh out loud.

My thoughts return to Trinity. Where the hell did I go wrong? Why can't we have a normal relationship? Why can't she be here instead of doing homework on a Friday night? I'm crazy about that girl, and I don't know why. She obviously doesn't feel the same way. She's not a groupie smothering me. She's for real.

That's what I wanted, right?

"And now, the dunk contest is about to begin! Get ready to be dazzled!" The announcer's voice blares through the speakers, breaking me out of my thoughts.

My excitement returns as I watch eight of the players—including Ronnie—make their way to center court. I already know a few of them won't make it. They're either too short or just plain can't dunk. I'm six-four, and as good as I am, I'm not much of a dunker. I prefer to take my shots from the outside. The competition begins, with each player given a chance at one dunk. A panel of judges sits on the sideline, holding up number scores. Ronnie is second to last, and with his six-foot height and mediocre jump, he manages to bang the ball off the front of the rim. The competition continues until there are only three players left. It's been forty-five minutes, and the winner—a six-nine freshman who did a spinning, behind-the-back-between-the-legs left-handed dunk—is announced.

The crowd goes crazy. I've been on my feet almost the entire time, clapping and cheering for my teammates as if I'm one of them. The players clear the court, and the cheerleaders and mascot return to center court to dance and rile the crowd again as the next event is about to begin.

To my right, Patrick and the other coaches are busy talking to each other or writing notes on their clipboards. Coach Langley is over at the announcer's table, speaking with someone there. He looks in my direction and then points, and the announcer leans over and smiles at me. He turns back to Coach Langley and nods. Their lips are moving, but I have no idea what they're saying. But something tells me I am a part of that conversation.

My phone vibrates in my pocket, startling me. I whip it out and check the screen. There's no way I'm going to be able to talk on the phone with all this noise.

It's a text from Dom.

where's trinity?

I frown. Really? Did he have to ask that?

busy.

I stick the phone back in my pocket, not bothering to see if he replies. I look across the court and notice Dom wrapping his arm around Denise and leaning in close to say something to her.

My mood lightens when the announcer mentions the three-point-shootout contest starting. I used to be an ace at this. I won every year. The team splits up again, six players going to one end of the court, while six go to the other. I keep an eye on Ronnie. He adopted my same three-point-release style that's earned him his place as the best shooter on the team.

Before the competition begins, the lights dim. I look around curiously. *Well, this is a first.*

"Ladies and gentlemen," the announcer says. "We have a special guest here tonight. He was a three-time all-star shooting champion and MVP for the Huskies and has helped take the team to the national championships, where they had two amazing consecutive wins. Stand and cheer for your very own Husky alumni, Kevin Jerard Anderson!"

Spotlights suddenly shine on me. I gasp and hop out of my chair. What the hell? Where'd all this attention come from? People are cheering. I even hear "DJ Kevitron!" And there I am on the jumbotron, looking up like an idiot because there's a TV camera right in my face. I snap my attention to the camera guy and smile. Guess I should wave, too. *Holy shit, I'm on national TV right now!* I wonder if Mama's watching? Or Trinity? I turn and wave to the rest of the crowd. The team and coaches are all on their feet, clapping and cheering, too. The last time I had this sort of recognition was at the championships, when I was named MVP. That was the last year I played.

Several camera flashes go off, blinding me. After a few moments, the arena lights brighten once more. The ovation fades, and the audience chatter and hip-hop music resumes.

Media cameras still surround me, and an anchorman moves in close, microphone in hand. "Excuse me, Kevin, do you have a moment for a brief interview?"

My mouth hangs open, and I look from the man to the cameras then over to the coaches. Langley stands near me, but he's smart enough to be out of the eye of the camera. He grins and nods at me, giving me an encouraging wave.

I'm supposed to talk? I haven't played in two years. I definitely don't want them asking about the gap in my enrollment. They may put two and two together and start getting personal.

"Uh . . . " I say to the eager middle-aged anchorman.

I feel a hand on the back of my shoulder and then hear a familiar voice. "That camera's not rolling now, is it?" It's Ben Madison. I didn't realize he was here, but thank God he is. I turn to him, relieved.

"No, not at the moment," the anchorman replies. "We will roll for the interview, if that's okay."

Ben tilts his head at me, his eyes narrowing, telling me in so many words that he'll handle it. He returns his attention to the anchorman. "I will answer whatever questions you have for my client, sir. I am his agent, Ben Madison."

The anchorman's eyes light up. "Ben Madison! Such an honor! I'd love to ask a few questions. Let's speak over here."

I watch them leave with the cameraman following, and I feel a great weight being lifted from my chest. Is this what agents do? If so, I can definitely learn to get used to that.

The vibrations in my back pocket are going crazy. I received over ten messages from friends and family, probably expressing their congratulations and excitement about my brief TV appearance.

But none of the messages are from Trinity. She must not be watching. Or maybe she doesn't care.

Realizing this, I don't bother opening any of the messages. I sit back down and try and enjoy the rest of the event as best I can. But it's hard to be happy, knowing that the girl I love doesn't seem to give two shits about me.

Chapter 23

It's Wednesday, the start of the long Thanksgiving weekend, and I'm sitting in my car outside Dom's place, waiting for him and Denise. We're all heading to Mama's place for the holiday. Well, all of us except Trinity. We've both survived our classes so far, but our relationship is practically nonexistent. She has stopped calling me every day like she used to, doesn't go to my club gigs, and we rarely hang out. I'm supposed to make my senior year the best year of my college life, but it's become the absolute worst.

I've been asking Dom for more advice, but it's like talking to myself. He pretty much gave me the same advice I gave him. Funny how that works. It's easy to give advice when the shit's not affecting you. I even tried asking Denise and her other friends, but it was like they were all sworn to secrecy or something. They didn't say much to me. Why do girls have to act so weird about stuff like that?

The fact is, I still love Trinity, and I don't think I can ever get over her like I need to. Like I probably *should*. I'm hopeless.

A steady rain falls from the overcast sky. Frowning, I honk the horn long and loud, wishing the two of them would hurry their asses up. The front door finally opens, and Dom and Denise rush out and down the walkway, their duffel bags in hand as they shield their heads from the pouring rain. Dom opens the back door of my car and helps Denise in before following. A whoosh of cold air fills the car, a constant reminder that winter's not far away.

"You two ready?" I ask, turning to face the backseat.

"Yeah, let's go," Dom says, nodding.

I glance up at the rear-view mirror, and I lock gazes with Denise, who wears a trendy brown-leather jacket. She gives me an apologetic look and a small smile then rests her head on Dom's shoulder.

Scowling, I crank up my music, not caring in the least if the two of them think it's too loud. It's my damn car. I cruise down the interstate as fast—and safely—as I can in the pouring rain. Traffic's pretty crazy on a Wednesday night with the Thanksgiving rush. Other than my music, the trip is silent. We pull up to Mama's house around nine, and the rain's finally stopped. We grab our bags and unload.

Uncle Adam opens the front door as we make our way up the walkway. He embraces Dom and me in his near-suffocating bear hugs.

"How's it going, man?" Dom says, once he's able to breathe again.

I stay silent and let Dom do the talking for a change.

"Great," Uncle Adam says. "It's good you two could make it for Thanksgiving. Your mother has been so excited about it." He pauses and grins at Denise. "And who is this lovely young lady?"

Denise smiles. Dom's right. She does have a beautiful smile. It reminds me of Trinity.

Damn it!

"Denise, this is my Uncle Adam," Dom says. "Uncle Adam, Denise."

"Nice to meet you," she says, extending her hand.

While the three of them go on with introductions, I head inside. The house already smells like spices, and they get stronger as I make my way to the kitchen. Mama's busy preparing a large turkey, so she doesn't notice me. Smiling, I watch her for a moment. She looks so focused and determined, caught up in the things she likes to do. She seems at peace. I move in closer and kiss her on the cheek.

"Hey, Mama," I say.

She stops what she's doing and raises her head. Her eyes go wide, and she reaches out as if to hug me but holds her turkey-juice-covered hands in the air instead. "Oh! Baby, you made it!"

Chuckling, I grab a paper towel, wet it under the faucet, and hand it to her. "Yeah. How're you doing?"

"I'm good, dear." She quickly wipes her hands and proceeds with the hug. "I've missed you so much." She pulls back and examines me. "You're looking healthy. You eating well?"

I laugh again. "Of course, Mama. Though not nearly as well as when I come home."

She beams. "I saw you on TV during Midnight Madness. It was fabulous! They even did a news recap the following day. My baby is a TV sensation!"

I rub the back of my head. "Naw, Mama. It was just a little recognition. That's all. I'm not famous from it or anything."

"But you still got your agent, right? I mean—"

"Yeah, I still got Ben in my corner. He submitted my name to next year's drafts. He says he's pretty confident I'll land a team."

Her eyes light up. "Ohh! Praise the Lord! My baby's gonna be a basketball star!" The front door closes, and Mama rushes out the kitchen. "Dominick! Hi, baby. How are you?"

I shrug out of my hoodie, lean against the wall frame of the kitchen, and watch the greetings and introductions all over again. Mama takes an instant liking to Denise. I knew she would. Denise is one of those people who don't give you a reason to dislike them. She has such a positive vibe about her that you just can't help but feel good inside.

While everyone else is chatting it up, I grab the bags and head down the hall. I drop Dom's and Denise's off in his room. Upon reaching my room, I don't feel like coming back out. I just want to stay in here all weekend until it's time to go. It sucks seeing my brother and his girlfriend together and wishing that Trinity were here.

Trinity. Taking my phone from my pocket, I plop down on the bed and lie back on the pillow that smells like azalea-scented fabric softener. I've gotten messages, but none are from Trinity. Sighing, I go through each one. More radio gigs, some meetups with friends on the courts, and conversations between members of my study group.

Finished, I send a text to Trinity.

Miss u.

I have no idea if she'll respond or not, but I hope she does.

"Kevin?"

I blow out a puff of air at the sound of Unc's voice. In my peripheral vision, I see him standing in my bedroom doorway, his bulky frame taking up every inch of it.

"'Sup, Unc," I say, not looking up from my phone.

"Hey, you all right?" He steps into the room.

"Yeah, man. Fine. Just tired."

"Okay." He nods. "School's going all right?"

"Yup."

He purses his lips as if he wants to say something more. I have a hunch as to what—*whom*—he wants to talk about, but I'm not in the mood. "I haven't talked to him since Dom and I were here last, so don't ask," I say, looking at him.

He blinks. "Ah . . . all right." He turns to the door. There's a moment of silence. "I'm fixing the turkey for tomorrow. Wanna help me set up the smoker?"

I glance back at the phone screen. Still no reply from Trinity. "Naw, man. I'm good."

His shoulders slump just a little. "Okay."

He leaves, and I toss the phone on the floor. *Fuck it all.*

I can't keep staying depressed over this shit. I have to move on. I'm sure she has by now. Are we even friends anymore? Why the hell can't I stop thinking about her? Am I truly, ridiculously love struck over this girl?

I hear Dom and Denise coming down the hall.

"The bathroom is this way," Dom says.

I see his shadow against the wall. All he has to do is lean over and look this way to see me, but he doesn't. His footsteps grow fainter as he leaves. I grab the basketball from under my bed and take practice shots. Minutes pass, and Denise exits the bathroom. Her shadow lingers on the wall a moment, and then she tilts her head back, peering into my room. "Kevin?"

I catch the basketball a final time and look over at her, forcing a smile. "Hey, Denise."

She stands at the doorway, peering into my room from afar. "So, this is your room, huh?"

"Yep. Since I was a kid. Mama didn't change anything except the bedding. And her usual mom tidying."

She chuckles. "That's cool. Your mom's really nice. She was showing me how to prepare the turkey to be smoked."

"Oh yeah. She'll talk your ear off when it comes to cooking."

"I'll say. I can see where Dominick gets his amazing cooking skills from."

"Yeah," I say with a sigh. All this small talk is driving me crazy. "Hey, you got a minute to talk?"

She raises her eyebrows, cautious, but I'm only being sincere. She finally nods and steps into my room, but remains a good distance from me.

I sit up in bed. "I'm not gonna bite. I just wanna talk. I'm . . . I've got some things on my mind."

She shoves her hands in her jeans pockets. Only she can do that and manage to make it look cute. "Trinity, I know."

I take a deep breath. "Look, Denise. You know I wouldn't be asking to talk to you like this if it wasn't important. I haven't heard from Trinity in so long, and I miss her. Is she angry at me or something?"

She bites her bottom lip, and her eyelids flutter as she turns her attention to the floor. "Kevin, I wish I could, but I promised Trinity I wouldn't say anything."

"Damn it, Denise." I clench my fists, trying to stave off my emotions. My eyes burn because it's so damn frustrating to be kept in the dark like this. "Can you at least tell me if she asks about me? Does she talk about me to you? Does she even care about me?"

She shakes her head. "I'm sorry, Kevin. She's just been stressed about things. But this isn't the first time she's been like this."

"When was the last time?"

"Back in high school, when a friend of hers died."

I nod slowly. "Did someone else close to her die?"

"No."

"So it's just personal problems? It's not me?"

"Kevin, I can't . . ."

So it is *me?*

Dom comes into my room. He looks to the two of us curiously then goes to Denise, looping his arm around her waist. "Everything all right in here?"

I stare bitterly at his arm around her and the way Denise relaxes to his touch. I wish I could hold Trinity like that right now. "Yeah, fine. We're just talking." I lie back on the bed.

Dom lifts an eyebrow. His eyes turn to the discarded phone on the floor. "Uh, you dropped this," he says, bending down to pick it up. The screen wakes up, illuminating his face in a white light. He scowls then turns to Denise and says, "Hey, can you give us a minute?"

Denise nods, and they kiss goodbye.

I shut my eyes and breathe out through my nose. The door clicks closed, and I open my eyes again. Dom looms over me at my bedside, holding the phone in one hand. My sent text to Trinity is showing.

"Dom, there's nothing to say, so get the fuck out of my room," I mutter.

"Like hell there's nothing to say. We're gonna talk. Now."

I groan. "It's been three months. Three fucking months, and I've watched our relationship go to shit. For what? Because she's so scared our relationship will crumble? She did this her damn self. I can't take this anymore, Dom. I want out. I just . . . " I stare blankly at the ceiling.

"Hey, man. Calm down. You're taking this way too hard."

I glare at him. "Easy for you to say. You and Denise are fine. Perfect. Not a fucking care in the world."

He purses his lips. "It wasn't always like that. You know that."

Yeah, I do, because I was the one who helped him out of his funk. "No one will say shit to me. I'm being kept in the dark, wondering like crazy what's up with Trinity." I can feel myself pleading. "Can you try talking to Denise again for me? Maybe she'll finally tell you something."

Dom shakes his head. "Man, she's been on to me about that since last month. She's not gonna talk to me. And to be honest, I don't think she really knows what's up with Trinity."

"But they're best friends. Why wouldn't she know?"

Dom shrugs. "Maybe it's something personal that Trinity's not ready to share with Denise."

"All I know is that Trinity has been scared of this relationship since before school started. She probably thinks I'm too busy with everything that's been happening to me recently."

"Are you too busy?"

"No! I mean, yeah, I've been busy with classes and deejaying and basketball and shit, but I try to make time for her. She's the one not reciprocating." Dom opens his mouth, but I continue. "And don't even say 'talk to her.' You see all those calls and texts I've sent over the past three months? How many times did she reply?"

He stares at the phone and cringes. "Not much."

"Exactly, bro. She doesn't want me. I have to convince myself of that. I have to move on with my life. I have to stop loving her so damn much."

"You obviously can't stop loving her, bro."

Damn, I know! "I'm gonna sound crazy for saying this, but I wish Trinity was a fangirl. At least then, I'd know she'd always want to be with me."

"Yeah, but like you said, fangirls aren't genuine. Is that what you want?"

I run my hand over my face, exasperated, and exhale.

Dom looks contemplative and then shrugs. "You once said, 'If she's not into you, then move on.' Well, I think you just need to try and move on. This funk is killing you, man."

I sigh.

Dom sets the phone on the night table and grabs my arm, tugging me out of bed. "C'mon, bro. It's Thanksgiving. Try to at least enjoy the holiday, all right?"

I jerk my arm out of his grip and get out of bed on my own. "I'll try."

I'm so pathetic right now. It must be a sickness. I've never felt like this before. It's almost six in the morning, and I'm lying in bed, still exhausted after pulling an all-nighter helping Mama, Dom, and Denise in the kitchen. I worked on anything that didn't involve using the stove, which meant peeling potatoes, grating cheese, and cutting up collard greens—and helping Uncle Adam outside with smoking the turkey. The strong smell of burned woodchips throughout the house made it hard for me to sleep.

It's not as if sleep matters, anyway.

I'm responding to e-mails when the screen suddenly switches to Trinity's name. *Holy shit, she's calling!* My heart pounding, I fumble with the phone as I answer it. "Hello?"

"Hi, Kevin." Trinity sounds so tired. So depressed. Not the happy girl I'm always used to hearing on the other end.

"Hey, I'm glad you called. What's wrong?"

There's a brief silence. "Kevin, I . . . I don't know how to tell you this, but . . . "

I bite my bottom lip. "Just tell me, Trinity."

"I think I'm going to have to drop out of school."

I blink. "Wait. What?"

"There's too much going on right now. My family needs me. I'm the only one who can keep things in line here. I don't want these kids hurt . . . "

"Kids? Hurt? What's going on, Trinity? Are you okay?"

"Yes, Kevin, I'm fine. But there's too much drama here. Too much for these kids to see. My family needs me."

"What's your address? I'll come see you."

"No, Kevin. I'll be fine. I just wanted to let you know what's up. In case you don't see me next week."

This has to be some sort of dream or déjà vu. "Trinity. Listen to yourself. You can't do this. What about your scholarship?"

"I know, Kevin. But it was either school or my family. I have no choice."

"Fuck that. Where do you live? I'm coming over there right now."

"No, Kevin. I don't want you involved in my issues."

I growl. "Listen, Trinity. I love you. I love you so much, and I'm going crazy here. I worry and care about you every day. I'm coming down there and making sure you're okay. You need to finish school. You have a future ahead of you."

"No, you of all people should understand since you had to drop out in order to take care of your family."

I was afraid she was going to say that. "I don't know what your situation is. Please let me come see you."

There's a pause on the other end. Then I hear voices. Several of them—some male, some female. Then Trinity says in a muffled voice, "I told you she's not here. I don't know what she owes you, but she's not here." She must have her hand covering the mouthpiece.

The voices continue then fade away. Trinity returns to the phone. "Hello?"

"Hey. Who was that?"

"Long story." She pauses, and a baby cries in the background. "Look, I need to go. Mikaylah is hungry. I'll talk to you later, Kevin."

I dry swallow as I hear the click on the other end. Not even an "I love you."

Thanksgiving with my family has to be put on hold for me this year.

I slide out of bed and slip on a pair of baggy jeans, a T-shirt, a hoodie over that, and my baseball cap and sneakers. I leave my room, taking only my wallet, phone, and keys. Stopping at Dom's bedroom door, I listen carefully. It's quiet in there, so I knock softly. The bed creaks, but other than that, there's no response. I let myself in.

"Dom," I whisper, blindly maneuvering my way through the dark room. The only light comes from the green numbers of his alarm clock, which read 6:25, and the muted moonlight filtering through the blinds. My hands extended, I feel my way toward the bed. My hand grazes a lump covered in bedding, and I hope and pray it's Dom I'm touching right now. The last thing I'd want to do is scare Denise out of her wits.

"Dom," I whisper a little louder, gently shaking the lump, which feels like a body.

There's a small moan, and to my dismay, it's *not* Dom.

Shit. I pull my hand back. I see movement in the darkness, and Denise moans a little louder.

"Dominick?" she mumbles.

There's more movement, and I see the silhouette of Dom's head slowly appear behind Denise. "What is it, baby?"

"Dom, it's me," I say in a low voice.

I'm certain I hear Denise gasp.

Fuck this. I make my way to the door and flip on the light. My eyes sting from the sudden brightness.

"Aw, Kev, what the hell, man?" Dom groans, squinting.

Denise shields her eyes with her hand.

"Dom, I need to go," I say.

Our eyes adjust to the light, and soon, we're no longer squinting.

"What are you talking about, man?" Dom asks.

"It's Trinity. I need to go to her. I think she's in trouble."

They sit up. Denise keeps the blanket hugged up around her chest, which I assume is because she has nothing on underneath all that bedding.

"Look, I gotta go. I'll probably miss Thanksgiving dinner. Tell Mama I'm sorry, okay?"

"Kevin, what's going on?" Denise asks, her eyes narrowed.

I scowl at her. "How the hell should I know? She wouldn't tell me anything. Neither would you."

She purses her lips.

"Hey," Dom warns. "Don't take this out on Denise. What's going on with Trinity?"

I shake my head. "I don't know. She wants to drop out of school because of some family shit."

"What?" they say in unison.

I glance at Denise. "You mean you didn't know?"

"Well, I knew she was having family problems, but I had no idea she wanted to quit school over it." Denise grabs her phone from the night table. "I'm going to call her right now."

I bite my bottom lip. "Please do. And let me talk to her, too."

She dials Trinity's number and waits a few moments. Her face is taut with concern. I cross my arms and wait patiently. Maybe Denise can get through to her. She's probably the only one who can.

"Hey, T," Denise greets, and I slow my breaths in anticipation. "What's going on? Kevin said something about you quitting school? What's going—oh. That's terrible."

I freeze. Dom and I exchange glances, and then I look back at Denise.

"Do you know where she went?" she continues. "Wow, I'm sorry, T. Do you need me to come down there? Okay." Denise shakes her head sadly at me.

My eyes widen. *What, dammit?*

"Okay, take it easy, girl," Denise continues, looking pensive. "I'll see you soon, right? We need to talk."

I extend my hand to her for the phone. She peers up at me then back at the bed sheets. "Hey, Kevin wants to talk to you. Do you—oh, okay. See you soon, girl."

I lower my hand. My face also falls.

"I'm sorry, Kevin. Trinity was busy. But she did tell me to tell you that she loves you." She smiles apologetically.

Even hearing those three words doesn't do shit for my anxiety right now. "Did she say what was going on?"

Denise frowns. "She said that one of her sisters went out partying and didn't come back. She left her kids at home. I'm sure there's more to it than that, but that was all she managed to tell me. She sounded very busy with the kids."

It's my turn to frown. "So she's gonna quit school to take care of her sister's kids?"

"Trinity's siblings are terrible. They made a lot of bad choices. Her parents are overwhelmed. I feel so sorry for that family."

I clench my jaw. "I'm going to see her, then. If that's what's stressing her out and the reason she's been acting like this around me, then damn it, I'm going. Do you know where she's staying?"

"Kevin, she doesn't want to see you right now. Please just—"

"No!" I yell, throwing my hands in the air.

Glaring at me, Dominick takes Denise's hand. "Hey, if you wanna go, then fucking go."

I take a deep breath, calming my nerves. "Look, I'm sorry, Denise. I really am. I just want to make sure she's okay. Please, just tell me where she's staying. I need to see her and make sure she's okay." My eyes burn. I know for certain I'll cry in front of them, but I don't care. I'm too fucking torn to care. "Please . . . "

Denise contemplates me for a long time and then sighs as she searches through her phone. "Fine. Fine, Kevin." She reaches over to the night table, finds a scrap piece of paper, and scribbles down Trinity's address. "She's at her sister Faith's place in the Kerr-Chester projects in Lakewood." She hands the paper to me.

I let out a breath. Lakewood. Less than an hour drive from here. "Thanks, Denise. You don't know how much this means to me." I turn to leave, adding, "Don't wait up for me for dinner, by the way. Sorry I can't be with you guys. I need to do this."

"Then do it," Dom says.

"Kevin, please be careful. Faith lives in a rough neighborhood."

I shake my head. Having traveled the country doing deejay gigs, I've seen my share of the roughest of the rough neighborhoods. "I'll be fine." I shut off the lights before I leave the room. "Happy Thanksgiving."

Chapter 24

I DON'T BOTHER SAYING GOODBYE TO MAMA OR UNCLE Adam. I don't need them worrying about me, and I trust Dom will come up with a good excuse. I punch in Trinity's address on my phone and map out the quickest route to get there. It's almost seven in the morning, and I'm not in the least bit tired. But I know it'll all catch up with me soon enough. I've got two hundred and fifty bucks on me, which was supposed to last me for the holiday weekend. Who knows how fast that money will go now?

In fifteen minutes, I'm pulling onto the interstate, headed south to Tacoma. I've passed through it many times, and I even have a couple of deejay friends who live out in Parkland, a suburb east of the city. Traffic's light this time of morning because of the holiday. My music cranked up, I cruise along, never getting Trinity off my mind.

Forty-five minutes later, I pull up to the curb in front of a run-down housing development. An old green car is parked in front of me. The car's paint is peeling and weather damaged—it almost looks like it's out of commission. Shutting off my engine, I remain sitting there a moment and gaze out at the neighborhood, taking in my surroundings. If this place is as bad as Denise says, then I need to plan for the worst.

A couple of old men two units down are sitting out front on rusted lawn chairs, smoking. A decrepit, scantily clad woman with rollers in her hair wanders over to the men, making rapid hand gestures at them. The erratic way she's moving makes me think she's strung out on some hard shit.

Beyond the block of units, I spot a lone, graffiti-ridden boxcar sitting on some train tracks, which run through an overgrown lot, and beyond that a distant line of bronze and gold lights that I'm guessing is an industrial park of some kind.

Denise obviously hasn't seen many "rough neighborhoods." This place is fucking Beverly Hills.

I adjust my ball cap and finally get out the car. I hear thumping bass music from a unit across the street. The windows of the second-story unit are open, and drab white curtains flutter in the wind like flags. The old men and decrepit woman stop talking and look in my direction. I can sense they know I'm not from around here. But I'm not afraid. I've seen the craziest of the crazy shit out there, and each experience has helped me to be a little more street smart. I tip my head to them, letting them know what's up, and I make my way up the short walkway to Trinity's unit. There's a rusted, turned-over shopping cart sitting out in the lawn amid some garbage and broken kids' toys. As I near the gaudy orange door, I can make out the faint sounds of a baby's cry inside.

I take a deep breath to regain my composure and then knock firmly.

I hear faint footsteps. "Who is it?" It's Trinity, and she sounds pissed.

My heart skips a beat at the sound of her voice. "Trinity, it's Kevin."

For a moment, all is silent except for the small sounds of the neighbors and the bass-thumping. Then, I hear a series of locks and chains being undone, and the door opens a crack. A whiff of musty, tobacco-tinged air filters out. Trinity peeks her head out, looking horrified. Her hair's frazzled, and she's dressed in sweatpants and a holey, stained T-shirt. I notice dark circles under her eyes.

Damn. She's a mess.

"Kevin! Oh my God. How did you find me?" she says.

I wedge my foot between the door and the frame to stop her in case she decides to suddenly close it on me. "Denise gave me your sister's address. I came to see you. I was worried sick."

Her eyes glaze over. "Kevin, you shouldn't be here."

"I shouldn't, but I am, and I'm not going anywhere until we talk. Can I come in?"

She bites her bottom lip and glances behind her before opening the door for me. "This is a bad idea."

"I'll tell you what's a bad idea," I say, stepping inside. "You dropping out of school to take care of your sister's kids."

"Kevin . . ."

I briefly take in the living room's interior. There are toys everywhere. The tan carpet is full of dark stains and cigarette burns, and the yellowed walls have cracks, holes—one looks distinctly like a bullet hole—and crayon scribbles on them. The TV's on and tuned in to a cartoon. Beyond the living room, I can see part of the kitchen and a pile of dishes stacked in the sink.

"When were you going to tell me?" I say. "You've been so scared of our relationship going to shit, and I've done every-thing I could to make sure that didn't happen. But you were the one keeping me in the dark about this. Why, Trinity? I love you. More than I probably should. I can't help it. I want to be with you."

The tears in her eyes fall, and she wipes them away, snif-fling. "Kevin. I couldn't tell you. I couldn't tell any of my friends, because I knew they would try and talk me out of it."

I sweep over to her and wipe her tears away with my thumbs. "Hey. I know what you're going through. But unlike you, I had to do what I did. Dom was emotionally unstable, and our own mother couldn't very well take care of him be-cause she was still getting over all that shit that happened."

Trinity places her hands over mine. "Kevin, that's exactly the situation I am in, as well. My sister, Faith is . . . she's hanging around with a bad crowd." She pauses. "She had her second child three months ago. I have no idea if one of those lowlifes she hangs out with is the father or what. She's barely home as it is to take care of her kids."

"Does she work?"

Trinity cringes. "Yeah, if you can call it 'work.' She's a drug runner."

I blink.

"You don't know the half of it. Anyway, Terrell stopped by last week to see her. She said she was going grocery shopping for Thanksgiving and asked if he could watch the kids. Of course, he agreed, and so she left, and still hasn't come back. When Terrell called and told me about it, I bought a bus ticket and came here as fast as I could."

"When did she leave?" I ask.

"Tuesday night."

"Where's Terrell now? Why isn't he here helping?"

Trinity shakes her head. "He's done enough for me and my family. I told him to go home to be with his family for the holidays. Anyway, these poor kids are my family, and therefore my problem."

"But they're not *your* kids. Are you honestly gonna take care of them for the rest of your damned life?" I ball my fists, pissed at her and pissed at her sister's laziness and neglect.

"I don't want them taken to Child Protective Services, Kevin. I'm the closest to a mother that they have right now. If the state gets a hold of them, they'll most likely go to foster care."

I exhale through my teeth. "You can't do this alone, Trinity. You have a life to live, too. Can't you talk to your parents?"

She shakes her head. "They're already burdened with Charity and her two kids."

Well, shit.

"Look, Kevin. I really appreciate what you've done, coming all this way for me and everything, but I have to do this for the sake of these kids."

"But I love you, and I want you back."

"I love you, too, but I have to do this. School has to be put on hold until things are better."

She sounds doubtful of that. I am, too.

"Why don't we talk to Faith, then?"

Trinity shakes her head. "Faith is so irresponsible. I can't get through to her. I don't think anyone can. There's nothing you can do right now, Kevin. You might as well go."

"I'll leave when you come with me."

"I can't."

"Then I'm gonna figure out how to change that."

A little boy comes out of the back room, rubbing his eyes sleepily. He's four, maybe five years old. He's barefoot and wearing long-sleeved superhero pajamas. Cradled under one arm is a toy basketball. "Aunt T, is Mama back yet?"

Trinity spins and gasps, rushing to the boy. "No, Pookie, now go back to sleep." She scoops him up in her arms.

The boy points. "Who's that?"

She purses her lips. "That's Kevin. Say 'Hi.'"

The boy smiles and waves. "Hi, Kevin."

Smiling, I wave back. "Hey, kid, what's your name?"

"Isaiah."

A sudden knock at the door makes me jump. Then a baby's cry follows from one of the back rooms. Trinity curses under her breath and paces back and forth with Isaiah in her arms.

"Tend to the kids. I'll get the door," I say.

She looks at me pleadingly then rushes to the back room. "Just tell whoever it is to leave."

I undo the series of locks and latches but leave the chain secured. I open the door a crack. A guy about my age stands there, dressed in too-baggy pants, a black jacket, and a backward ball cap. He's built—*chiseled*. He sports a goatee and a silver chain necklace, and the tops of his hands are covered in tattoos, which appear to continue under the sleeves of his jacket. He tilts a pair of sunglasses down at me and studies me with narrowed eyes. I stand rigid. I'm sure this thug-wannabe punk knows I'm a new face in the neighborhood. But he doesn't intimidate me.

"Need som'in,' bro?" I ask, my street slang naturally coming to the forefront.

He pushes his sunglasses back up. "Yeah, 'bout two g's worth. You Fi's new contact?"

Fi? That must be Faith's street name. I scowl. "No. Now get the fuck outta here." I proceed to close the door on him, but he wedges his combat-booted foot between it and the frame.

He rips his sunglasses off and glares. He has a nervous twitch in his right eye. "Maybe you didn't hear me the first time, so I'll say it again, *bro*. I need two g's worth."

"And maybe you didn't hear *me* the first time, so I'll say it again, *punk*. Get. The fuck. Out of here."

He slips his fingers down one of the deep pockets of his baggy pants and reveals the butt of a gun. I'm not at all surprised to see it, as I've dealt with my share of drug runners before—much more dangerous ones than this amateur.

"Don't mess with me, man," he warns.

I hear footsteps behind me and glance over my shoulder.

"Kevin? Who is it?" Trinity approaches and cranes her neck to see around me.

"No one important." I turn back to the guy, who slips the gun back into his pocket. But Trinity pushes past me and confronts him. "Trinity, wait—"

She puts her hand up, shakes her head at me, and then glares at the guy. "Jovan, I told you not to come around here anymore."

Jovan tilts his head at her. "She owes me some, T. You know where she is?"

"No, I don't know where she is, and even if I did, I sure as hell wouldn't be telling you. Now get the hell out of here before I call the cops!"

He looks her up and down and just laughs—a disturbing, sadistic laugh that makes me pull Trinity back and behind me.

"Yo, T, it's Thanksgiving! Supposed to be givin' an' shit, right?" He laughs again and unwedges his foot from between the door and frame. He takes a few steps back, shoving his hands in his pockets. "I'm comin' back later. She better be here by then." He pauses and glares at me. "An' tell your ol' boy to back the fuck off."

I bow up to him like a bulldog and then feel Trinity grab the back of my shirt. I watch him like a hawk as he heads down the street.

I shut the door and reset all the locks.

"Kevin, don't talk to him again, please. He's bad news," Trinity says.

"No shit," I say, turning to her. "How long has he been coming over here?"

Trinity shakes her head. "I don't know. Weeks, months, maybe. Faith doesn't say much about that stuff with me."

I scan the room. "She stashes drugs here?"

Trinity shrugs. "I don't know. I hope not. I haven't seen any drugs. Believe me, I've turned this place upside down, looking."

I purse my lips. Searching for them would probably be a waste of time—if there are any drugs at all. "We need to leave."

"Not without Faith."

"You said so yourself. Faith won't listen."

"Then I have to make her listen. She's going to get herself killed at this rate. I don't want to lose my sister, Kevin."

"From what it sounds like happened to her, it seems like you lost her a long time ago."

"No! I won't give up on my sister!" Her eyes well up, and she turns away. "Kevin, please. I can't leave right now."

"You need to leave, or else these drug runners will keep coming up here and giving you more of a problem. Eventually, they'll just force their way in."

She says nothing and begins busying herself with clearing the coffee table of used plates and an ashtray.

I raise an eyebrow. "You smoke?"

"No, Faith does." She heads to the kitchen.

I rub my hand over my face as I think. I need to find Faith, wherever she is. Trinity won't budge from here without her. I head to the kitchen and find Trinity at the sink, washing the dishes. I approach and circle my arm around her waist, but she flinches, so I draw my hand back.

"Hey, when was the last time you heard from Faith?" I reach for a dish towel to dry the newly washed dishes, but she snatches it away from me.

"Last night," she replies, tossing the towel aside. She scrubs and scrubs at the dried, crusted food and stains on a plate. "She called from some motel across town, near the highway. Sunnyside Motel, I think it was called."

Not much to go on, but it's a start, at least. I lean over and kiss Trinity's cheek. "I'll be back."

Heading to the door, I hear a plate clunk in the sink, followed by hurried footsteps. "Kevin! Please don't!"

I say nothing and unlock the door.

Trinity tugs at the back of my sleeve. "Kevin!" There's sadness in her voice.

A lump forms in my throat, and I shrug off her hand. "I can't stand to see you like this, worried about your sister," I say, not turning around. "I'll bring her back."

"Kevin, you're going to get killed out there. These guys have guns and who knows what else!"

"If it means I'll get to see you smile again, then I'll take that risk." I march out the door, slamming it behind me. My heart aches as I hear Trinity's muffled cries beyond.

CHAPTER 25

I MUST BE OUT OF MY FUCKING MIND DRIVING HELL KNOWS where to face hell knows what. But the sight of Trinity's misery drives me to keep going. And those kids . . . I may not know them, but I can't let anything happen to them with punks like Jovan coming around there.

By ten in the morning, the Sunnyside Motel comes into view, and I slow down. This side of town looks about the same as Trinity's neighborhood. The motel's rusted, neon sign, which looks like it's straight out of a retro movie, blinks its few remaining letters that strain to work. Pulling into a vacant parking spot, I observe the two-story structure and am surprised it's not condemned yet. Graffiti is scrawled across some of the paint-peeled walls. Iron bars cover the bottom-floor windows, and I notice a bullet hole in the glass of one of the windows.

I've no idea where to begin searching—or how. It's me against punks with guns—or whatever they have. If drugs are involved, it's most definitely guns.

What the hell am I doing? Helping Trinity and her family, that's what.

Getting out of the car, I check the rest of my surroundings. A familiar sound nearby piques my interest.

Feet scuffing asphalt.

A basketball bouncing.

There's a court near here. Wandering around the motel, I discover the small, two-goal court out back beyond a broken metal fence. A group of guys are hard at play among a small crowd.

But there's something odd about these people. Drawing closer, I discover that most of the women are scantily clad. They weave through the spectators, and as they get close to some of them, they engage in some discrete activity that I'm unable to see. The expressions on the women's faces are desperate, almost nervous. Like they're strung up on something.

I've no doubt there's some illegal shit going on over there. It's hidden in plain sight, masked with an innocent basketball game.

Maybe Faith is there. I'm not sure. I pull out my phone and text Trinity.

hey can u send me a pic of Faith?

While I wait for her to respond, I casually head toward the court. The crowd is pretty lively. I stop at the metal fence and peer at the six players. All of them are tall, built, and rough, and seem focused on the game in progress. My adrenaline pumps as I see the intensity of the game, but I suppress it. I came here for a purpose. I can't get distracted.

My phone vibrates, and I quickly pull it out. I study the picture Trinity sent me of her sister. She looks a lot like Trinity, only a shade darker and much thinner. But still gorgeous. It's a shame that she has to get caught up in this scene. With the picture etched in my mind, I put the phone away and scan the crowd. A woman saunters up to me, smiling crookedly, her hair a mess. I can't tell if she's a prostitute, a drug runner, or both. Pursing my lips, I nod. If I'm going to get close to Faith, I'll have to blend in.

"Hey," the woman says, threading her fingers through the open holes of the metal fence.

"Hey." I look her up and down, feigning my interest in her. But honestly, this girl makes me want to gag. She's stick thin with sagging tits, visible veins on her legs, and a nonexistent ass.

She raises her eyebrows. "You coming in or what?"

"Yeah, sure." I make my way to the entrance and flip up the latch to the gate. The woman meets me there and shows me to a vacant seat on the bleachers. I follow without protest while my eyes take in the surroundings.

She sits next to me, and I snap my attention to her. She smiles a yellowed, gap-toothed smile then scoots a little closer. I can smell cigarettes and a hint of weed under her strong, cheap perfume. She curls her arm around my waist then moves her hand across the top of my thigh. I flinch, trying desperately to hide my disgust.

"Good game, hm?" she whispers, tracing her finger up and down my bicep.

I wrinkle my nose. Ugh. Smoker's breath. "Yeah. You think they'll let me get in on that?"

She looks at me, surprised. "Yeah, but . . . " She leans in my ear. "There's a fee."

I grunt. "Yeah, I know." I scan the crowd again. "Give me a minute, okay?"

Her hand squeezes my thigh, and I flinch again. "Sure thing, baby," she says with a wink. "I'm Clair if you need anything."

She leaves, to my relief, and heads to her next victim.

My eyes zero in on a woman on the other side of the court, sitting on the top row of bleachers with a man in a button-down shirt. Her legs crossed, she's leaning over, whispering something in the guy's ear as she runs her fingers down her cleavage. Squinting, I get a good look at her face when she turns toward me. She's definitely Trinity's sister.

Shoving my hands in my pockets, I wander around the court to her. The three-on-three game's going strong, and the guys on the court don't pay attention to me. I sit on the bottom row and keep Faith in sight, glimpsing a small plastic baggie that she pulls out from her shirt and discretely hands to the well-dressed guy, who exchanges it for a wad of cash. He nuzzles her cheek as if he's kissing her, but I can tell he's whispering something in her ear. She giggles and whispers something back, but I can sense a hint of doubt on her face.

The guy catches my gaze, smirks, and nods before getting up and making his way down the five-level bleachers. I move up to his spot and sit beside Faith. She's even more lovely in person. Not thin and frail like Clair or some of the other women walking around. She smells like lemons, which does its best to hide the hint of tobacco on her. She smiles at me, and for a moment, she almost looks like Trinity.

"Hey," she says in a soft, sweet voice. I still can't believe this girl is a drug runner.

"Hey . . . Faith, right?" I murmur, directing my gaze toward the court.

"How did you know that?" she asks with a hint of edginess in her tone.

I raise my eyebrows at her. Her smile fades, her lips forming a thin line. *Damn.* What was her street name again? "Uh, a little birdie told me. I'm Kevin, by the way."

She checks me out and then her eyes narrow. "Did my sister send you here?"

"Nope. I came here on my own. But speaking of your sister . . ."

She scoots away. "No. I don't wanna hear it. If you're not here to buy, then get the hell out of here."

"Faith." I reach out for her hand, but she slaps it away.

"I said go!"

A few of the guys on the court look my way, as do a few more on the bottom bleachers.

Shit. I can't give myself away. "Sorry, I'll buy. Whatcha got?" I say loud enough to hopefully defuse the situation.

To my relief, the players and onlookers resume their activities.

Faith looks skeptical but scoots back closer to me. I notice her right forearm is scarred and bruised in a few places.

Like she's been sticking herself.

"Hey," I whisper, reaching for my wallet. "Just talk to me, okay? Please?"

She eyes my wallet like a hungry wolf. "Money talks."

"Yeah, yeah." I pull out a twenty.

"So what do you want?"

"I want to talk." I hold the twenty to her, and she takes it, but I don't let go. Not yet. "If I give you this, will you talk to me?"

She frowns and tugs on the bill. "Maybe. What's it to you?"

"A lot. You've got an older sister at your house worried about you. And she's taking care of *your* kids." I let go of the bill.

She takes the bill sadly. Then she looks nervously toward the court and begins slipping her fingers down her shirt. She's pretty well endowed and probably has a huge stash down there.

"Hey, I don't want any drugs, I just want to—"

She leans her face closer to mine. Her breath is sweet and citrusy. "I gotta do what I gotta do to pay these bills."

I freeze. Was this some sort of charade? Did she really want to be here? I notice the guys on the court are finishing up the game. One of them looks my way, narrowing his eyes, and I hastily pull out another twenty and slip it to her. The guy turns back to the game.

"You don't need to be selling drugs to pay bills, Faith," I whisper. "You deserve better than this. And what about your kids?"

She nestles the twenty in her cleavage. "I make over nine hundred dollars a day. I can afford everything my kids need."

"Not with drug money."

She raises an eyebrow. "Are you a cop?"

"Naw. I'm just a deejay." I crack a smile.

"A deejay, huh." She uncrosses then crosses her legs.

"But how long do you think it'll be before the cops find out? Because sooner or later, they will. Then what? Your kids get taken away from you. You're left with nothing. There's already some suspicious people coming around your place."

She wrinkles her nose. "Was it Jovan again? That mother-fucker. I told him a hundred times not to come around there." She looks toward the court, where the guys begin to break for water. A new group takes the court. She looks at me again and rubs her fingers together. "Keep 'em coming."

I reluctantly hand her another twenty. "Hey, I need money to get back home, y'know. I live in Seattle."

"Yeah? I like that city. But it got too expensive for a high-school dropout like me."

"So go back to school. Get your GED. It's not too late. You're, what, eighteen?"

"Nineteen, thank you."

"Right. Well, that doesn't mean you still can't get your GED. Why don't you take online classes or something?"

She rolls her eyes and snorts. "Why the hell are we talking about my education, anyway? I'm happy doing what I'm doing now. It pays the bills."

"Bullshit." I scowl. "Your ass and tits are what's paying the bills."

"Yeah, God blessed me with some nice ass and tits." Smirking, she rubs her fingers together for more money.

"I've been around enough druggies to know when someone's enjoying doing this shit," I say, slipping her another twenty. "And you are definitely *not* enjoying yourself."

She raises her eyebrows. "Oh? And how do you figure that, mister deejay?"

"You don't look fucked up like the rest of these chicks out here." I gesture to Clair and a few of her other comrades swarming more customers. "Though, I'm worried about your arm. Was that recent?"

She gives a light shrug. "Eh, I tried it once, didn't like it. Hurt like hell and made my arm numb. Gave me a nice buzz, but not enough to want to keep doing it, so I gave it up. Unfortunately the bruises and scars don't go away that quickly."

Well that's a bit of a relief. But that doesn't mean she's out of danger. "Hey, that's good that you're not addicted to that shit, you know? It fucks with your head, makes you look like an idiot. Like Clair over there."

She follows my direction and chuckles. "Clair? She's a sweet girl. Doesn't bother anyone."

I shudder. "I'm just saying that you're way too good for this. Come back with me. I'll . . . I'll take you to Seattle. Find a way to get you set up with something."

"Sweet, but no. I'm happy here."

The bleachers shake, and I look over. One of the guys from the court stands over us, sweaty and glaring.

"'Sup," I say casually.

Faith leans back from me and flicks a lock of her hair from her face. "Hey, Vince."

The guy looks between us suspiciously. "Pretty long transaction goin' on here." He focuses his gaze on me. "You having problems deciding, bro?"

"Naw, we're just finishin' up. I was actually waiting to see if I could get in on a game." I smirk.

His eyebrows rise. "You play? Sure, man. The guys are about to start in a few. Hurry the fuck up here."

"Yup."

He leaves, and I turn back to Faith, my heart pounding faster and harder with adrenaline and fear. *What the hell am I doing?* "Okay, so here's the deal. I'll play for a bit while you get your pretty ass out of here and back to your kids."

"No way," she says. "Vince's my boss. No one fucks with his money. Or his stash."

"Leave that shit here. You don't need it anymore. You never needed it."

She raises her eyebrows. "You gonna pay my bills, then?"

"No, I can do better than that, but you gotta let me help you."

Vince looks impatiently toward me from the court, and I shift my gaze back to Faith. "I gotta go."

"So do I," she says, frowning.

I move my face close to hers until our cheeks touch. "I wouldn't be doing this if I didn't care about you, Faith."

"Whatever. You don't know me."

"No, I *don't* know you. But I *do* know that you have a sister who's worried sick about you. I'm Trinity's boyfriend. That means you're every bit as important to me as she is. Please come with me." Not waiting for her response, I pull back. She regards me with intrigued, ebony eyes.

While I can't resist a good b-ball game, I hope she gets the hell out of here.

I'm on a team with Vince and one other, Rodney, who like most of the guys playing, easily towers over me with his tall, burly frame. As I suspected, all that muscle slows these guys down. I easily run circles around them, handing off a few assists to my teammates and scoring a few outside shots myself. After each scored goal, I glance over to the bleachers to see Faith in her same spot, only with a different customer. I sigh. I was hoping my stalling would give her time to leave this place unnoticed.

Toward the middle of the game, I notice her get up and join Clair and the other girls. She whispers something to Clair, holding her forehead, and she hands off her stash. A guy comes up to her and checks her out, feeling her up—probably making sure she's not smuggling—and then sends her off with a smirk and a pat on her ass.

"Get better soon," he calls, waving to her. "I'll let Vince know."

She responds by blowing a kiss to him and then wandering away from the court, toward the motel.

Pursing my lips, I return to the game. We're only four points away from twenty-one, and I anticipate an easy win for us. These guys may be tough drug runners, but they suck at basketball. I single-handedly wrap up the game by grabbing two steals and driving to the basket, leaving my opponents and teammates in the dust. I've barely broken a sweat when it's all over.

"Holy shit, man, that was sick," Vince says, holding his hand out for an offhand shake.

"Thanks, man." I shake his hand.

A guy on the opposing team bounces the ball to me. "Never seen skills like that. Good game."

I take the ball and bounce it a few times. "You too. Thanks for lettin' me get in on it."

Vince raises his eyebrows. "Time for one more?"

I shake my head. "Naw. Got some shit to take care of. I'll be back tomorrow." I rub my nose with my thumb, hinting to him that it wouldn't just be for b-ball.

To my relief, he takes the hint and smirks. "Yeah, sure, man. Do what you gotta do."

I nod. "Later." Shoving my hands in my pockets, I leave the court and head toward the motel. I discover Faith standing at a bus stop across the street, smoking a cigarette. Smiling, I hop in my car and drive over to her.

Her eyes narrow at me as I pull up, as though she's trying to make out who's driving.

I roll the passenger-side window down and smile. "Get in here, babe. I'll take you home."

She exhales a long stream of smoke then taps ash from her cigarette. She smiles back crookedly and leans into the window. "And what if I say no?"

"Then I'll carry you over my shoulder caveman-style."

She laughs and finishes her cigarette. "I'll have to think about that one."

"You left 'work' early, I see."

"Yeah, well . . . " She purses her lips. "I had a headache."

"Bullshit. Did you think about some of what we talked about?"

"Maybe, maybe not." She pauses and looks across the street. I follow her gaze and notice several figures moving about the upper balcony of the motel. She opens the passenger-side door and hops in. "Go."

I blink, but the urgency in her voice doesn't let me hesitate for too long. I put the car in gear and speed off.

Chapter 26

"YOU KNOW WHAT SUCKS?" I SAY, AFTER SEVERAL MINUTES of silence.

"Hm?"

"It's Thanksgiving, and I'm gonna totally miss dinner at my mom's place. How the hell can you 'work' on Thanksgiving?"

"Work is work. Don't matter what day it is."

"Fuck that," I say. I keep my eyes focused on the road. "So, who's the father? Why isn't he around?"

"Don't know, don't care. He's probably dead or locked up. My kids are doing just fine without him."

How many times have I heard that? It stings deep, because I get where she's coming from. "Okay, here's the deal. I'm gonna take you home, we'll get Trinity and the kids, and we'll head for Renton tonight."

"Renton? I thought you were going to take me to Seattle."

"I will, but, my family is in Renton, and I bet my uncle can hook you up with a job or something. He knows a lot of people. I'm gonna help you get you on your feet, Faith."

She bites her bottom lip, in a gesture similar to what Trinity does. *God, I miss Trinity.* "Why are you doing all this for me?"

"Because I actually give a damn about you, Faith. And I'm keeping a promise I made to your sister."

She averts her gaze. "You're weird, but I guess I can see how Trinity can snag someone like you. You kind of remind me of her in some ways."

"Are you done with this shit? Done running drugs for Vince? 'Cause we're not coming back here."

"Technically, I can leave whenever I want. Vince knows I don't steal his shit. And I was never really his big seller."

I blink. "Even with your ass and tits?"

"Yes." She smirks. "I may have nice T 'n A, but I suck at business, and he knows it. Girls like me are expendable."

"So you never did like what you did, huh. Why were you doing it in the first place?"

"Because it was good money! And it gave me a roof over my head."

"So you own that place?"

"Well, technically, Vince owns it, but I pay him," she says.

"Seriously?"

"Yup. And my kids have everything they want because of me."

I shake my head. "It's dirty money, Faith. You're doing your kids a disservice."

She glares at me. "You got kids of your own?"

"Nope."

"All right. Then shut the hell up. You better know what you're doing, by the way, dragging me like this. Because if I find out all this is bullshit, I'll call Vince and send his guys on you to fuck you up."

I roll my eyes. "Right." *Empty threats.*

It's after two o'clock by the time we arrive at her apartment unit. Taking Faith's hand, I walk her to the door. I knock and Trinity answers. She holds Mikaylah, who's asleep over her shoulder.

Trinity's eyes widen. "Oh my God," she says in a loud whisper. "Faith!"

Faith reaches for her daughter as she steps inside. "Hey, thanks for watching them for me."

Staying silent, I follow. Isaiah is lying on the couch in a superhero T-shirt and basketball shorts, his little toy basketball cuddled in his arms and his thumb in his mouth. I smile, the sight of the little runt reminding me of me as a kid.

Trinity frowns and hands Mikaylah to Faith. "We need to talk."

"I'm sure we do." Faith rubs the baby's back and rocks her gently. "But it's Thanksgiving. I didn't even get a chance to eat any turkey. Can't we do it tomorrow?"

Trinity shakes her head. "I don't give a damn what day it is. Your life, your *kids* are more important right now."

"Hey," I finally say. "I told Faith I'd get her out of here. I'm gonna take her to Renton."

Trinity gapes. "You what? Kevin, you can't do that!"

"Why not? She doesn't need to be here. I'm gonna see if my uncle can find her a job or something. And rent's pretty cheap around where they live, so I'm sure we can set her up with something a little better than this." I gesture to the messy place.

Trinity looks from me to Faith. "Did you agree to this?"

Faith shrugs and heads toward the back room. "I didn't agree to shit. Your boyfriend's bent on getting me away from Vince, and well . . . " She glances at me. "He *is* kind of cute, and he's a beast at basketball. Should've seen the way he spanked Vince. I had to leave before I died laughing."

I raise my eyebrows. "You saw?"

Faith nods with a wink. "Yeah, I saw. More than I probably should've. It was embarrassing." She disappears into the back room.

Trinity puts her hand on her forehead. "Wait. Wait. Am I missing something here? You played basketball with that damned drug runner?"

"Yup, and he sucked. But I only did it to stall long enough for Faith to get out of there." I loop my arm around Trinity's waist. "That's why we gotta get out of here and head to Renton. There's plenty of room at my mom's place."

Trinity bites her bottom lip. "But there's so much to pack, and—"

"Fuck that," I interject. "Pack what you need. Leave the rest of this stuff behind. Vince owns it all, anyway." I say to Faith as she returns to the living room, the baby no longer in her arms, "That goes for you, too."

Faith sucks her teeth. "I'm not leaving my shit. You out of your mind? I paid for all this!"

"With drug money. Look. You're getting out of here. Starting a new life. Leave this old shit behind. You're not a runner anymore, got it?"

She glares and crosses her arms, surveying the room.

There's a sudden pounding on the front door, making the three of us jump. I can only suspect the visitor is either a cop or another damn druggie. My bet's on the latter.

"Open up, Fi!" says a muffled male voice.

Scowling, I march toward the door, but Faith bolts in front of me. "No." She puts her hand to my chest, stopping me. "I got it."

Trinity comes up beside me, grabbing my arm and holding it tight. She looks at her sister worriedly.

Faith flings the door open and scowls at Jovan, who stands with his hands shoved in the pockets of his baggy jeans. A cigarette hangs from his lips. His eyes are focused on Faith, and he seems to not notice Trinity and me behind her.

"'Sup, Fi. You done workin' today?" he asks in a smooth, poisoned tone.

Faith folds her arms over her chest. "Depends. What do you want now, Jovan?"

He plucks the cigarette from his mouth and grins a set of yellow-stained teeth. "Supplies are getting low, so . . . " He finishes his cigarette and adjusts his ball cap. His eyes flick to mine, and he frowns. "What's the punk doing here?"

I yank my arm from Trinity's grasp and push my way past Faith. "Listen, asshole." I point my finger in his face. "I told you to get the fuck out of here. And *stay* away."

He glares at me then flicks his gaze over to Faith, then to Trinity. His left eye twitching, he suddenly yanks a gun out of one of his pockets. Holding it shakily with both hands, he aims it straight at me. "Back off, motherfucker!"

"No! Stop!" Trinity cries.

My heart drops to my stomach. He's liable to shoot Trinity or Faith on accident with those shaky hands.

Faith gasps behind me, and I can tell that she's backing away from the door. Good. I want her away from me. Trinity, too.

I hold both hands up in surrender. It's not the first time I've had guns pulled on me like this, and fortunately, I'm able to keep my cool.

Jovan presses the gun to my forehead. The barrel's cold steel makes me shiver.

The main thing is that you don't panic. Michael's words resonate in my mind at that moment. Why the hell am I thinking about my fucking brother right now?

Maybe because I was the guinea pig for his self-defense practice when we were kids. I was always getting beat on, and I knew practically all of his routines.

"Jovan, stop," Faith says. "He has nothing to do with this. I don't have any more powder. You'd have to go to Sunnyside for that. I'm sure they're still playing out there, so—"

"No!" Jovan cocks the gun. "You gimme what I came here for, or I'll blow your ol' boy's fucking brains out!"

Don't panic. I take a deep breath. I shut my eyes for a moment then look back at Jovan. I've felt this before, only the gun to my forehead was fake and made of rubber instead of carbon steel. And the one holding the trigger was two inches shorter than me, a scrawny kid with goofy glasses.

Remember, K, it's just another lesson. That's what my master always told me. Another lesson. There are *several* lessons I need to teach this punk. And I only have one chance to do it.

Opening my eyes, I grab the gun and simultaneously weave to the side while pointing it away from the doorway, anticipating it going off. The deafening *bang* that follows startles me. I'm still aware of what's going on around me, so as far as I know, I haven't been shot. But what about . . .

My hearing gradually returns. I hear women screaming and children crying.

Oh my God.

But I can't tend to them until I deal with Jovan. The training lesson with Michael Jr. from back in the day is clear in my mind. *Now's my chance.* My left hand grabs the top of the slide to keep the gun from cycling while my right hand grabs Jovan's wrist, my fingers wrapping over the bottom meat of his thumb. Jovan stumbles forward and makes a startled grunt.

I twist Jovan's wrist sharply. There's a snap. Jovan shrieks in pain, and the gun dangles limply in his fingers.

I see eight-year-old me tapping my hand repeatedly on the foam mat when Michael Jr. had me in the same position. *Holy shit. It* does *work!*

Faith and Trinity scream, and their footsteps scuffle away from the room and into the back of the apartment. I hope to God they're okay.

Alone with Jovan, I yank the gun from his grip and toss it far away from his reach. I seize him by the collar and shove him out the front door.

"You're crazy, man! You're crazy!" Jovan cries.

I glower. "Damn right."

Holding his collar with one hand, I slug him across the jaw with the other. His head whips to the side, and then I knee him in the gut. Hard. He coughs and gasps for air.

"Don't you *ever* mess with me or these women again, you understand?" I say through clenched teeth.

His mouth opens like he's about to say something, but he gurgles instead.

I land my foot square in his nuts. I have no shame—not for people like him. Not when he comes around here with drugs and guns with those kids so near.

I release my grip and watch him crumple to the ground, barely conscious, curling in a fetal position. He whimpers and bawls like a baby, holding his nuts with his one good hand. I stand over him. "And if you, or any of your punks come around me, those women, or those kids, I'm gonna kill all of you. Understand? I'm gonna fucking kill each and every one of you drugged-up bastards!"

He's barely moving at this point. I've no idea if he's alive or dead, nor do I care. I retrieve the gun, empty the cartridge, and head back inside with them. I set the items on a high shelf and hustle to the back room.

I discover Trinity, Faith, and Isaiah all huddled together in the closet. Mikaylah, who's in Faith's arms, bawls, while Isaiah looks out in awe.

"Jesus Christ." I help them out of the closet. "Are you all okay?"

Trinity nods then looks at Faith.

"I'm okay," Faith says, her face reddened and tear streaked. She holds her baby protectively against her chest.

Isaiah watches the three of us. "You're crying, Mama."

Sniffling, Faith moves to the crib and lays Mikaylah inside.

Trinity rubs Isaiah's head. "Your mama's okay, Pookie. Everything is okay." She looks at me. "We'll leave."

I nod, and she heads to the hallway closet and pulls out suitcases.

Isaiah continues watching her curiously. Then he turns back to me. "We're going bye-bye?"

Smiling, I kneel down to peer into his eyes. "Yeah, li'l man. We're going someplace cool. You'll like it."

Isaiah beams. Then he looks at my hands, and his brow pinches. "Blood." He points.

I look down and realize I scraped some skin off my palms when I grabbed the gun. Minor scratches. "I'm okay. I had to beat up a bad guy."

His eyes grow wide. "Ooh, are you a superhero?"

I grin. "Naw."

"But you're tall like a superhero. And you got muscles. And you beat up bad guys." He moves closer and gives me a hug.

My whole body freezes. I've never had a kid do that to me before. I try to stand, but he hangs on. Does he want me to pick him up?

After a few moments, I comply with his unspoken demands and heft him up in my arms. He wraps his arms around my neck and rests his head on my shoulder. "I wanna beat up bad guys, too," he murmurs sleepily.

I relax a little, rubbing his back. "Maybe when you're older, I'll teach you a little something." I glance over at Trinity, who looks back at me, smiling. God, I missed that smile.

Trinity opens the closet and drawers and begins stuffing clothes into the suitcases.

"Need some help?" I ask.

"No, it's okay," she replies, eyeing the dresser.

I hear soft breathing. Isaiah has dozed off.

"He really likes you, Kevin," Faith says, sitting on the daybed as she fidgets with a pink knitted baby bootie. "He only clings to people he really likes."

I give a half smile. "He thinks I'm a superhero."

"I wonder if you really are," Faith says. "I mean, after what you did."

"It's just gonna get worse the longer we stay here. We need to go now."

Faith nods. "I know."

Remaining silent, Trinity zips up the first suitcase and starts packing another.

"Thank you, Kevin, by the way," Faith says. "Jovan's never gotten that crazy before. I mean, he knows I have kids. He never pulled a gun out like that around here before."

"It was because he felt threatened," I say. "Because I was here. He doesn't know me. He thought I was one of your contacts."

Her eyelids flutter downward. "I'm sorry that you got all caught up in this."

"I'm just glad we're going to finally get you and the kids out of here," Trinity says, stuffing baby items in the suitcase.

Faith bites her bottom lip. "I still can't believe you risked your life like that. I mean, it's unreal." She looks at Trinity. "You've got a good man, sis."

Trinity grins at me. "I know."

Chapter 27

We spent the rest of the day packing. We even took some time to have our own version of Thanksgiving dinner by way of turkey sandwiches, raisins, and apple juice. It certainly wasn't the most extravagant, but I loved it nonetheless since I got to spend it with Trinity. And Isaiah was excited about it, too. I'm really starting to like that kid.

It's ten at night when I pull up to Mama's house. Only a few lights are on in the house. I called Uncle Adam before we left, letting him know what was up, but I didn't tell him much. I couldn't really explain everything on the phone at the time.

We unload the car, and I grab the suitcases while Trinity and Faith carry the sleeping kids. I knock quietly on the front door, and footsteps approach. The porch light comes on, the door creaks open, and Uncle Adam's large frame appears in the doorway. He squints at us sleepily.

"Hey, Unc," I whisper, careful not to wake the kids.

He nods and rubs his eyes then opens the door for us.

As we file inside, I can smell the remnants of Thanksgiving dinner. But I'm too damn tired think about food right now.

Unc looks us all over, then his eyes turn to me expectantly.

"This is my girlfriend, Trinity," I begin, gesturing to her. "That's her sister, Faith. And these are Faith's kids, Isaiah and Mikaylah. Everyone, this is my Uncle Adam."

Unc, who's a little more awake now, nods to the girls. "Hi."

Trinity smiles graciously. "Thank you so much, sir, for allowing us to stay here."

"Of course," Unc says. "There's a spare room in the back with a bed you can use."

I say to Trinity, "You can stay with me, if you want."

Trinity nods. "Okay."

I pick up the suitcases and lead the girls back to Michael's room. At least his room is useful for something. We pass by Dom's room, but his door is closed, and I'm not sure if he and Denise are asleep already. Michael's room is big enough to accommodate Faith and her kids, and the bed is just as large.

While I set the suitcases down, Trinity lays Isaiah on one side of the bed and tucks him in.

"Is there anything you need right now?" I ask Faith.

Faith sits on the edge of the bed, cradling her baby. "No, I think that's all for now. Thanks, Kevin." She looks at me with eyes on the brink of tears.

"Try to get some sleep tonight, sis," Trinity says. "We'll be right across the hall if you need anything."

We leave the room, and I show Trinity to mine. My arm around her waist, I lead her to the bed. She stops there but doesn't sit.

"Kevin," she says in a small voice.

I wrap both arms around her and pull her to me. I'm exhausted, but I feel like I've not held her like this in months. "Hey, it's over and done now. Your sister will be okay. No need to dwell on the past." I lean in to kiss her, but she presses her fingers to my lips.

"Kevin, thank you. For everything." She swallows. "I'm so grateful right now. So grateful that you would care so much to risk your life like that." Her eyes glaze over, and she bites her bottom lip as if trying to stave off tears. She lowers her fingers from my lips.

"Hey, your family's just as important to me as you are. I love you, Trinity." I press my lips to hers in a gentle kiss.

I've missed her taste, her touch. Everything about her. But as much as I want to jump in bed with her right now, I really need to talk to Uncle Adam. I reluctantly break the kiss. "Hey, I need to talk to my uncle for a bit. I'll be back."

She nods and pulls away from my embrace. "Okay," she says, kicking off her shoes and pulling off her shirt.

My eyes zero in on the way her tits almost spill out of her black lace bra. She plops down on the bed, her belly doing a little jiggle.

My cock stiffens. *Damn it*, I need to get out of here before I devour this girl. I hurry out the room, shut the door, and exhale, trying to think thoughts that will ease my hard-on.

When I reach the living room, I discover Uncle Adam nodding off in the recliner.

"Hey, Unc," I whisper, gently shaking him.

He jumps with a snort and looks up at me with half-open eyes. "Huh? Oh, h—hey, son."

I collapse on the couch and rub my hands over my face. I pause and observe the room. "Is Mama still awake?"

He yawns and slaps his cheek to wake himself up. "Nah, she was exhausted after dinner. It's been a long day for all of us."

I swallow a lump in my throat. I still feel guilty for not being with my family for Thanksgiving. In a way, I'm no better than Michael.

Michael. *Damn.*

"We need to talk, man," I say.

"Yeah. Yeah, sure. What's up?"

"About what I mentioned on the phone."

Unc's fully awake now. "You mean the drug runners? Jesus Christ, Kevin, you could've gotten killed doing what you did."

"Unc, this was my girlfriend's sister we're talking about here. I couldn't just stand around and do nothing."

He sighs and nods. "Right. Right."

"I was wondering if you can help Faith get a job. Help get her on her feet."

"A job? Unless she knows how to fix up antique cars, then no."

"C'mon, Unc. There's gotta be something. Data entry, inventory, answering phones. She needs something so that she can afford a place to stay and take care of her kids."

"You act like she's the only woman in the world in that situation. I can't help her."

I clasp and unclasp my hands, staring at the floor.

"But," Unc continues, and I look up. "If she's good with numbers, I can try talking with a couple of friends who run a local grocery store. Last I heard, they are looking for a bookkeeper."

"That'd be great, man. She seems to be good with numbers, with the amount of time she spent doing what she was doing." I grimace. "Don't let 'em know about that, eh?"

Unc shakes his head. "Don't worry about it. They prefer to hire people like her—those who decide to turn their life around. They're really involved in the community. Faith sounds like she might be a good fit."

"Thanks, Unc. This means a lot. And it's not just because she's Trinity's sister."

"Yeah, I know. Like I said before. You're a good kid."

I shift on the cushion. "You know what's really weird, Unc?"

"Mmm?"

"When I had that gun pulled on me, all I could think about in that moment was Michael."

He blinks. "What?"

"Yeah, man. I could hear his voice in my head, telling me how to disable the guy. And it worked."

He purses his lips sternly at me for a moment then averts his gaze. "I remember those days when you boys used to come visit on weekends. You two were what, five and six? Your mother was worried sick about the two of you brawling and wrestling and doing hell knows what else. I figured you were just being boys, doing what boys do."

I manage to smile. "I'm glad you didn't try to stop us."

"Pain is life's greatest lesson. Especially for a kid. But it's good that no broken wrists and arms came out of all that." He rubs his chin. "Son, you know what this means, right?"

My throat tightens as I try to swallow. "Uh, not really."

"It means you owe Michael Jr. a great deal of gratitude. He practically saved your life by teaching you those skills. You need to call him, tell him about this."

I scowl. "Unc, I can't." *Especially after I practically kicked him out of the family.*

Unc crosses his arms. "Then you make things pretty easy for me, son. You either talk to Michael, or take Faith with you on your way back to Seattle. Let her find a job on her own."

"But she couldn't make it in Seattle."

He raises his eyebrows. "Is Faith's well-being worth less than giving your own brother a call?"

"That's cold, man." I roll my eyes. "Fine, damn it. I'll talk to him."

"Good." He nods curtly.

I clench my jaw. I guess this was bound to happen sooner or later.

Breakfast the next morning feels a little awkward, but Mama doesn't seem to mind that these strangers and their kids have practically invaded her home—at least, not after Uncle Adam has explained who they are.

Her plate cleared, Faith leaves to tend to Mikaylah.

Mama looks at Denise and Dom, then to Trinity and me, and smiles.

Trinity dabs her mouth with a napkin then sets it on her empty plate. "Thank you for breakfast, Mrs. Anderson." She nudges Isaiah beside her. "Say 'thank you' to Mrs. Anderson, too, Isaiah."

Swinging his legs in his chair, Isaiah beams wide. "Thank you, Miss Anderson!"

Mama smiles at the boy and rubs his head in the same way she used to do to my brothers and me when we were his age. "Oh, you're welcome, baby." She turns to Trinity then to Denise. "You are all welcome, including Faith and her adorable little girl. Please stay as long as you like. There is plenty of room for you all."

Uncle Adam, who sits on the other side of me, sips idly at his coffee. "I made a few calls earlier to some friends and got Faith squared away with some job interviews on Monday."

"That's great, Unc," I say.

Trinity beams. "Thank you so much, Mr. Anderson. You don't know how much this means to me to see my sister out of that bad situation and doing something worthwhile with her life."

"Praise the Lord she's out of that environment," Mama says.

"Kevin is a superhero, Miss Anderson!" Isaiah pipes.

All eyes zero in on him. Mama raises her eyebrows. "Oh?"

Isaiah nods. "Yeah, he beat up a bad guy."

She looks to me for confirmation, and I cringe, scratching the back of my head. "Yeah, uh, just some guy giving Faith and Trinity a hard time. It's all good now."

Mama nods thoughtfully. "Okay."

Trinity helps Isaiah out of his seat. "Why don't you go see your mama now."

The little boy runs down the hall and disappears into Michael's room.

Uncle Adam catches my eye and raises his eyebrows, his silent expression questioning whether or not I held up my end of the bargain.

Not yet, but I will. To be honest, I don't know what to say to Michael. I've got too much pride to come groveling at his feet. Who knows if he'll end up hanging my apology over my head until the day I die?

Turning back to Mama, I change the subject. "So, how was Thanksgiving dinner yesterday?"

"Wonderful, though I wish you and Michael could have been there, too," she replies, a hint of sadness in her voice.

I frown.

"You missed out on Denise's awesome mac 'n cheese," Dom adds. "That shit was *goooood*."

"Language, Dominick," Mama warns, glaring at him.

"Sorry," he mutters. Denise nudges him with her elbow and gives him a wry smile.

"Well, I'll have to remember to get an extra scoop of leftovers before I leave, then," I say.

Uncle Adam finishes his coffee, then stands and begins gathering the dishes. "He didn't save any for you, unfortunately, Kevin."

Son of a bitch. I get up as well.

We all help clear the table then go our separate ways. Dom joins Uncle Adam outside to do some yard work, while Mama, Denise, and Trinity talk in the living room. Mama decides to embarrass me and Dom by showing the girls old baby pictures of us and telling stories of our mishaps. Their giggling is relentless.

That's my cue to get the hell out of the living room. I know what I need to do, but I don't feel ready to do it. I decide to check on Faith, instead. The bedroom door is open a crack, and I knock softly. "Faith?"

"Ah, just a minute," she says, and I glimpse her shifting on the bed.

Isaiah opens the door wide, grinning. "Hi."

I smile back at the kid. "Hey, li'l man." Behind him, Faith has a blanket draped over her chest, covering a bundle.

I blink, realizing Mikaylah is under that blanket. "Uh, I didn't mean to distur—"

"It's okay," Faith says, removing the blanket. Her shirt's on—no boob flashes. "She's had her fill."

I scratch the back of my head. "I, uh, just wanted to make sure you were okay."

Faith lays the sleeping baby on the bed. "I'm fine. Don't you have better things to do than to worry about me?"

Yes. Like calling Michael. "Uh, not really. Well, you know. You're a guest and all."

She retrieves her purse by the bed and fishes through it. "By the way . . . " She pulls out some bills, gets up, and approaches me. "I guess I should give this back." She stuffs the money in my hand.

I look down at the wad of cash. Sixty dollars—the same amount I gave her at the park yesterday. "Keep it," I say, handing it back to her.

She shakes her head. "Think of it as rent. For your mom letting me and my kids stay here." She returns to the bed.

I pocket the money with a sigh. "If you insist."

Isaiah taps me on the thigh. He's smiling big.

"Can you fly like Fresh Davis?"

I raise my eyebrows. "Fresco 'Fresh' Davis? What do you know about him, li'l man?"

Faith scoffs. "You kidding me? Every time there's a damn basketball game on and Chicago is playing, he's glued to the TV, looking for Fresh Davis."

I chuckle. "Well, he's the best player in the league. What kid doesn't idolize him?" *Myself included.* What a dream it'd be if I managed to get drafted onto Chicago's team and play alongside a legend. I rub Isaiah's head. "Naw, I can't fly like him, but I sure wish I could."

Isaiah hugs my legs. "That's okay. You beat up bad guys. That's cool, too."

Damn, I love this kid.

My phone chirps, and I slip it out of my back pocket. It's a message from Russell:

gr8 news! Call me asap!

I pocket the phone and pry the kid from my legs. "Hey, I gotta take care of something. Later, Faith. Bye, li'l man."

Isaiah waves. I make my way out, across the hall and to my room.

More giggling erupts in the living room as I shut my bedroom door. Well, at least the girls are enjoying themselves. I call Russell back, and he answers on the second ring. "Great news, Kev!"

"Yeah, you texted that already," I say flatly. "What's going on, man?"

"Remember the Portland gig on KMSC some months ago? Well, Mr. Jamison, the owner, is starting up two more stations online that will be streaming from the radio station's main website. He's dedicating one of those stations to be twenty-four seven Underground House music!"

I blink. "No shit? That's great, man!"

"That's not all. He wants to block out a few hours on the station especially for you. You're gonna get your own radio show, man!"

My jaw drops. Radio show? "Wait. What?"

"I know, Kev. I said the same thing. Just think, you'll be broadcasting all over the world! And you're gonna make some mad money from this, too. We just need to get you set up with some new equipment so that you can deejay from home."

This is all happening way too fast. Did Russell already agree to all this on my behalf? "Russell, wait. I need to process all this."

"Well, hurry the hell up! Mr. Jamison has been doing casting calls for more deejays to fill in the various time slots. But he's asked for you specifically."

"I dunno, man. There's a good chance I might get drafted next year. If I do, then I won't have much time for deejaying anymore."

"That's the beauty of the Internet, Kev. Just make a couple of mix tapes and play them on the show while you're away."

I scrunch my face. "Hell no. If I'm gonna deejay on the radio, then I'd rather do it live."

He sighs. "Look, Kev. This is your big break. You need to decide what you wanna do." He pauses a moment. "I'll stand by whatever choice you make, though."

"Thanks. I really need some time to think about this. I'll be back in Seattle tomorrow, so maybe we can talk about it, then."

"Yeah, sure, man. Drive safe."

"Thanks, man."

I stare at the screen. *This has to be a dream.* I never considered having my own radio show. I always dreamed of owning my own club, spinning my stuff, but this might be even better. I decide to call up some of my deejay friends to see if they heard the news, as well.

As I'm scrolling through my contacts, I encounter Michael's number. My throat tightens. I still haven't called him. Best I just get it over and done with so it doesn't keep haunting me. Sighing, I dial his number. His phone rings and rings, but he doesn't pick up. Either he's off fighting again, or perhaps he's ignoring me. Just as well. At least I can say I tried. Hanging up, I stare at his number on the screen and decide to text him. I need to get this off my chest.

> never thought I'd have to use the stuff u showed me when we were little, but I did and it saved my life last night. Thanks.

I toss the phone on the night table and lie back in bed. My eyes cut to a large bag hanging from the doorknob of the closet. I can't believe I haven't noticed that before. There's a note attached to it, written in Dom's handwriting. Curious, I get out of bed and retrieve the semi-heavy bag. I pull off the note.

As I sit back down on the edge of the bed, I flick my eyes over the paper.

Fixed them for you while you were away.

— Dom

Smiling, I peek inside the bag at my old mixer and turntable. Good as new.

CHAPTER 28

Sunday night, the four of us return to Seattle. Faith and her kids are staying at Mama's for another week or so until she gets a job and her own place to stay. I drop Dom and Denise off at their homes and stop by Trinity's so that she can pack some new clothes to spend the night at my apartment. How long has it been since she and I actually had some time alone? All I want to do is shower and lie in bed with her in my arms. It's nine o'clock by the time we arrive at my place and unload.

"I'm going to call Faith." Trinity takes out her phone.

"Okay. I'll hop in the shower while you do that."

When I finish in the bathroom and emerge all cleaned and shaved, I find Trinity in the kitchen, rearranging the food in the fridge as she makes room for the foil-covered plates of Thanksgiving leftovers. I approach from behind and hug her around her waist. My fingers sink into the softness of her belly. She's so squeezable. So sexy. Her ass presses into my groin, which is shielded by the polyester-mesh basketball shorts I'm wearing.

"Are you done in the bathroom? I want to go shower," she says playfully.

"Then go shower," I murmur into her ear. Then I plant gentle kisses along her neck.

She chuckles and rubs her hands over mine.

Reluctantly, I set her free, and she goes off to do her thing. I smile, fantasizing about her in the shower. As much as I want to join her, I'm too exhausted. These past four days have been crazy, and my nerves are only just starting to calm. Besides that, school starts up again tomorrow, and it's going to be a bitch to get up in the morning if I don't take a rest now. Sometimes I hate Sundays.

I finish in the kitchen then return to my room to unpack, shoving a bundle of my dirty clothes in the closet. I'll get around to doing laundry eventually. I climb in bed and stare at the ceiling. I can't stop thinking about Russell's news from yesterday. *My own radio show. Damn, this is awesome!*

The idea really starts to set in now that my mind is a little more relaxed. It's great—the best thing that's ever happened to me in my music career. I dial Russell's number.

"'Sup, Kev!" Russell greets on the second ring.

"Hey. So, I've thought about the radio show, and I've decided to do it."

"Seriously? That's great! I'll call Mr. Jamison first thing tomorrow morning."

"Thanks." I pause, scratching the side of my head. "I'm thinking I'm gonna need some new equipment. Of the portable kind. When basketball season starts—"

"Don't worry, man. I've got you covered. I have a friend in London who owns a music store. He can definitely hook you up with what you need."

"And I'm gonna need a good laptop that'll handle all the music programs, and—"

"Kev, seriously. Don't worry. I've got it. I'm ordering the stuff as we speak. You'll be more than ready for your debut."

My debut. That's what I'm worried about. What if no one tunes in? My fans are all about seeing me and experiencing my music in person, not listening to some online radio station. It's not often I really play on the radio.

"All right, man," I say after some moments of silence. "I'll leave you to do your thing. Thanks again."

"No, thank *you*! So if this takes off, then I can officially be your manager, right?"

I scrunch my brow. "Technically you've sorta been acting like my manager all this time."

"Yeah, but those were more like favors for a friend. Now we're getting into some serious business, man."

"If you say so. I got class tomorrow. Later, man."

As we hang up, Trinity enters my room, a towel wrapped around her damp body. The scent of my soap emanates from her. Smiling, I shut off the phone and toss it to the floor. I'm suddenly not so exhausted anymore. Seeing her perfectly curvy body cinched in a towel makes my senses—and my dick—spring to life. The exhaustion in my body is replaced by lust.

She looks down at the tent in my shorts and smirks.

"C'mere," I murmur, extending my hand to her.

She moves closer to the bed and then drops the towel.

I lick my lips hungrily as I trace every inch of her curves with my gaze. She crawls into bed on top of me—on top of my hardened dick—and kisses my lips. My hands move to her ass, where I grope her, moaning against her lips. God, I've missed touching her like this. I've missed these moments. She rolls off me and snuggles beside me, draping one of her legs over mine. Her hand strokes my chest, and I close my eyes.

"Kevin," she murmurs in my ear, "I can't thank you enough for everything you've done for me and my family."

I open my eyes. Thoughts of the stressful Thanksgiving break cause my erection to go down. "I didn't do anything, Trinity. It was your sister's choice to give up that life. I only hope that she'll stay straight."

"I think she will. She likes you. Isaiah likes you, too. I bet he'll be your number-one fan if you make it in the pro leagues."

I smile. "I like the kid. He reminds me a lot of me when I was his age." I stroke the side of her cheek. "Hey, it's over now. Tomorrow, classes start back up. And this time"—I kiss her lips tenderly—"no more running off. No more distance."

She kisses back and smiles. "No more distance." Her hand drifts down my abs, over the bulge in my shorts. She slips her hand under my waistband, grabs my dick, and kisses the side of my neck. I squirm, not from being kissed near my scar, but from how awesome her hand feels.

"God," I whisper in heated breaths.

She kisses along my jawline as she slowly strokes my length. My eyelids flutter closed out of pure bliss.

"Since class starts tomorrow, let's make the most of tonight," she whispers in my ear.

"Mmm." My mind starts to drift. I feel my shorts and boxers get tugged down and the cool temperature of the room whisking over my dick.

I open my eyes.

Trinity hovers over me between my legs, her face drawn to my abs as she kisses down the line toward my groin. I suck in a breath, reaching down to run my hands through her hair.

Holy fucking shit. "T—Trin—" Before I can say anything more, she takes me in fully, my pulsing dick pressing deep into the back of her throat. A loud moan escapes me, and my body shudders. Her mouth is incredible. I think she's done this before—or maybe she's just naturally good. She grabs my balls while she sucks me hard, and I inadvertently thrust my hips into her. Her hands run across my abs as she sucks and slurps, her tongue swirling over every inch. My mouth open, I breathe hard, feeling close to climax.

"So . . . good . . . " I say between breaths. "So . . . good . . . "

She moans in response, her head bobbing.

I pump her mouth harder and faster as she sucks, my cock painfully hard and ready to explode. A girl's never gotten me this worked up so fast before. But Trinity—*holy shit*, she's amazing.

My fingers get tangled in her hair, and I push her face into me as I feel the sudden hot rush of my sexual high fill her mouth. Moaning, she sucks it all away—the pain, the stress, the fear, every bit of me—and I'm left feeling buzzed. My body collapses. I pant, letting go of her hair.

"That—that was good," I whisper.

She peers up at me as if she's drunk and licks her lips. She seems wholly satisfied. "I like the way you taste."

Damn, she swallowed.

She slides off me and heads to the bathroom to clean up. I lie in bed, too stunned to move, too relaxed to care.

I'll never stop loving this girl.

Chapter 29

I STARE OUT THROUGH THE SEA OF HUNDREDS OF BLACK mortarboards at the raised platform where UDub's president is making his speech. His voice reverberates throughout the massive football stadium, where hundreds—perhaps thousands—of parents, family, and friends fill almost every seat on another overcast day.

This is it. I can't believe it.

A lot has happened in these past six months. Faith got hooked up with a full-time bookkeeping job at Uncle Adam's friends' store, and she found a really nice condo for her and her kids. Isaiah is my shadow. He's really into basketball, and I even taught him a little basic dribbling and shooting skills. He's a fast learner. He clings to me like glue and listens to everything I say. Kind of like how Dom looks up to me. I seem to have this effect on people.

The radio station gig turned out better than I thought. Russell promoted the hell out of the station and my show, posting flyers everywhere around town, sending out e-mails, and hitting up tons of social media sites. As a result, there were almost five thousand worldwide listeners on the first night. That was way better than Mr. Jamison was expecting and was certainly more listeners than any of the other shows he had lined up. Since then, my radio nights have been gaining more and more listeners, and the groupies at the club gigs are worse than ever. But that's okay. I've learned to deal with it. It's all part of the game. I never thought in a million years that I'd become an Internet sensation.

Things are looking great for my basketball career, too. Most of my weekends were spent flying to different cities around the country with Ben to visit some of the teams that were interested in me. I got to participate in their basketball camps and had a chance to show off my skills. Ben insists there are at least seven teams who want me, and it's going to be an interesting draft. I can't wait. I'm more than happy to know that my chances of going pro are pretty much guaranteed. David and the rest of the guys are happy for me, too. David even made it into the D-league. That's no surprise, as good as he is. It'll be cool if we end up playing on the same pro team one day.

Trinity did job interviews for several schools and educational facilities across the country. She wants to start up her own teen-pregnancy center once she has the money. It'll be a lot of work, but I'm going to support her every step of the way.

As for me, I don't know if or when I'll ever put this soon-to-be business degree to any use. Maybe when Trinity is ready to start that center. For now, at least, I'll have it as a backup. It's like what Michael Jr. always said when he used to teach me self-defense: "You're learning something you may never use in your lifetime. But aren't you glad you got it in your back pocket?"

For a son of a bitch, Michael was certainly wise in his words. Unfortunately, however, he and I haven't talked since I blew up at him during Thanksgiving break. He never even texted me. Maybe he finally took the hint and decided to leave me alone. But the thought of shutting him out of my life still nags at me.

My hand gets squeezed, bringing me back to the present. I look beside me at Trinity, who smiles. The president's long speech becomes a dull buzz as I lean over and kiss Trinity's cheek. Some students sitting behind us give us a low whistle. Ignoring them, I drape my arm around Trinity's shoulders. Denise sits on the other side of Trinity.

"Do you see them?" Trinity whispers, her eyes turned to the stands.

I follow her gaze. The spectators look like colorful dots from where I'm sitting, but I know Mama, Uncle Adam, and Dom are all up there somewhere. "Nope," I reply. "But that's okay. It's all about us right now." *And all about you.*

She plants a kiss on my cheek then turns to Denise. The two of them whisper something I can't hear and break out into random giggles.

"Pomp and Circumstance" begins playing from the speakers, and the sea of students stands as faculty and administration begin announcing names.

"See you on the other side," Trinity says, and she merges in with the rest of the line.

Spectators cheer as each name is announced. Some cheer louder than others. I shuffle closer and closer to the stage, where I'll soon walk across the threshold to a new life of opportunity.

"Trinity Imani Brown, Magna Cum Laude," the Dean of Educational Studies announces, and applause fills the stadium along with loud cheers from a small section of girls. I can only assume those are Trinity's friends. Squinting, I can make them all out, and my family is sitting beside them.

"Kevin Jerard Anderson," the Dean of Business announces. My heart pounds as my name reverberates in the stadium. Explosive cheers fill the place. The cheering is not just from friends and family, but also from fans. These are people who knew me two years ago as the Huskies' all-star. I walk across the stage, my chin held high. The Dean shakes my hand, presents my diploma case, and flips my white tassel to the left. Turning out to the crowd, I pump my fist in the air, and the cheers and applause grow louder. I even hear some of the girls yell "Kevitron!" As I walk off the stage, I glimpse my family, who are all still on their feet, waving and cheering.

And Mama looks so happy right now, waving her hands in the air. It makes my eyes burn. I haven't seen her so excited like this since Dom was born.

Returning to my seat, I wait until the rest of the names are called. Trinity places her hand on mine, grinning. I lean in to kiss her, but she stops me.

"Wait," she says, her smile never leaving.

"Denise Nakia Ramsey, Summa Cum Laude," the Dean of Arts and Sciences announces. In the bleachers, Denise's family members, who are seated near mine, stand and scream like crazy. Trinity claps over her head and yells while I let out a loud whistle. Denise turns, the sparkly lettering on her mortarboard glinting with her name and major. Trinity's is decorated the same way.

As the last student sits, the college's president returns to the podium. He orders the graduates to stand, and as we do, Trinity squeezes my hand tighter.

"And under the authority vested in me by the State of Washington and the Trustees of the University of Washington, I hereby confer upon you the degree for which you have qualified, with all rights, privileges, and responsibilities appertaining. Congratulations, graduates!"

At that, some of the graduates toss their caps in the air. Trinity, Denise, and I just wave ours around a bit since we don't want to lose them. The stadium erupts in cheers. Trinity plants the biggest, juiciest kiss on my lips. I ignore the fact that "Pomp and Circumstance" has started playing again, and I wrap my arms around her.

"Hey, lovebirds, time to get a move on," a student says behind us. I suddenly realize the lines are moving, filing out of the stadium. Taking Trinity's hand, I catch up with the rest of our line.

The graduates and faculty spill out into the stadium's lobby, where they meet their friends and families. Trinity and I scour the sea of people, searching for ours.

"Look, there's Alexis," Trinity says, pointing near the doors that lead out of the stadium.

I follow her direction and immediately spot Alexis's purple hair, tattoos, and ghostly-white skin. Her friends stand near her, and next to them are Dom, Denise, Mama, and Uncle Adam. Mama's all dressed up, but not like the way she dresses up for church. No, she looks a good ten years younger—like that beautiful woman I remember from when I was a kid.

She rushes to me and gives me a big hug. "Oh, Kevin, baby! You did it!"

I return the hug, inhaling her azalea scent. "Yeah. Thanks, Mama," I murmur in her ear.

She kisses me on the cheek then stands back and looks me over. Uncle Adam hugs me, followed by Dom.

"Good job, bro," Dom says as we do our special handshake.

"Thanks, man. You're next."

He grins and goes to hang out with Denise and her parents.

I glance over to Trinity and her family. Her two sisters, Faith and Charity, are there with their kids. Her parents smile at me and wave. They love me like a son, especially since I treat their daughter like gold. But she's worth so much more than gold. She's worth everything to me.

I grab Trinity's luggage as she exits the cab, and pay the driver. It's chaos outside the hotel in the heart of Manhattan with guests, valets, and cabbies everywhere. We make it through the revolving glass doors of the front entrance and find a place to sit in the lobby. I plunk down on a heavily cushioned chair, releasing the luggage beside me. I exhale. Who'd have thought this trip would be so exhausting? And the draft hasn't even started yet. It was hard to say goodbye to everyone, especially Dom, but it was also exciting to know that I was one step away from living my dream.

Unlike me, Trinity is excited and ogles everything around her. She'd hasn't been outside of Washington, so she's a first-class tourist.

"I can't believe we're actually here!" Trinity says, tugging my arm excitedly. "New York is such an awesome city!"

I smile weakly. I haven't been back here in years, but this city still feels like home. It's more 'home' than Washington. Maybe that's because there are too many bad memories in Washington. Memories I'd rather forget.

"Did Mr. Madison call yet?" she asks.

I whip out my phone from my pocket. No missed calls. It's nearing four in the afternoon, and that's when we should be expecting Ben. He's already been here for the past two weeks, dealing with this draft stuff. He got me set up in this sweet hotel only a few blocks away from the arena where the draft is going to be held tomorrow night. "Not yet," I reply.

"I sent him a text on our way from the airport. He should be by soon."

She nods. "Okay. I'm going to call Denise, then, and tell her how much fun she's missing."

I grin. Maybe one day Dom will bring Denise here, too.

While Trinity's gabbing away on the phone, Ben enters through the revolving doors. My exhaustion lifts, and I pop up from my chair. Ben comes over. "There you are, Kevin." He shakes my hand and nods to Trinity, who's still on the phone.

"Sorry. She's too excited to be here."

Ben waves his hand dismissively. "No need to apologize. This is something new for the both of you. You, of all people, should be very excited. I've got a good feeling about this draft."

"Any of them involve Fresco Davis?" I laugh.

"I don't know about that. Rumor is, you're one of the top five picks. Chicago played pretty well last year, so they're most likely not going to get the first-round pick. But any-thing can happen." He pulls two key cards from his pocket. "Here are your room keys. You're all set to go. Eighteenth floor, room 18-24. I'm heading back to the arena. Call me when you're all settled, and we can talk more over dinner. Your girlfriend is welcome to come along, too."

I take the keys. "Thanks."

He leaves, and Trinity ends her phone call. I hand over her key then heft the luggage. We take the elevator to our floor and make our way to our designated room. I open the door and freeze. I stare, openmouthed. I'm a little afraid to touch anything.

"Oh my God!" Trinity exclaims. "This place is amazing!"

Plush carpeting, separate kitchen, dinette, and living areas, and posh cedar furniture greet us as we make our way inside. A large window in the living area overlooks the city. We're pretty high up, and I can see New Jersey across the Hudson, and Brooklyn and Queens across the East River.

Trinity scours the rest of the suite, gasping and swooning over every inch of the place. "Come see the bedroom, Kevin! Oh! Check out this shower! I haven't seen so many knobs and shower heads like this!"

I bring the luggage into the bedroom and set it beside the massive king-size bed that looks as though it has about five layers of blankets and sheets on it. I mean, seriously, I might get lost in it. I join Trinity in the bathroom and observe the odd shower that I'd only seen in movies and those network home-improvement shows. "I guess they spray you everywhere at once?"

"I guess." Trinity smirks. "Maybe we can explore that tonight."

I smirk back. Oh, *hell* yeah.

Chapter 30

The arena is packed Thursday night. I haven't been paying much attention to the league commissioner's speech. Instead, I survey the dozens of round, black-covered tables at center court and the prospective players and their friends, families, and agents. Each of the tables has, as a centerpiece, a basketball sporting the league logo and colors.

Ben sits across from me and Trinity, speaking with two other men I've never seen before. I guess they are agents, too. Two prospective players dressed in suits and ties sit on the other side of me. I've not talked to them much, but found out they are recent graduates from Auburn and Colorado State, respectively. Nervousness fills their eyes.

A cameraman slinks around tables, focusing the lens in my direction. My heart thumping away, I adjust my tie with a nervous twitch. *Everyone's probably watching at home. At least, I hope so.*

Trinity's hand touches my lap, and I jump out of my thoughts. She smiles at me then draws her hand into mine, squeezing it. She's so beautiful in a sparkly purple gown that makes her look like a curvaceous princess. Her hair's done up and adorned with a matching purple barrette. She wears a hint of makeup, and she smells like vanilla. She leans over to me and plants a tender kiss on my lips. Not caring who around us is watching, I return the kiss.

"And now, the first pick of this year's draft will be made by Milwaukee, who have five minutes to make their decision," the league commissioner says.

There's a mix of cheers and boos among spectators and fans of other teams. I pull back from the kiss and look toward the stage as the commissioner disappears behind a curtain. The giant screen on the stage shows the recent picks, the logo of the team who has the current pick, and the names of the next four teams who have upcoming picks. Milwaukee had a shitty season last year, so I'll most likely be among their top choices for first-round picks.

I glance across the table at Ben, who nods and winks at me. He once asked me the top three teams I'd love to play for. My list was simple: New York, Seattle, or Chicago alongside the legendary Fresco Davis. I had the honor of meeting Fresco during pre-draft training four months ago. He's an amazing guy on and off the court. He has so much integrity. It's no wonder he's a legend and loved by all.

Trinity squeezes my hand again and whispers, "Here we go."

I hold my breath and focus on the stage. The commissioner comes out from behind the curtain, and the crowd cheers. Then the arena goes quiet.

"With the first pick in this year's draft," he announces, "Milwaukee selects Shaun LaVelle from the University of Kentucky."

The crowd goes wild as spotlights shine on a guy two tables over. He's dressed in a suit and has his dreads tied back. I join in with the applause, despite the small niggling feeling in my gut. As good as I may think I am, these guys are at the top of their game. And unlike me, many of them did their full, four-year athletic tenure in college. At this point, I'm just a streetballer. These guys deserve a better chance than me.

I watch Shaun go to the stage to shake the commissioner's hand and pose for pictures. Then, as he leaves the stage, a sports commentator and a cameraman stop him.

An hour goes by, and the top ten picks have been made. One of the guys at my table was the seventh pick made by Philadelphia.

Nothing, so far, for me.

I slump in my chair and sigh softly. This night suddenly feels very long, and there are still about three hours left to go. I stare at the stage as the commissioner makes his announcement of the next team—Seattle—who is up for making their first pick of the night, the eleventh overall pick of this year's first-round draft.

Seattle didn't have too bad of a season, but it was bad enough to earn them four picks. It'd be cool if I played for them. I'd be close to family and friends.

Trinity strokes my arm, her touch bringing me out of my thoughts. She smiles at me reassuringly and kisses my cheek. But the kiss doesn't do much to lift my spirits at this point.

"Ben was certain I'd be among the top ten," I murmur.

"Well, Ben doesn't know everything. Besides, the night's not over yet. There's still a chance."

Across the table, Ben sits calmly, speaking with another agent beside him. He doesn't acknowledge me.

Maybe Trinity's right. Maybe there's still a chance. After all, some of the greatest players in history were higher picks. Back in the day, before Fresco Davis, Cedrick Marron was the biggest name in the league. And he was the thirty-seventh overall pick in the draft.

The commissioner's voice is a dull buzz as my mind continues to wander. If I end up not getting drafted, then I need a Plan B for my career. I'll use that business degree and work alongside Trinity to help her get that teen-pregnancy center up and running. Then maybe I'll make a full-on effort with my radio deejaying.

Tonight won't be a wasted exercise. If anything, it'll help me realize what I need to do with my life.

"Kevin Anderson from the University of Washington."

I tumble out of my thoughts and back to reality. *Did I just hear my name?*

Suddenly, I notice my arm being tugged and Trinity screaming in my ear. I blink several times and look around.

Spotlights shine down from above and cameras surround me. The crowd is going wild, and I exhale, jumping out of my chair. *Holy shit! That* was *my name!*

Ben pops up as well, applauding.

"Oh my God, Kevin!" Trinity exclaims, jumping up and down. "You did it!"

I hug and kiss her and sense a camera lens close to my face. But I don't care. I will kiss this girl on national TV, letting the whole world know how much I love her.

One of the many well-dressed staff members standing near the tables approaches me and hands me a blue baseball hat with New York's team logo embroidered on the front. *New York.* I got drafted to New fucking York!

Ben, with a tilt of his head, gestures for me to go to the stage. Without hesitation, I slip on the baseball hat and snake my way through the sea of tables as I head to the stage where the commissioner is waiting. I glimpse the big screen and notice that I'm the eighteenth overall pick. I hurry up the shallow stairs and stride across the stage, feeling the hot spotlights and camera flashes. My hands are sweaty, and the black dress shirt sticks to me.

The commissioner extends his hand, greeting me when I approach. He's grinning. The crowd cheers louder. We shake hands and exchange a brief hug.

"Congratulations, Kevin," he says in my ear as we pull away.

"Thanks." I can't stop smiling.

Placing his hand on my shoulder, the commissioner turns me toward an unseen person at the foot of the stage.

I assume someone down there is taking pictures, so I give them my best smile. There's a flash, and the commissioner pats me on the back. "Thank you, Kevin," the commissioner says then steps away to let me take my exit.

I wave at the audience and cameras. As I'm headed back to my table, a sports commentator holding a microphone stops me.

"Excuse me, Kevin, do you have time for a few words?"

I open my mouth then glance over to my table, where Ben's already up and headed my way. He nods and gestures with his hand that it's okay.

"Sure," I say, returning my attention to the commentator.

A cameraman nears and points the big camera at me.

"As this year's draft's eighteenth contender, what was going through your mind as you sat there, waiting for the commissioner's announcement?" He points the microphone at me.

I take a deep breath, gathering my thoughts. "My mind was blank, to be honest. I didn't think I'd make it. But I'm glad I did, and I'm glad my hometown of New York chose me. It's an honor to have the opportunity to play for them and help them win—hopefully—a championship next season."

"And how do you intend to prove your skills as the eighteenth pick once you start with this team?"

Out of the corner of my eye, I notice Ben standing nearby, away from the camera's line of sight. He waits for me patiently, his hands behind his back. "I'm gonna go in strong,"

I say to the commentator. "I'm gonna play hard like I always do, and show my future teammates I have what it takes."

The commentator smiles and shakes my hand. "Thank you, Kevin. And congratulations again." He leaves.

I return to my table with Ben. The rest of the night is a blur as I continue reliving the moment the commissioner said my name. The moment I walked on stage and shook his hand. The moment when my life got a little better.

My phone vibrates like crazy. I get more than ten text messages from friends and family. I look for Dom's and read it.

GREAT JOB KEV!! U DID IT!!!!!

I smile.

thx. was mama watching?

I get a reply almost instantly.

yeah me denise and uncle adam are all here at her house.

My heart brightens. And to think almost a year ago I had to fight tooth and nail to get him to see Mama. We've all come a long way, and for the better.

"I'm so proud of you, Kevin," Trinity says, and I snap my attention from the phone to her.

Words can't describe how fucking awesome I feel right now, so I kiss Trinity repeatedly, deeply, not caring that others might be watching. Trinity's going to live with me in New York, follow through with the job interviews she got lined up here for the public school system, and eventually start that teen-pregnancy center.

With the success of the online radio station, I'll be keeping up with my deejay sessions from anywhere.

Trinity and I are going to live a new life—a happy life—together. I wouldn't want to spend it with any other person.

Because Trinity is, and will always be, my number-one fan.

Estranged from his family, Michael Anderson quells the anger and demons of his past through the dangerous world of underground fighting. But his reckless world comes to a halt when he encounters a mysterious computer hacker, Alexis Richards. Knowing Alexis has access to his deepest, darkest secrets at her fingertips, Michael must find a way to redeem himself for his past mistakes.

Please see the next page for a preview of

Scorned

Chapter 1

I BOUNCE ON THE BALLS OF MY FEET, MY ADRENALINE pumping. A refreshing breeze sweeps across my face, bringing some relief from the dry September air. I inhale the stench of sweat and burned rubber, and I can smell the coppery tinge of old metal. The noise of the crowd echoes from beyond the long corridor of rusted shipping containers. My heart races.

Dante—my trainer, mentor, and most trusted friend—pats me on the shoulder. "Ready for this?"

I nod as I undo the silver cross I wear around my neck, kiss it, and tuck the chain in a pocket of my jeans. I flip up the hood of my black sweatshirt and proceed through the makeshift passageway, which is lit only by the moon.

"Don't fuck up," he says.

Of course I won't. Because I want to do more West Coast fights. If I prove myself here in Los Angeles tonight, then Dante will get off my ass about me not being ready.

Hell, I'm almost twenty-six. Been fighting full-time since I was eighteen. You would think my 23–2 streak this year would convince Dante, but no—he keeps me fucking hand-cuffed to the smaller venues on the East Coast. I can't be mad at him. He saved my life. I owe it to him to work hard no matter where he has me fight.

But this past week, Dante has gone out of his comfort zone and landed me a headline fight. And here I am, some-where in LA in the middle of an abandoned fucking rail yard on a Sunday night.

I'm not expecting to steamroll my opponent. Not this time. I looked him up a couple nights ago. Craig Stiller, aka Atomic—twenty-eight years old, six-nine, and three-twenty. His rap sheet included attempted murder—which got him locked away for nine years—drug possession—the hard shit—and aggravated assault. I'm sure he's out to prove a point just like the rest of them. I need to be on my game to-night—more than ever.

At the end of my walk, I stare out at a crowd packed into an open-ended, abandoned warehouse, which is dimly lit by several strategically posted citronella torches. In the midst of the crowd stands a raised platform constructed of metal grat-ing. Distorted music starts blaring from a pair of small speakers at the base of the platform. It's screaming death metal. I have no idea what the artist is singing—if you'd call it that—but the music riles the crowd to a violent level. People roar death threats, head bang as they flash hand signs, and jump around, acting crazy. I take a deep breath. Glancing over my shoulder, I notice that Dante is no longer behind me. He's found his way into the crowd, out of my line of sight. Thank God. It'll rattle my nerves if I see him watching me with that "don't fuck up" look on his face.

Craig emerges from the crowd, a muscled, tattooed—way more ink than me—freak of nature with short, spiky hair. He raises his arms in the air and makes his way to the platform, waving for the crowd to scream and cheer louder. And they do. This crowd is out for blood. Craig walks around the ring, flexing his bare chest and arms as he eyes random people, perhaps looking for me. His face is hard and mean, as if he's ready to chew a hole in the metal grating.

I smile under the hood. *He's trying way too hard.* I've fought plenty of people like him. They put on the tough-guy front and end up getting their bells rung with one solid punch. But I can't assume that's the case with Craig. Underestimating my opponents was what caused this year's two losses.

The death metal fades out—thank God—and my theme song, "C.R.E.A.M.," starts to play. People crane their necks and look around with curious looks on their faces, probably expecting to see a tall, muscly guy. There are few cheers as I quietly snake my way through them and onto the platform. I mostly hear murmurs.

I shrug off my hoodie and toss it out of the ring. I'm only six-one and weigh one fifty-five. Muscular? Pfft. Yeah, right. I'm definitely some kind of genetic failure because I can't seem to gain much muscle despite all the intense workouts I do. Or maybe God just hates me. Either way, it fucking sucks.

Craig stops his flexing, looks me over, and then smiles, the flickering torchlight winking off platinum from one of his bottom teeth. I stare back at him, emotionless, hoping my not reacting to his display fucks with his head. That usually works with my opponents, but I think he's onto me.

My theme song fades out, and a guy in a flashy red-and-gold jacket and wearing sunglasses comes between us. He waves a handful of betting slips over his head and addresses the crowd in a thick Asian accent. "All bets are in! All bets are in!" He points to me. "Knox from da Bronx!" There's barely a murmur in the crowd. Then he points to Craig. "LA's own 'Atomic' Craig Stiller!"

The cheering shakes the floor. I might have a bigger fight on my hands if I end up beating this guy. I stare out at the spectators, assessing how much of a challenge this is going to be. Lots of guys in the crowd look as if they might be contenders, too. But for a moment, my eyes settle on a girl standing in the front, her arms crossed, chewing gum, not engaging in the wild craziness around her. She's silent, and she's looking straight at me as she blows a pink bubble.

The announcer runs out of the ring and yells, "Fight, mothafuckas!"

My attention immediately snaps to Craig. I position myself in a fighting stance. Craig's hands are up, and he stands almost like a boxer, keeping light on his toes. He throws a jab at my face with such speed it's almost a blur. I weave to the side and land one of my signature roundhouse kicks to his solar plexus. My foot stings. *Damn, he's solid.*

But even so, he groans and bends forward from the blow. I may be small, but my feet are like sledgehammers. At least, that's what Dante always says whenever we spar.

As I advance, he moves as if he wants to try and take me to the ground. He swings wildly with a right hook. His fist makes contact with my ribs. I groan, but in that split second, his face is wide open. In one motion, I move in and uppercut him in the chin. His head snaps back. He staggers backward. Blood trickles from his mouth, and he immediately grabs it with his hand.

Sweet. He has a glass jaw. I come at him with a fury of punches to his face and kicks to his ribs. The boos rise from the crowd.

Growling, Craig rushes me like a bull, breaking my combinations. I sidestep away from his line of destruction. I don't anticipate his arm extending and clotheslining me.

With a grunt, I'm slammed to the ground. The back of my head hits metal. Something shiny glints across my line of sight then disappears. Craig pins me down and whips his fist across my face. I'm seeing stars, the looming image of him becoming a blur.

The boos are replaced by cheers, whistles, and other shit in Craig's favor. They quickly start to sound distant. I don't even hear Dante. Hell, I don't *want* to hear Dante. I need to get my shit together fast. If I end up losing, Dante will never let me fight out west again.

For a few moments, my vision goes clear, and I see that girl again. She's not too hard to spot because of her purple hair, which is styled like a Mohawk with the sides cut short and the top untouched and tied back. She's kneeling down, focused on something on the floor. She must be bored out her mind. I guess her boyfriend dragged her here.

Craig moves into my line of sight, and all my attention is back on his blurry image. The image moves. Anticipating he's drawing back for another punch, I pull my legs up, move one of them around the side of his neck, and force his head to whip to the side. Bending my knee, I have half of his neck pressed against my calf and thigh. I squeeze, applying a little pressure to the artery. His face starts to turn red and purple. While he coughs and gasps, I shift my body out of the lock but keep him in my control. I swing my other leg under his torso in a half scissor then finally yank one of his arms up and across the top of my thigh. It's a perfect setup for an arm break. Pressing against the joint, I hear him cry out in pain.

Tap, damn it. This guy's stubborn. It's going to take me actually breaking his arm or snapping his neck for him to tap out.

No, I won't snap his neck. Instant death. And that's one thing I can't do—one thing I *won't* do: kill. My vision clears again, and I watch the rowdy crowd yell like the savages they are. Except for Goth Girl. She's back to standing and looking at me.

With Craig still tangled like a pretzel, I squeeze my legs harder against his torso and that artery in his neck, intending on putting him to sleep instead. His head turns a deeper purple than that mysterious girl's hair. His body flinches in my hold and finally goes limp.

The crowd boos, and some scream obscenities as I unwrap myself from my opponent and stand. I bounce on my toes and watch him, ready, in case he's just playing opossum. After a few moments, I know he's not.

The announcer comes rushing back in the ring and holds up my arm in victory. "Winner! Knox from da Bronx!"

Three young guys swarm Craig, trying to wake him up. As I turn to leave the ring, Dante's standing there, holding my discarded hoodie. He pats me on the shoulder and casually leads me through the thick, angry mob as if nothing's wrong. But *everything* is wrong. The look of death is in all their eyes as I walk past them. They lost a shit-ton of money tonight. And I think I just earned one of the biggest payoffs of my career.

We snake through the maze of rusted shipping containers as we head back to where Dante parked the car. The adrenaline wearing off, I can feel the stinging pain in my jaw and ribs. I bet my right eye is swollen as fuck.

"You did good," Dante says, grabbing his keys out his pocket.

"How much did we win?"

"Two Gs." He unlocks the door. "Get in."

Relieved but exhausted, I slump down in the passenger seat with a sigh. The softness of the seat feels great in comparison to that metal grating. The absence of the noisy crowd makes my ears ring. I wipe away sweat and dirt from my face and chest then grab my glasses, which are sitting on the dashboard. I slip my hand down my pocket and pause.

I blink. *Where's my necklace?* "Dante, we need to go back."

Dante raises an eyebrow at me. "For what?"

"I lost something important. I need to go back and—"

"Kid, did you *not* see that pack of angry wolves back there? They're ready to chew your head off."

"I don't give a fuck, man! I need to find it!"

Grumbling, he starts the car but doesn't put it in gear.

I smile slightly at him. "Thanks, man. I'll be right—"

"Shit, they're already here." Dante nods toward the passenger-side window.

"Huh?" I follow his gaze toward the silhouette of a female figure rapping on the glass. Dark purple streaks glint from her hair. *Holy shit—it's that girl again.*

"I'm getting us the fuck outta here," Dante says, throwing the car in gear.

"Wait." I don't know why, but something about her tells me that she's not part of the angry mob. I flip on the overhead reading light and roll down the window.

She leans on the edge of the rolled-down window, tapping her black-painted fingernails against her biceps. She studies me with light-brown eyes accented with thick lashes and shadowed with black powder. *Shit. What if she's a cop? Naw. If she were a cop, Dante would know.*

"Yeah? Whatdya need?" Dante says in an annoyed tone.

She looks from Dante to me. I check out the tattoos that run down her neck and arms and across her exposed cleavage. My God, she's got a nice set of tits. Lip, nose, and eyebrow piercings cover her pasty-white face. Two metal gauges cover her earlobes. She dresses completely in black—and here I thought all that gothic shit was just a phase in high school.

She wears black lipstick on that nice set of lips. Around her neck is a black choker with a thorny rose entwining a skull. I bet she's a very pretty girl beneath that angsty facade. "Knox." Her voice is rough, but there's a hint of sweetness in her tone. She sounds like a girl I would definitely never underestimate.

I scrunch my brow. "Uh, yeah, that's me."

She nods, slips two fingers down her shirt, her large tits giving a happy bounce, and presents my silver necklace. "You dropped this."

I widen my eyes. I don't know which is more amazing: her tits or the fact that she found my necklace. In the end, my reasonable side prevails over my lust, and I take the necklace. "Thanks. I thought I lost this."

She smiles and then turns to leave. "Be more careful next time, eh?"

About the Author

Marie Long is a novelist who enjoys the snowy weather, the mountains, and a cup of hot white chocolate. She's an avid supporter of literacy movements like We Need Diverse Books (WNDB) and National Novel Writing Month (NaNoWriMo). To learn more about her, visit her website: www.marielongauthor.com.

www.ingramcontent.com/pod-product-compliance
Lightning Source LLC
Chambersburg PA
CBHW050523110726
47899CB00005B/1574